ANNA SCHUMACHER

This book is dedicated to Johnny Irish,
who would probably tell me I'm doing it wrong.

Penguin.com
Razorbill, an Imprint of Penguin Random House

ISBN: 978-1-59514-752-3

Printed in the United States of America

1 3 5 7 9 10 8 6 4 2

Interior design by Vanessa Han

A translation of the Aramaic text carved on a stone tablet discovered in an excavation on Elk Mountain, Carbon County, WY:

When the true Prophet reads this message, the era of the Great Divide is at hand. For on the eve of the Great Battle, seven signs and wonders shall come to pass, each in turn and none without the others. And these shall be:

CLARION

BLOOD

FIRE

PLAGUE

RELIC

DEATH OF A FIRSTBORN

PROPHET

And yea, once these seven signs and wonders appear, there shall be a Great Battle between the Children of God and the Children of the Earth. The Children of the Earth shall sow evil and discord wrought from the pits of Hell, while the Children of God turn to the heavens for strength from the One True Deity. The victor shall rule the land and the sky, the earth and the heavens, and forever hold dominion over the soul of humankind, and the loser shall be cast out forevermore into Eternal Nothingness—while those who fail to choose sides shall perish. Heed, for when this warning is uncovered and the true Prophet comes to light, the era of the Great Divide is at hand.

The Rite of Air

Facing east, we raise our swords

And murmur these enchanted words:

Gods of Air, where'er ye roam,

Blow our siblings swiftly home.

1

DARKNESS HAD FALLEN OVER CARBON County by the time Daphne pulled her compact Subaru to the side of the dirt road. Up ahead she could make out strains of raucous laughter, and the acrid smoke of charred meat drifted down to her on a sharp breeze.

She pulled her boyfriend's worn flannel shirt around her shoulders, trying to ward off the early autumn chill, and double-checked that the doors were locked before slipping the key into her pocket. There wasn't much to steal in her car—after splitting her earnings from working the oil rig between her ailing mother in Detroit and the collection plate at church, she could only afford an ancient clunker with a perpetually jammed cassette deck. Still, she couldn't trust the drifters who had taken up residence in the abandoned motocross track parking lot. They were rough-and-tumble oil prospectors with not a lot going for them and even less to lose, and it was rumored that they'd steal the shirt off your back, if given the chance.

The night noises sharpened as she approached: gas generators hacking out watts of power, hot dogs sizzling on portable barbecues, and plastic tarps erected as haphazard shelters crinkling in the wind. The parking lot where the Carbon County locals had once come to race dirt bikes, drink beer, and swap bragging rights was now a makeshift village of weather-beaten tents and rusted pop-up trailers, the track itself shut down.

None of the locals had wanted to set foot there since the horrible night just three months before, when Daphne had helped deliver her cousin Janie's stillborn baby on the cold metal bleachers overlooking the track. Too many of their own had died there: first Trey, who had wrecked fatally during a race, and then Jeremiah, the baby who never took a breath.

Now the gate to the track was permanently shut, its padlock caked with rust, and the parking lot was transformed into a drab tent city of desperadoes. Only one thing could send Daphne there almost nightly to pick her way through the narrow paths between tents, stepping over mud-caked work boots and pots still crusted with last night's beans. It drew her there despite the drifters' unsavory reputation, despite the rumors of their rough-handed, heavy-drinking ways. She went because beyond the gate, on the eroding hills and turns of the track itself, was the only place where she could meet her boyfriend, Owen, in secret.

Owen was the best thing that had ever happened to her, but also one of the worst. He was the last person she'd expected to find in Carbon County, a rural town in the Wyoming foothills where she'd taken refuge with her extended family, the Peytons, after an especially rough winter in Detroit. But instead of the peace and quiet she'd been craving, she found oil on her uncle's land and a strange ability to read the ancient Aramaic words on a stone tablet discovered beneath the earth, an ability that some said marked her as a prophet. She found all that, and she also found Owen, a green-eyed stranger who somehow wormed his way into her heart despite her general distrust of everyone, especially guys.

As soon as he arrived, it felt like Owen was everywhere: on the oil rig where she worked and at the motocross track, where he quickly destroyed the locals in competition, instantly making him the least-liked guy in town. It didn't help when Trey, a popular local boy, died in a race against Owen—or that later, he and Daphne were the only two present when her pregnant cousin, Janie, went into sudden, early labor, delivering a stillborn infant on the bleachers overlooking the motocross track.

Maybe the townspeople hated Owen because he was there at all the wrong times, or maybe it was just because he didn't say much to anyone besides Daphne, didn't have the gift of small-town small talk that put them at ease. Whatever it was, she knew exactly what they thought of him . . . and what they would think of *her* if they knew he was her boyfriend.

Now, more than ever, she needed the townspeople's approval. She'd fallen from their graces once before, when her cousin's jerk of a baby daddy, Doug, revealed that she'd stood trial for her stepfather's murder in Detroit. It had been in self-defense, after he tried to rape her at knifepoint, and she'd been acquitted—but Doug didn't tell anyone that part. Instead, he'd accused her of not only killing her stepfather, but he and Janie's infant son as well. He'd implicated Owen, too, and the townspeople had rallied behind Doug, threatening to throw both Daphne and Owen out of town.

It was only after Pastor Ted learned that Daphne could read the Aramaic tablet and declared her a prophet that the townspeople grudgingly allowed her back in their good graces . . . but by then, it was too late for Owen. The town needed a scapegoat, and he was the most convenient target.

If it weren't for her aunt and uncle, Daphne wouldn't have cared what anyone thought about her personal life. But Uncle Floyd and Aunt Karen meant everything to her: They had taken her in when she had nowhere else to go and taught her the true meaning of family and faith, and she would rather die than upset them. They had never trusted Owen and still believed that he may have had a hand in their grandchild's death—and until they had a little more time to heal, Daphne didn't want to upset them further.

So, to avoid suspicion, she and Owen met on the abandoned motocross track after sundown, where fear of the drifters kept the gossipy townsfolk away.

Gravel crunched behind her, and Daphne froze. But the path through the camp was deserted, with the drifters gathered around a fire at the other end of the parking lot. An unsecured tarp scratched at the ground, echoing the sound that had made her panic. Exhaling in relief, Daphne turned and made her way out of the camp.

She slipped past the padlocked gate and onto the dark trail leading to the motocross track. Even when she wasn't sneaking out to meet Owen, their clandestine relationship made her jumpy and anxious, always looking over her shoulder and trying to wipe the traces of their secret from her face. If she could have resisted him, she would have. But their bond was too strong, too powerful, to ignore.

The dark drew itself around her, only the pale comma of a moon punctuating the sky, and she heard the crunch again, closer than before. But she wouldn't turn and look, wouldn't let her paranoia get the better of her.

Stones skittered across the path behind her, and the wind panted in her wake. Although it was too dark for shadows, she thought she saw something flicker across her vision. Her stomach clenched as she felt the sudden presence of a stranger behind her, his skin emanating a dank rot.

She whirled around, but it was too late. Yellowed nails dug into her shoulders, the force knocking her to the ground. She got in one good scream before his hand clapped over her mouth, filling her lungs with the sickening scent of decay. Adrenaline flew through her veins as she kicked the air, praying for her steel-enforced boots to connect.

The stranger covered her body with his, stilling her legs and pinning her to the ground. Greasy strings of hair fell onto her cheeks, and he laughed a grating chainsaw laugh, reaching into the folds of an oily trench coat to reveal a blade that turned the weak beam of moonlight to ice. The world pulsed, and terror screamed through her, her vision condensing into a single point of light. Her eyes rolled back in her head as power gathered in her stomach, spreading from cell to cell until she was charged like a battery, electricity fighting its way through her skin and making her writhe and quake under his weight. She looked straight into his eyes—one gray, one brown—and saw, with horror, their true intent.

She'd had a knife to her throat and a grown man's unwanted body on hers before. She knew what that man, her stepfather, Jim, had wanted: to force himself inside of her, debasing her body until it no longer felt like her own.

But this man didn't want that. He didn't care about her body. He wanted her life.

She jerked and seized beneath him, and the power rocketing inside of her forced her hands around his neck, choking off his windpipe with a python grip. For a moment, everything was black. Then she heard a voice in her head, and all she could see was fire.

The Vision of Fire

And yea, there will come a day
When ye stand before the derrick
That pumps oil from the earth
And a wall of flames consumes the sky.

These shall be no ordinary flames
But the hellfire of damnation,
Wild with hunger to destroy
All that is holy and good.

And ye shall see, as the fire approacheth
And crude oil boils inside the earth
And the heat peels trees from land
And skin from bone

Ye shall see a shadow
With shoulders wide as mountains,
Arms raised, fingers outstretched,
Coaxing the fire ever closer.

Slow as boulders forming
The dark figure turns
Until he looks down upon you
And you fall to your knees.

For this figure has a face you know,

A face you have touched.

You have seen these eyes

Flash serpentine green.

These eyes have deceived you,

These hands draw down fire to burn the land,

This heart serves only the dark lord

And this soul is as black as the devil.

Your limbs shall tremble

And your heart shall tear in two,

For this is a face you know—

A face you love.

OWEN CROUCHED IN THE DARKNESS, his body sizzling with need. Being at the motocross track was both a torture and a release: Torture in the jumps and berms that made him miss his dirt bike the way an amputee misses a limb. Release because it meant time alone with Daphne, whose touch raced through him faster than any motor and cut like the sharpest hairpin turn.

With the track shut down, she was the only thing keeping him sane. She was a reason to get up and go to work on the oil rig each morning and his last thought before falling into a fitful sleep every night. But even the cool relief of her smile, the kisses stolen on their lunch breaks, and their electric evenings alone on the motocross track weren't enough to staunch the dreams.

They came thick and furious each night, the same nightmares that had driven him to Carbon County so many months before. Dark figures danced around a bonfire, but now he could see them more clearly, eleven pairs of emerald eyes glowing like fireflies, only one face still dark. They danced and chanted, hands clasped and limbs gleaming in the firelight, and as their voices crescendoed to a wild shriek and the fire flung itself into the sky, the earth began to shake, threatening to open up and release a mighty and powerful god, the God of the Earth.

The dreams always ended with a voice of thunder and lighting, of molten gravel pouring from the earth's core. *Find the vein*, it had whispered to him long ago, terrifying and seducing him, sending him back and forth across the country until he found his sister, Luna, and together they let it draw them to Carbon County like gravity, an elemental force.

That voice was the God of the Earth, Luna had explained to him, and the God of the Earth was their father. At first he thought she was crazy, a lost hippie child who'd probably taken too many substances at the music festivals where she performed with her glowing hula hoop. The only evidence that they were even related were their identical green eyes and her stories of growing up on the commune where he was born, a commune called Children of the Earth. But when the Aramaic tablet told of a great battle between the Children of God and the Children of the Earth, he began to reluctantly believe his sister. If she was right, that meant that he and Daphne were on opposite sides of a great battle between good and evil—a battle that the tablet had threatened could destroy the world.

He didn't want it to be that way, but the predictions on the tablet had all come true, from the fiery wreck that had taken Trey's life at the motocross track to the flock of birds of paradise that had dropped dead from the sky on the day of Janie's wedding. Now the second part of the prophecy was coming true: The Children of the Earth were arriving in Carbon County.

He'd noticed others with the same green eyes trickling into town, other children of the God of the Earth, and he knew from the faces in his dreams that all but one had arrived. Like him, they'd been drawn there by dreams of fire and destruction that ended with the gravelly voice of their father urging them to "find the vein." And Luna, in that half-cheeky, half-ominous way of hers, had made it easy for them.

She had her own place now, a brand-new nightclub that was full to bursting with roughnecks and prospectors each night. All Children of the Earth were guaranteed jobs there, as bartenders and busboys, bouncers and cocktail waitresses and kitchen crew. And just so there wasn't any question about where they should go, she had named it the Vein.

So far Owen had managed to stay away, gritting his teeth and gripping the bottom of his chair as Luna packed her costumes and hula hoops and urged him to move across town with her to the loft above the club, tears filling her eyes and her words wrapping around him like a serpent as she begged him to join her.

He'd refused. He had to stay away from her, from all of them, to protect his love for Daphne. If she knew, just as the tablet had predicted, that most of the Children of the Earth were already in town, she'd be forced to choose between her loyalty to him and her duty as the prophet of the Children of God. He knew that he'd have to tell her eventually, but he couldn't bear for her to have to make that choice just yet.

So he stayed far away from the Vein despite Luna's text messages and the voice in his dreams, which pulled at his blood like a magnet at metal shavings. His will was strong, and his love for Daphne stronger. But each day that he held out was harder than the last, and he was terrified that someday, by his will or against it, he would end up among them. As much as he fought it, the need to go to his brothers and sisters grew stronger every day.

A scream cut through his thoughts with the white-hot immediacy of lightning, making the hair on his arms stand on end. He was on his feet before he could catch up with his body, racing down the face of the jump and calling her name. He knew that voice and knew it could only be her.

Daphne.

He shouldn't have let her come alone, he thought, furious at himself as his feet pounded the track, kicking up dust and splattering his pants with mud. Daphne was tough, but the path through the drifters' camp was dangerous, the squatters unscrupulous in their quest to get what they wanted—and what if what they wanted was a girl? Owen never should have put her in that kind of danger, and Daphne never should have agreed to it. Their desire for one another had grown huge and reckless; something had to change before it was too late.

Unless it already was.

A thin layer of sweat clung to his skin by the time he reached the messy circle of squatters who had gathered at the bottom of the dark path down to the track. "What happened?" He shouldered past the men, ignoring the sour scent of their beer breath and unshowered bodies.

"Looks like she's having a seizure," someone grunted.

"But I wouldn't get too close," another cautioned. "Lookit what she did to him."

Ignoring the warning, Owen stepped to the front of the crowd.

Daphne convulsed on the ground, flopping like a minnow in the bottom of a rowboat. Her eyes were narrow white slits, and her lashes beat furiously against her cheeks. A few feet away, a man lay unconscious, stringy hair feathered around his head. His eyes, one gray and one brown, were open but unseeing, the red still draining from his face and a patina of bruises decorating the stubbled skin of his neck.

A knife marked the ground between them, its blade throwing slices of light from the drifters' headlamps and gas lanterns.

"Daphne!" Owen rushed to her even as crooked hands reached for his arms and tried to hold him back.

"You don't wanna do that," someone warned. "We pulled her offa him, but it wa'n't easy. Girl's got a demon grip."

"Call an ambulance!" Owen broke free and rushed to her side. He wasn't afraid of her, even if the rough-and-tumble drifters were.

He knelt by Daphne's convulsing body and slipped a gentle hand under her head. She stiffened at his touch, and her eyelids flew open. But the eyes that bored into his weren't hers—they were barely even human. They blazed with fear and distrust so sudden and unexpected that he snatched back his hand.

Daphne's body jackknifed, her legs spasming as her hands flew to his throat. Steel-strong fingers closed over his neck, crushing the air from his lungs.

"I told 'im not to go in," he heard one of the squatters say, but it sounded like it was coming from far away, from another continent on another planet in another lifetime.

He sputtered for breath. He was losing air, losing consciousness. The world telescoped inward, its edges black and fuzzy, static filling his ears like sand.

He was going to die. The realization shot a cannonball of adrenaline through him, and with the last shred of his waning strength he brought his hands to his neck and closed his fingers over Daphne's. He imagined strength pouring up his arms and through his hands, pictured Daphne's vice-strong grip turning to jelly under his fingers. The vision squeezed through the choked-up passageways of his windpipe, rushing from nerve to nerve.

My fingers are steel, her fingers are jelly. These words would be his last thoughts, he realized through a thick film of panic. If only they were true: if only Daphne's strength really were waning, if only the crushing tension in her muscles would relax into flesh and beyond flesh, into jelly so soft he could spread it on toast. As he pried at her fingers, gasping for breath, he thought he felt her hands loosen under his, her strength give millimeter by painstaking millimeter.

A sliver of air rushed to his lungs, just enough to give him a better grip. The refrain of *my fingers are steel, her fingers are jelly* pounded in his brain. He breathed in again, the sound raspy and desperate as he wedged first one, then two, then all of his fingers into the growing gap between her hands and his throat. With a final burst of strength, he freed himself and threw her aside.

Daphne's arms flopped in the dirt. Black dots floated in Owen's vision as he rubbed his throat, the bruises tender beneath his fingers. Air had never tasted sweeter, and he sucked in giant lungfuls of it, the pain in his windpipe a stabbing reminder of how close he'd come.

"Damn." A nearby prospector shook his head, whistling air through his teeth. "That was close. How'd you do it?"

"I don't know." Now that he was out of immediate danger Owen could feel power surging through his body, sparking from his mind down to the tips of his fingers in electrical currents that made his skin seem feel hot and too tight. His brain was on overdrive, the echo of *my fingers are steel, her fingers are jelly* dancing there like a song that had stuck in his head. It almost felt like those thoughts, rather than his own strength, had saved his life.

Daphne shot to sitting like a zombie rising from the grave. Her eyes flew open, and she looked around wildly, taking in the knife and the man lying unconscious and the circle of drifters. When her gaze reached Owen, she shrieked and scuttled back in the dirt. Her face was drawn in terror, and she whimpered as if the sight of him caused her pain.

"Daphne." He kept his voice low and gentle, knowing she must be disoriented. "It's okay. It's me, Owen."

"No!" She turned her back to him and clutched her knees, curling into a ball and rocking back and forth.

Still gasping for breath, he crawled over and wrapped his arms around her trembling shoulders. She shrugged him off at first, still whimpering into her knees, but as the keening wail of the ambulance grew closer and the drifters began to scatter he tried again.

"You had a seizure, Daphne," he said softly, his lips close to her ear, soothing her the way he'd soothed his little sister after a nightmare in his previous life back in Kansas long ago. "I know it's scary, but you're okay. You're going to be all right. I'm here."

She relaxed and let him envelop her, wrapping herself in the scent of earth and motor oil that never left his skin, resting her head against his chest and drying her cheek on his T-shirt. This was Owen, the *real* Owen. That other Owen, the one who'd blazed huge and evil in her vision, didn't exist. He couldn't. She'd been hallucinating, her mind riled up in self-defense and playing terrible tricks on her.

But as the siren swam closer and the sky pulsed red and she sobbed into Owen's shirt, another thought nagged at her, one she couldn't ignore. Because, whether or not she wanted it, she was a prophet—and prophets didn't see mistakes or hallucinations. They saw visions from God.

3

THE DOG WAS BARKING. BELLA stood on the pink lump that Janie made under her sleeping bag, pawing at her shoulder and yapping in her ear, awakening her from a heavy nap dotted with restless dreams.

"Shut up, Bella." Janie swept the dog onto the floor, but Bella landed on her cream-colored paws and went right on barking, dancing back and forth from the couch to the TV and making the cherry vodka on the milk-crate coffee table slosh in its plastic bottle.

As she struggled out of the depths of sleep, Janie slowly realized what the dog was fussing about. Someone was knocking on the door, the pounding echoing through the empty halls of the half-finished mansion atop Elk Mountain.

"Crap." She sat up, throwing off the sleeping bag, and ran a hand through the rat's nest of her hair. She dimly remembered something about Hilary coming to visit, a text message exchange from yesterday or the day before—it was easy to lose track of time when all you did was sleep and watch *Teen Mom.*

"Janie, it's for you!" Deirdre Varley's nagging trill floated up from the lobby and bounced off the vaulted ceiling.

"Coming," Janie called back. But it came out sounding like a croak.

She found her slippers and padded down the hall, tightening the drawstring on her sweatpants as she descended the stairs.

"Hey, girl!" Hilary's voice was unnaturally bright, the brightest thing by far in the towering, empty lobby of the half-finished chateau. She wrapped Janie in a hug that smelled like baby powder and fresh laundry, making Janie wonder what had happened to her old best friend who had always reeked of cigarettes and Rihanna's Rogue perfume.

"Close the door, you're letting cold air in," Deirdre admonished. She gave Janie a pinched glare. "I wish you'd remembered you were having company," she sniffed. "I had to come all the way down from our wing to let her in."

"Sorry." Janie looked down at her slippers, threadbare Smurfettes staring mournfully from her toes. "I'll remember next time."

Like there would be a next time. It's not like anyone ever came to visit her—even her mom had gotten sick of Deirdre's sniping and stopped coming round, choosing instead to nag Janie by phone.

"It's good to see you." Hilary smiled and pushed away a stray corkscrew curl that had fallen over her eye. "It's been too long."

Janie didn't know how long it had been, exactly. Lately she'd been losing track of time, whole days disappearing between commercial breaks and fitful dreams. But it must have been a while, because Hilary didn't just smell different, she looked different, too. She'd put on some weight, and her face was rounder, the skin taut and glowing and her old acne pockmarks nearly gone.

"Yeah, well." Janie gave a vague shrug. "I guess we should go upstairs."

She led Hilary up the wooden skeleton of a wide, sweeping staircase that would one day be finished in marble, past doorways with no doors that peeked into rooms whose only decoration was yellow sheets of insulation stapled to the walls. With the lawsuit against Janie's father stalled and the Varleys hurting for cash, they'd sold their ranch house in town and moved the family to the chateau on Elk Mountain before it was finished—and judging from the way money had been lately, it seemed like it may never get done at all. Vince Varley swore they'd get it fully insulated and heated before winter, but there had been no workers for days, maybe even weeks. The Wyoming air was chilly even in early September, wind whistling through the cracks in the walls like lost children crying to come home.

"Brrr." Hilary hugged her arms and shivered as they entered the den. It was the only room in the west wing—Doug and Janie's wing—that was fully furnished, but the old leather living room set from the Varley's ranch house still seemed dwarfed by the vast expanse of plywood floor. "It's cold in here."

"I'll build up the fire." Janie dredged logs from a cardboard box and poked at the smoldering coals, watching them jump and hiss before licking at the wood and filling the room with smoke. "At least there's plenty of wood on this land."

"Remind me to bring you a space heater next time I come." Hilary perched on the end of the couch and looked around, slowly taking in the panorama of the Savage Mountain Range from the huge bay window. "Sure is some view, though."

Janie guessed it was okay, but she preferred to face away from the lonely peaks, staring instead at the fireplace or the flat-screen television Doug had propped somewhat precariously on a milk crate.

"Want a drink?" Janie held out an economy-sized plastic bottle half-full of the cherry vodka she'd taken to sipping throughout the day. The strong, clear liquid burned sweet trails down her throat and kept her mind hazy and soft, away from the thorny edges of thoughts that caught and ripped at her brain: memories of the birds that had fallen dead from the sky on the day of her shotgun wedding to Doug, of Daphne holding her stillborn infant son in her arms, of Doug pushing her into the dirt and screaming over her as she sobbed, blaming her for their son's death. "It'll warm you up."

She realized that maybe she should go to the kitchen for glasses (it's what a good hostess would do, what her mother would do), but that meant a long trip down the cold stairs and dark hallways, and possibly meeting Deirdre Varley's disapproving face over the vast kitchen island, silently judging her daughter-in-law while she attempted a new casserole with some phony-sounding French name.

But Hilary shook her head. "I don't really drink anymore," she said. "I know—crazy, right? Me, turning down a drink? But, well, ever since everything happened, with Trey going to God and them finding that ancient tablet and—well, you know . . . what happened to you." She averted her eyes, color creeping into her cheeks. Janie knew. Sometimes, it felt like it was *all* she knew.

"Anyway, I've been trying to live a little cleaner since all that," Hilary went on. "Pastor Ted says the Rapture's coming any day now, and we all have to get right in the eyes of God. That means no drinking, no swearing, no getting down before marriage—which is great for me, 'cause now Bryce keeps talking about putting a ring on it." She grinned wickedly, a flash of the wisecracking old Hilary superimposed over the clean, shiny new one.

Janie took a swig from the bottle, seeing as how Hilary didn't want any anyway. Maybe it wasn't exactly polite, but what did it matter? It wasn't like Hilary was the queen of England. As the liquid warmed her insides, she looked up and saw concern flash in her old friend's eyes.

"We miss you at church." Hilary sounded like she was trying to coax a scared dog out from under the bed.

"Yeah, well," Janie shrugged. She already wanted another swig—it seemed like she needed more and more to take the edge off lately. "I've been real busy up here."

Hilary's eyebrows knit, and for a moment Janie saw herself through her friend's eyes: hair matted around her face, bundled in her old Carbon County High sweatshirt and a cheap pair of sweatpants that, honestly, she hadn't changed in a few days. She must look pathetic, like a washed-up housewife who couldn't even get it together to do laundry. Not that the laundry hookup was even close to ready in the Varley mansion, and Deirdre, being too proud to let them go to the laundromat in town, insisted they hand-wash their clothes in the sink. Screw that: Janie had better things to do. Like sleep. And watch TV. And drink.

"Well, we'd all love it if you could find time to come see what we've been up to at the church!" Hilary sounded too upbeat, too positive—the very opposite of her sarcastic former self. Had Janie been that annoying when she was on her big Jesus kick? She couldn't remember. Everything about the past, the time before she married Doug and lost her baby and moved into the house at Elk Mountain, seemed so far away, like it had happened in another lifetime to another person. A happier person.

"So many people have moved into town since Pastor Ted got that show on the Christian channel," Hilary continued. "There are all these great new folks now, we've started a youth group and everything, and the Sunday sermons are packed. Seriously, Janie, you would not believe it: standing room only! It's a good thing your folks are donating the money for a new church, and that's close to done, too, so we'll have room for everyone who's ready to be saved."

Hilary leaned forward on the couch, eyes glowing. "Just come to church this Sunday, Janie. It would mean so much to your folks, and to Pastor Ted, and . . . well, to *me*."

Janie couldn't hold out anymore. She grabbed the bottle and took a good, long gulp. The vodka burned, but it was so much easier to swallow than Hilary's words. She'd believed in the church—in God, in Jesus, all of it—with all her heart before. But where was God when she'd cried out to him to let her baby be delivered safe and sound? Not listening, obviously. So why should she put her faith in him now?

She set the bottle down and wiped the back of her mouth with her hand. "I'll go," she said.

"You will?" Hilary scootched forward on the couch and wrapped her arms around Janie, a hint of her old fierceness in her grip. "That's so great! Pastor Ted will be so excited—and Daphne, too! She's there every Sunday now, and you wouldn't believe the fuss people make about her. I guess not every congregation gets to have its own real, live, honest-to-goodness prophet."

"That's . . . awesome." Janie tried to force a smile, but it just wouldn't come. It wasn't that she didn't love Daphne, not exactly.

Just that she didn't buy into all that prophet baloney. A real prophet would have been able to save her baby. A real prophet wouldn't have let an infant die in her arms.

Hilary sat back on the couch and kept talking, her chatter rapid and meaningless. Janie tuned out, sneaking occasional nips from the bottle and nodding along numbly as Hilary gossiped about their old friends and raved about Pastor Ted and waxed on about clean living and the Rapture and that weird new club in town, the Vein, which Pastor Ted said was a hotbed of sin they all must avoid if they wanted to be swept up to heaven in God's golden light. It was a relief when her friend finally ran out of things to say and Janie could escort her downstairs to the door, the naked worklights strung through the hallways yellowing their skin as they said goodbye.

"So you'll really come to church on Sunday?" Hilary asked for what seemed like the millionth time, clasping one of Janie's cold hands in both of her warm ones.

"Yeah." Janie nodded thickly, knowing it was a lie. But if a promise would get Hilary off her back, then she was more than glad to make it. The vodka had worked, finally, and the world was sleepy and slippery around her, a snowglobe filled with static. "I'll see you there."

"Great. I can't wait!" Hilary kissed her cheek, and then she was gone, and Janie was blessedly alone again, her footsteps ghostly echoes in the huge, silent halls. She trudged upstairs, swaying, a little off-balance thanks to the booze, and tipped another shot into her mouth as she turned on the TV. A little girl's face filled the screen, lips pink, eyes rimmed in fake lashes. One of those child beauty-pageant shows. Perfect. Janie loved those.

Bella leapt onto her lap and snuggled into her, the dog's cuddles one of the few honest pleasures still left in her life. Janie felt her head tip sideways and her mouth fall open, the booze and couch and the dog's tiny patch of warmth pulling her eyelids shut into a heavy, troubled sleep.

↔

An arrhythmic thumping jerked her awake. She didn't know how long she'd been asleep, only that it was dark outside and her head was pounding, her mouth dry and scratchy from her lips all the way down to the sour slosh of old vodka in her stomach.

The thumps grew louder, suddenly familiar. It was Doug, stumbling down the hall. So it was late, then. He always came home late, and often drunk—not that she had any right to judge. She held her breath, wondering if it would be one of those nights he wanted something from her or if he'd just pass by, heading to the large, lonely bed in the master bedroom they supposedly shared.

Things had been different with Doug since that night, the night of Jeremiah's funeral, when he left her sobbing in the dust by the bonfire. He'd apologized, of course: Doug was good at apologizing.

He'd gotten down on his knees and said he was out of his mind with grief, so broken up about their baby that he didn't know what he was doing. And she'd forgiven him, because she didn't know how else to respond and because she loved him and wanted things to go back to the way they were.

Not that they had. Now they were ghosts orbiting each other in the giant house, Doug finding as many excuses to leave as Janie did to stay. She didn't know where he went. All she knew was that he came home drunk, sometimes wanting her body and other times wanting nothing more than bed.

The footsteps stopped, and he appeared in the doorless doorway, weaving slightly on oversized feet, his big head blocking out the work lights from the hall. Disgust and desire welled up in her, battling for control as he lumbered toward her and lowered himself to the couch with a heavy grunt. Even as the whiskey on his breath repulsed her, she found herself arching out of the sleeping bag to meet his groping hand.

He didn't say a word as he unbuckled his belt and grasped her hand roughly, guiding her to him. She didn't either, although her breath quickened and she felt herself lean toward him, anxious for even the quickest, sloppiest kiss, the most fleeting connection to what their life and their love had once been.

Her cell phone jangled on the coffee table, startling them both. It was late, she knew—too late for anyone to call.

"Mom?" Her voice was rusty with disuse. "What's up?"

She listened, her eyes widening, before hanging up and slipping the phone into her pocket.

"What?" Doug fell back on the couch, staring woozily at the mournful sliver of moonlight outside the bay window as Janie chased her shadow around the room, looking for the boots she hadn't worn since her last trip out to gather kindling.

"It's cousin Daphne." Her voice was hollow. "She had an accident or something, and she's in the hospital. I gotta go."

She found her imitation Uggs under the couch and mashed her feet into them, sweatpants and all. She fished the keys to Doug's truck from his pocket and looked down at him one last time, at the blanket of sleep that had already fallen over his face and the gently snoring mouth that had once declared his undying love. She didn't know whether she wanted to kiss that mouth or kick it, and so she did neither.

Instead, she let herself out of the house and started his truck, shivering as she drove off into the night.

4

MUSIC THROBBED THROUGH LUNA'S BODY, pulsing the blood in her veins and making her skin feel warm and alive. The tips of her multicolored dreadlocks brushed her bare back, tickling the sensitive skin where a tree tattoo sprouted from her root chakra and spread over her back and down her arms. She threw back her head and closed her eyes, letting the music roll over her shoulders and trace trails in the air from her fingertips.

Even in the darkness behind her lids, she could feel them watching her, hungering for her. Their eyes left hot retina prints on her hips, which swirled lazily, keeping the twinkling circle of her LED hoop aloft. From time to time she sensed a grubby hand reach for her, desperate to stroke even the tiniest patch of skin on her calf, but it was easy enough to send the hand's owner stumbling backward with a well-timed kick of her vegan leather boot.

The Vein was packed, the music deafening, the air thick with crushed dreams and frustrated desires. Her Earth Sisters Freya and Abilene moved like panthers behind the bar, green eyes flashing as they poured shots down the prospectors' throats and tucked their ample tips into holsters slung low on their hips. Orion winked at her from the DJ booth while Aura sent fog creeping across the floor and lasers dancing over the walls, and Gray and Kimo moved silently through the crowd, clearing glasses and mopping up spills, their lithe bodies no more than shadows that left the Vein's patrons feeling inexplicably cold and empty as they passed, making them shiver and curse and hurry to the bar for another drink.

Oh, how the prospectors could drink! It took gallons of booze to fill their vacant souls each night. Their greed was massive and oppressive, their desire for easy money and cheap thrills so strong that sometimes Luna found herself forcing back bubbles of nausea while she twirled her hoop atop her go-go platform, above it all.

Radio signals of want radiated from them, so loud at times that Luna wanted to scream at the prospectors that these desires would leave them even emptier in the end, just as the alcohol drained not only their wallets but also their souls. She wanted to force them to see the beauty in the earth, the blinding happiness in a simple life spent worshipping the land, the incomparable joy of respecting every living thing. She wanted to make them understand the damage they did each day when they went tearing up the foothills looking for oil.

But she knew that route didn't work. Her people had been trying to turn the tides for centuries, from the druids of Ireland to the monks of Tibet to the gentle hippies who had raised her on a commune called the Children of the Earth. Their warnings never worked. People were just too greedy, just too blind.

With the earth on the verge of destruction, the planet's veins bled of oil, its airways choked with smog, and the water in its cells polluted with toxic chemicals, it was Luna's responsibility to tap into the ancient power of the earth and take action. She had to stop the destruction before it was too late.

But she couldn't do it alone. She needed the Children of the Earth—*all* of the Children of the Earth—at her side.

Somewhere below the go-go platform, a fight broke out. Glass shattered, and an arc of blood sailed through the air, the sound of fist meeting flesh exploding over the music's driving beat.

Luna put down her hoop and leapt to the floor, landing silently on the thick rubber soles of her boots. She flowed through the crowd like steam, and it automatically parted to let her pass. In a moment she was between the brawling men, the solid center in a swirl of flying fists and hamburger-meat faces, of bloodied lips and bloodshot eyes.

"Stop." She held up her hands, a palm facing each of them. She felt the magic build inside of her, the indigo-colored force that started in her throat chakra and roared to life in her veins. It sensed the men's desires radiating off of them like a foul smell, knew by instinct that their fight wasn't really over a spilled mug of ale but because they were frustrated, their thirst for approval and women and riches never slaked.

She fed on them, these desires, and now she knew what to do with them. The men may have thought they wanted to fight and win, but she sensed the need underneath: to feel completely safe and protected, the way they'd felt as infants in their mothers' arms.

Luna glanced from one man to the other, the buzz of power pulsing through her. Up in the DJ booth, Orion cut the music, and the Vein fell silent.

"You don't fight in my club." Her voice was quiet, her eyes cool. "Understand?"

"Yes'm." The men murmured, bashful, staring down at their muddied shoes. Their anger fizzled and seemed to leak from their suddenly unclenched fists. They didn't dare meet her gaze.

"Now get out." She raised her face to the teeming crowd, meeting all of their eyes at once, making them blush all the way to the roots of their greasy hair. "All of you. We're closing up for the night."

Moving as one, the staff of the Vein pushed the mob of prospectors toward the exit. Within minutes the bar was empty. Only the Children of the Earth remained.

"Are there any left?" Luna asked Kimo as he slipped by with a push broom.

Her Earth Brother stopped. He tilted his head to the side, so that his stiff black Mohawk almost disappeared, and sniffed the air delicately. His eyes went a shade greener, glowing incandescent in the bar's gloom.

"There's two in the bathroom," he said. "You don't even want to know what they're doing."

Luna nodded. "Get them out."

Kimo hurried away, and she grasped the railing of the spiral staircase and took the steps two at a time. Orion paused from packing up his turntables to give her shoulder an affectionate squeeze as she wafted past him and through a black door.

Ciaran sat at a desk in the management office, counting the night's earnings. His fingers were dragonfly legs dancing across the backs of bills as he sorted them into piles. They didn't stop as he looked up.

"Evening, Earth Sister." He tossed a long, honey-colored lock of hair from his eyes.

Luna kissed his golden cheek. "We do well tonight?" She perched on the edge of his desk, swinging her legs.

"We cleaned up, like we always do." He punched numbers into a calculator, his smile never losing its glow. "If those prospectors knew how to make money like we do, they'd stop looking for oil in all the wrong places."

She tapped him on the nose. "If they knew how to make money like we do, we wouldn't make money like we do."

"Touché." He opened a safe in the wall and placed the bills inside. "But you're not happy," he observed. "Something's bothering you."

Her legs stopped mid-swing. Ciaran was the first of her Earth Siblings to arrive in town after Owen, but she still wasn't entirely used to the way he could see inside her mind. It was his power, just as manipulating desires was hers.

She got up and closed the door, then leaned in close and whispered in his ear. "He isn't back yet."

Ciaran's brow wrinkled. "That guy? The one who was supposed to take care of Daphne?"

"Yeah." The word tasted dark. "Something happened. Something bad. I can feel it."

Ciaran scratched his knee through a hole in his jeans. "Maybe it's a sign," he said finally. "From our gods. Telling you that this is wrong."

Frustration simmered in her throat. "How can it be wrong? I've tried everything else: reason, begging, magic. Owen won't leave her. I know that deep down he wants to be with us—when I sleep, I can feel him reaching for us in his dreams. But that girl has a hold on him, and until we get her out of the picture, he won't come back. And without him, we can't—"

She broke off, unable to face the enormity of what it would mean to lose this war. It meant that the greedy and ungrateful would go right on pillaging the earth until their beautiful planet was nothing but an empty, smoking husk hurtling through space. It would mean that she had failed.

Ciaran placed a hand on her shoulder. His compassion broke something inside her, and she felt the lump of frustration move up her throat and push against the back of her eyes.

"I just miss him." Her voice trembled, and she glanced down at her knees. Ciaran held her by the shoulders, his hands soft and soothing.

"I *need* him," she continued. "We can't do this without him. Without all thirteen of us, we won't have the full strength of the circle, and we can't call the Earth God to heal the planet."

"I know." Ciaran's voice was like cool moss on an open wound. "It's okay, Luna. He'll come back, and we'll be able to work our magic. We'll do what needs to get done."

She looked up at him. She hated feeling this vulnerable, this lost, but Ciaran understood. He understood, and he didn't judge.

"Yes." Their eyes locked, green on green. "I promise, Luna. Owen will come back, and our circle will be complete."

5

AT FIRST ALL SHE SAW was white. The shapes were fuzzy and indistinct, overlaid with horrific remnants from her vision like slides held up to the light. She saw the man with stringy hair and different-colored eyes, the knife glinting in his grasp. She saw flames clawing their way into the sky around the oil derrick, and the unbearable hugeness of the shadow drawing them closer. She clawed at the air, trying to grasp the visions and tear them apart, and as she swam into consciousness, her eyes cleared and the white came through, antiseptic and safe.

"Daphne!" Uncle Floyd flew to her bedside. "You're awake."

Concern dragged at the leathery folds of his face, but the weight of his hand on hers was a relief. Beyond him, other figures blurred into focus: Aunt Karen, Cousin Janie, and Pastor Ted.

"Where am I?" She looked around at the white walls and perforated ceiling tiles, the IV trailing into her arm and the rails on her bed. "The hospital?"

"You had a seizure." Aunt Karen smoothed back her hair. "But you're fine now. See? Your whole family's here with you, me and

Floyd and Janie, plus Pastor Ted and, uh . . . Owen from the rig, too."

"I was asleep . . ." Her head felt heavy and dull, like someone had stuffed cotton between her ears.

"They gave you a sedative." Owen leaned against the wall, his face half-hidden by oil-colored hair. "In the ambulance. You were still kind of freaking out."

Floyd narrowed his eyes, and Daphne wished she could tell her uncle how good Owen truly was, how much he meant to her. He wasn't the monster everyone in Carbon County thought he was. If only there was a way to make her family see.

"Oh." She shook her head. "I was having such weird dreams."

"You've been through a terrible trial, Daphne." Pastor Ted stepped forward, his round, smooth face solemn under uncombed hair. He must have woken up in the middle of the night to come to her bedside, she realized guiltily—and he was so busy with his new TV show and growing congregation as it was. "The man who attacked you may not have been an ordinary man. I suspect he was an agent of the devil, sent to erode our faith by murdering our prophet. It's only by the grace of God that you were able to defend yourself."

"You did a darn fine job of it, too." Pride percolated in Floyd's voice. "Put 'im in a coma, using just your own strength."

"But Floyd." Pastor Ted turned to her uncle. "It may not have been just *her* strength. You see, when someone is touched by the

Lord, they sometimes become a sort of conduit for divine power. God saw that Daphne was in trouble and channeled His own power through her to vanquish the evildoer."

"Thank goodness He did." Tears brimmed in Karen's eyes. "Can you even imagine . . ." she sniffled, unable to finish the thought.

"Now, Daphne, this episode you had . . ." Pastor Ted gazed down at her intently. "Do you remember anything from the time you were out? Did you hear or see anything, maybe receive a message?"

"I—" Daphne gulped, her mouth suddenly dry. She couldn't help sneaking a glance across the room at Owen, remembering the way he'd appeared in her vision: eyes burning with evil, his giant hands coaxing flames from the foothills to engulf the oil rig.

"Go on, Daphne." Pastor Ted leaned forward. "You can tell us. You're in a safe place."

Her voice came out in a rough, hoarse whisper. "There was a fire at the rig. It was huge—it swallowed the whole sky."

Pastor Ted gripped the railing on her bed, his knuckles growing pale. "That's from Revelations 8:6!" His voice turned deep and sonorous as he quoted the Bible, but he couldn't quite mask the glee that always crept into his speech when he talked about the Rapture. "'When the first angel sounds his trumpet, there will be a mixture of hail and fire that will burn up a third of the earth.'" He turned to Daphne, face flushed. "Anything else?"

"Well . . . there was a shadow, like the shadow of a man. He was holding his hands up to the flames. It looked like he was controlling the fire . . . like he was trying to bring it closer."

She knew she should tell the whole truth: that the "shadow" was Owen and that she saw nothing but evil blazing in his eyes. But how could she? If she confessed what she'd seen in her visions, the already-suspicious townspeople might drive him out of town.

Plus . . . it was Owen. Owen had held and soothed her while the bruises from her hands were still fresh on his throat; he'd traveled in the ambulance with her and even braved her disapproving family, just to stay by her side. How could she possibly admit, even to herself, that the evil figure in her vision had been *him*?

Pastor Ted gasped. For a moment, he was speechless.

"What?" Daphne sat up straighter. "What does it mean?"

The pastor shook his head slowly. "Of course, I can't say for sure, but when a prophet sees a dark figure controlling fire—well, it can really only be one thing." He took a deep breath, and everyone in the room leaned forward. "The devil."

Before they could react, a raspy voice jerked their attention to the door, where a portly cop stood scowling. "This Daphne Peyton's room?"

"Why, yes, Sheriff Bates." Floyd still looked dazed from Pastor Ted's words. "She's right here."

"Great. I'm gonna hafta ask you some questions." The sheriff barged past Pastor Ted, his bulk devouring the rest of the space in the already cramped room. He was a large man, soft around the middle, with thinning hair and a doughy chin. Beside him, his head just level with the cop's ample stomach, hovered a boy of no more than six or seven years old.

"Well, hello, Charlie." Pastor Ted knelt and ruffled the boy's otter-pelt hair. "Are you helping your dad fight crime?"

The sheriff glared at him. "He's here 'cause I got nowhere else to put 'im when I get a late-night call. Now, if you don't mind, I got questions to ask, and it's gotta be witnesses and family only. So Ted, you can go ahead and skedaddle."

"I see." The pastor straightened. "Daphne, please don't hesitate to call if you remember anything else. And Kenneth," he nodded at the sheriff, "you know you're welcome back in church anytime. We've missed seeing you since Ellen passed."

"Missed me, or missed the extra coins in your collection plate?" The sheriff sniffed. "Thanks, but no thanks. With all those drifters stirring up trouble, I got no time for church these days anyhow."

The pastor shot him a wounded look, but Sheriff Bates had already turned back to Daphne.

"So you were attacked, huh?" He towered over her bedside.

"Yes," she replied. "I just—"

"I'll ask the questions around here, if you don't mind," he interrupted. "Now, tell me everything: where it happened, what time, who was there."

Daphne squirmed. She knew that being at the motocross track would arouse suspicions, but that's where the ambulance had found her. There was no point in lying, but no way to tell the truth without revealing her relationship with Owen.

"Um." She paused to gather her thoughts.

"Could you maybe hurry it up?" The sheriff butted in. "I got a kid here who oughta've been in been in bed hours ago."

She glanced at Charlie, who regarded her with curious, chocolate-colored eyes.

"Hey." Owen straightened from his slouch against the wall. "Go easy on her. She's still sedated."

The sheriff turned to him with a piggish glare. "And who are you?"

"Your witness," Owen said evenly. "I work with Daphne at the rig, and right before our shift ended, I noticed she was acting strange. I followed her when she left, up to the old motocross track—"

"*That* place?" the sheriff burst in. "What are you, nuts? She'd be crazy to go there alone at night."

"I *said* she was acting strange," Owen hissed. "Obviously she wouldn't have gone there otherwise."

Daphne sank back into her pillow, weak with gratitude. Owen may have been stretching the truth, but he was doing so to protect her and to keep the secret of their relationship safe. He went on to recount the way he'd "followed" her through the drifter's camp, losing her briefly but rushing to her side at the sound of her scream.

"I didn't see the whole thing," he finished truthfully, "but the man who attacked her had a knife. Whatever she did to him, it was in self-defense."

The sheriff nodded, frowning, and jotted things in a notebook. "What she did was put him in a coma," he said finally. "He's just down the hall, on life support—and until he comes out of it, he ain't talking. Now you're sure that's all you saw?"

"That's it," Owen shrugged.

The sheriff narrowed his eyes. "Does this corroborate your version of events?" he asked Daphne.

"Yes," she insisted. "All I remember is being attacked at knifepoint. And even that's kind of a blur."

"And you're sure you don't know why you were at the track in the first place?" Suspicion hovered in his voice.

"I'm sure," she said. "I wish I could remember. But I can't."

"Now listen here." Floyd's face had gone from its usual ruddy red to the mottled fury of a bruised plum. "Daphne's had a terrible shock. According to our pastor, she was just face to face with Beelzebub himself. So if you don't mind, I think she could use some rest." He glowered at Sheriff Bates, rage steaming his glasses.

"Fine." The sheriff glared back. "I was just about done anyway. If I think of anything else, I'll be back. C'mon, Charlie."

He turned and trundled out the door, the linoleum floor tiles sighing under his bulk. Charlie stood silently, appraising them all with solemn brown eyes, before scurrying after his dad, nearly tripping over his small legs in an effort to keep up.

Gratitude surged through Daphne. The sheriff's presence in the room had been harsh and jarring, a fluorescent light too bright in her eyes. Now that he was gone, she felt flattened against the hospital bed, limbs heavy and head stuffed with sand.

"You should get some rest." Karen was by her side again, patting her hand. "But don't you worry: Between us three Peytons, we'll keep you company tonight till you're ready to go. Floyd and I will just run and get some coffee down the hall, won't we? Janie, honey, can I get you anything?"

"Coffee's fine." Janie sank into a chair, watching the tiles on the floor blur and drift back into focus. Exhaustion kept throwing fuzz into the evening's events, scrambling everything her dad and Daphne and the sheriff said like a bad TV signal. She could see the emotions running between them, the way if you turned a sweater inside out you could see the mess of loose ends and scraggly knots behind the picture on the front, but she couldn't make out the words—or why anyone even bothered to talk. From where she sat, it seemed like they all just liked the sound of their own voices.

"I guess I should go, too." Janie felt Owen's glacial green gaze on her, like being splashed by water from Hatchett Lake. A moment later it was gone, and he was looking back at Daphne, just like he'd been doing all night. The only times he took his eyes off of her was when he was raising his voice in her defense.

"I guess." Daphne sounded soft and far away. "Thanks for . . . you know. Everything."

"Of course." Owen went to her bedside and dropped a hand on her shoulder. His eyes cut back to Janie, and he coughed nervously. "Happy to help."

Janie pretended to study the wheels at the bottom of a hospital cart. But from under the fringe of her lashes she saw the way Daphne's hand snuck up to meet Owen's, the brief but intimate touch as their fingers intertwined. It was only for a second, but that second was like a punch in the gut, a reminder of how it had once been to reach for someone and know he'd be there.

"I'll see you at the rig," Daphne breathed.

"See you." Owen's voice was heavy with meaning. Janie watched him lope out of the hospital room, leaving the faint scent of metal and earth in his wake.

Once he was gone she leaned her head against the too-shiny white wall, thinking that the sedative would drop Daphne back under and she could finally get some rest herself. Her parents would come back and see her like that, realize she was tired, and send her home to the dull safety of her faded pink sleeping bag on the couch in the Varley manor. Maybe she'd sneak into the echoing terra-cotta chef's kitchen first and grab a nip or two of Deirdre's cooking brandy, just to make sleep come quicker.

"Janie." Daphne watched her cousin's head loll against the wall. She'd smelled alcohol on Janie's breath, noted the puffiness below her eyes and the sallow tone of her skin. "Are you okay?"

Janie started, her eyes blinking slowly into focus. "Shouldn't I be the one asking you that?"

A laugh scratched Daphne's throat. "I feel like I haven't seen you in ages," she tried again.

"Yeah, well, you made it pretty clear you didn't want me moving in with Doug." Janie studied the spots of mud on her boots. "Even though, y'know, we're *married.* So it's not like I expect you to come and visit."

Daphne opened her mouth, but words evaporated on her tongue. It was true that she'd tried to talk Janie out of moving up to the Varley mansion, had even suggested that she file for divorce. But it was crazy that her cousin had stayed with that monster after he'd threatened to sue Janie's entire family, and it was obvious to everyone in town how miserable Doug made her. Everyone, it seemed, but Janie herself.

"Anyway, it doesn't matter." Janie scuffed her boot against the floor. "You're too busy with all that bogus prophet stuff anyway."

"What?" Daphne croaked. "What do you mean, bogus?"

Even through the fog of her sedative, Daphne could see how jaded her cousin had become. Once upon a time, Janie would have been the first to believe in Daphne's visions from God. But it seemed like her cousin, who used to insist that everyone had a guardian angel and that prayer really could cure all that ails you, had left town for good, replaced instead by this cold stranger with dead blue eyes.

"Oh, c'mon." Janie weaved a little as she stood, and Daphne caught another flash of booze on her breath. "This prophet crap's just a cover-up. You're hiding something. Or maybe some*one*."

She glanced meaningfully in the direction of the doorway, where Owen had just left. Daphne watched her heart rate spike on the monitor next to her bed. Had Janie guessed that there was still something going on between her and Owen? She'd seen them flirting when Owen first came to town, and she'd tried to put a stop to it, but Daphne and Owen had kept their relationship private since.

There was a flat, sick-sounding slap as the sole of one dirty pink boot hit the linoleum, then another. Janie was halfway to the door by the time Daphne located her voice. "Janie, wait!" she called.

Janie stopped, her shoulders tensed under a sagging hoodie. She turned and regarded Daphne, her eyes narrowed to slits. "What?" she asked.

Daphne ached to confess the truth: not only to get her secret off her chest, but to rekindle the closeness she and Janie had lost.

But how much could she risk telling? Janie didn't approve of Owen any more than her parents did. What if she passed Daphne's secret on to Floyd and Karen? They were vulnerable enough that it seemed like the news could break them.

But maybe she just needed to bite the bullet and tell. Janie would understand—she'd been in love once, or maybe she still was. And even though they'd drifted further apart since Janie had lost her baby and slipped into her depression, Daphne still considered her cousin her closest friend.

Her silence stretched on as she tried to formulate the words, and then the moment was gone.

"Yeah, that's what I thought," Janie sighed. She turned back to the door, her feet falling into a slow, sad shuffle, hair trailing down her back like the tattered trim of a cheap, grubby blanket.

"Tell my folks I had to go," she said woodenly.

Before Daphne could respond, Janie was a silhouette, then a shadow, then a watery reflection in the hospital window as she hurried down the hall.

HEATHER ANDERSON SQUINTED INTO THE sunset. She'd been wearing her sunglasses for most of the drive west, to protect her striking green eyes from a sun that felt like it was growing closer and brighter with every mile she put between her and the leafy passageways of her hometown in rural New York state. But even polarized lenses were no match for the glare of the sunset, pricked by the peaks of Wyoming's Medicine Bow mountain range so that it spilled like the runny yolk of a soft-boiled egg across the sky.

The west, and her future, felt wide open, full of possibilities. She'd spent most of the drive picturing the University of Arizona's sunbaked quad, weekend Wildcats games and field trips to buttes and faults and canyons, the cool slosh of beer in a Saturday night Solo cup and the ring of study-break laughter with her first-ever roommate. There would be midnight Lucky Charms from the cafeteria and toothy kisses with tall, tanned boys, pickup soccer and, best of all, weeks on end without snow, clouds, or rain.

Arizona's endless sunlight and crisp, dry air would evaporate the darkness that sometimes permeated her nights, the dreams that woke her gasping and drenched in sweat. She blamed northern New York's upstate gloom and long winters for her moodiness—because it wasn't *her*, she knew that. Heather Anderson was as solid and sensible as the rocks she planned to study, a declared geology major who'd chosen her college as much for its Earth Sciences Department as for the warm winters. She was student council secretary and captain of the Oneonta varsity girls' soccer team, doting big sister to Matt and Jessica, beloved daughter of Mira and Frank. She wasn't the dark figure chanting and dancing around bonfires in her dreams, goaded and cajoled and strangely, horrifyingly attracted to the gravelly voice urging her to "find the vein."

Her stomach rumbled, and she checked the GPS on her dashboard. Six hours to Moab, a long and lonely hump until she could check into the motel she'd booked online the week before. She'd decided to take the scenic route to Tucson, planning her trip around a handful of geological oddities: the Tripod Rock in New Jersey, Missouri's Ozark caves, the cannonball concretions in Theodore Roosevelt National Park in North Dakota, Arches National Park in Utah, and then finally down to the University of Arizona and her brand-new college life. Her mom had wanted to come, but Heather talked her out of it: There would be a lot of driving and a lot of rocks, and her mother would start fidgeting in that distracted way she had. It was better for her to go alone.

Another, more forceful groan rumbled her gut, and the sun slanted sideways through her windshield, temporarily blinding her.

"Okay, okay, fine," she said to the Jeep Cherokee's interior, slowing to a crawl and squinting into the horizon. "We'll get off at the next exit and find a diner, wait for the sun to go down. But then on to Moab."

A sign loomed ahead, its stark white letters barely visible in the glare. "Looks like we're going to Carbon County," she said to the voice warbling pop songs on the radio. "And, note to self, stop thinking out loud. Your new roommate's going to think you're a freak!"

The talking-out-loud-to-nobody thing was new, and she blamed the solo cross-country road trip. All that time to herself, the hours where the cliffs along the side of the highway started to develop personalities in her mind, the nights alone in chain motel rooms that smelled of mold and disinfectant and hard, sad little soaps, the sleep streaked by yellow parking-lot lights and broken by recurring dreams—all of it was starting to get to her, and in a way she regretted refusing her mom's offer to come along.

The road dipped into a valley sprinkled with lights, and she passed a sign so new she could see the mounds of fresh dirt where it had been planted. *Welcome to Carbon County: Home of Miracles!* it declared cheerfully, next to a seal that appeared to contain an oil derrick and something that looked like the Ten Commandments.

"It'll be a miracle if I can find something to eat besides McDonald's," Heather joked, tapping the brakes and falling in line behind a slow-moving water truck with Global Oil logos on its mud flaps. She followed the truck at a glacial cruise past a flashing sign advertising Elmer's Gas 'n' Grocery and onto a bustling main street lined with shops just closing up for the day. Idling at a traffic light, Heather noted the parking spaces packed with mud-splattered pickups and a sign in a real estate office advertising one-bedroom apartments starting at $1,800. She saw throngs of scruffy, tired-looking men waiting for tables in the well-lit windows of restaurants with names like Pat's Steakhouse and Manic Manicotti.

The businesses along Main Street thinned out, replaced by a vast trailer park packed with mobile homes that were squat and uniform as headstones. A sign at the gate informed her that it was the Lucky Strike Community—*Prospectors Welcome! Hookups start @ $200/wk!*

"I should turn around," Heather declared. The sun had disappeared behind the mountain range, leaving only a rusty stain in the sky, and the spaces between the trailer homes were thick with shadows. Yet she kept driving, telling herself she'd hit the next turnaround and maybe just grab a slice of pizza somewhere, eat it in the car, and hustle down to Moab. As the sky darkened and the water truck turned off onto a dirt road and her stomach gave another long, low moan, Heather kept driving. She had an inkling now that there would be more up ahead, felt promise in the way the road curved up into the foothills. None of the restaurants along Main Street had been quite what she was looking for, she reasoned, but soon she'd find the perfect spot for a bite.

As the last greasy trails of sunset smeared across the sky, she noticed a sign glowing red in the distance, its molten glare fire-bright in the quickening dark. Her stomach clenched—not with hunger, she realized, but with anticipation. Even though the sign was still far off, she knew from the strong twist in her gut that it was the place.

Her body seemed to pick up speed even as the Jeep slowed. She felt the racing patter of her pulse and her blood flowing faster in her veins. The sign was closer, almost close enough to read, and her turn signal was already on. She was halfway into the parking lot, pulling up in front of a long, low building with a peaked roof and blacked-out windows, when the words on the sign registered, and she slammed on the brakes and cut the engine, shuddering along with the Jeep as its power ticked away.

The words on the sign sat black and somber against smooth plastic that glowed scarlet from within, as if lit by fire. They were words she felt she'd known forever, words whispered to her night after night in a voice like tumbled pebbles, broken and granite-hard and flecked with shavings of glimmering mica, words that filled her with darkness and dread and longing.

The Vein.

She sat for a moment, hands useless in her lap, unable to unbuckle her seatbelt.

"It has to be a coincidence," she whispered. "It just . . . there's no way . . ."

She knew she should turn back, turn around, get out of that parking lot and as far away from Carbon County, Wyoming, as possible. She knew, somehow, that once she stepped foot inside the Vein, everything would change. She thought about her life, her future down in Tucson, the mirage of college life shimmering in the distance. But she was already unbuckling her seatbelt, stepping out into the early evening chill. Dry mountain air caught in her lungs, and her heartbeat was a drum marching her to the door, matching the pulse of music thudding faintly through the walls.

She pushed open the door and stepped inside, into a room glowing with the dim intensity of an underground cavern.

"Sorry, we're not open yet." A guy with a chiseled chin and massive shoulders stopped her with a gentle tap on the arm. He had a long, dark ponytail and a serious mouth, but his eyes were all Heather saw.

His eyes. Gazing into them she forgot where she was, forgot where she'd been or where she was going, almost forgot her name. His eyes were green in a way that had seemed, for all of her life, impossible to duplicate, green in a way that made strangers on the street stop and stare and her friends ask, in hushed and giggling tones at countless slumber parties, if she wore colored contacts. It was like staring into a trick mirror, like her eyes had been transplanted into the bouncer's face.

He looked up at her, and his expression changed. "You're here." He stretched his arms wide, showing the callused ridges of massive hands. "Welcome home."

Heather's feet felt like concrete. "What do you mean? I've never even been here before."

The bouncer ignored her, cupping his hands around his mouth. "She's here!" he called in a voice that echoed through the empty bar: "She's here!"

Suddenly, people began to appear. A head popped up from behind the bar, and she heard shuffling footsteps, felt the presence of bodies hastening toward them from hidden back corridors.

"She's here." The voice was throaty, rich as turned earth. A door opened behind the bar, revealing a girl with wild, colorful dreadlocks, wearing a backless green top and tattered bell-bottoms that rode low on her hips. Her eyes met Heather's from across the room and sent sparks prickling up and down her arms, shorted her breath, and spread heat up the back of her neck. "Welcome," she said with a honey-slow smile. "I'm Luna. I'm your Earth Sister."

Heather's mouth fell open. She couldn't take her eyes off the girl, couldn't look away from those eyes. They were the same green as the bouncer's, the same as her own.

"Yes," Luna glided toward Heather, grinning like a cat. "You're finally here, Earth Sister. Welcome home."

"Hold up." Heather's voice came out shrill, shaky. Not the way she wanted it to sound. "What's going on? Why are you all freaking out about me being here? I've never met any of you before."

"But that's not true." Luna spread her arms, which dripped in bronze bangles. "You're our Earth Sister. You've known us since the day you were born."

She indicated the small crowd of bar staff that had gathered behind her. A chill trickled down Heather's spine as she saw their eyes: all the same shocking shade of emerald. Even in their strangeness, there was something familiar about them, something almost comforting.

She took another step back, so the cool steel of the door pressed into her spine. "I only have one sister," she said. "And she's not here."

Luna's laugh was a silvery tinkle in the silent room. "It's not that simple, Heather. Don't you know where you were born?"

Heather went cold all over. "How do you know my name?"

"Because I'm your sister," Luna explained patiently, as if speaking to a child. "We were conceived on the same night, at a place called the Children of the Earth, during a beautiful ritual under the full moon. We were born side by side and took our first breaths and our first milk together. We came into this world as a family, as Children of the Earth, and now we're all together again, a family once more. At last."

The others nodded somberly behind her.

"But . . ." Heather began. She couldn't find the words to continue. If what Luna said was true, it would explain why she had never seen a photo of herself as a baby, why her parents were always vague about her birth and jokingly referred to that time as "our hippie phase." It would explain why they didn't get married until she was three years old, when she toddled down the aisle in front of them in an itchy blue dress carrying a basket of flower petals.

"You were named after the grasses that blew like waves in the fields," Luna continued, her voice a seductive singsong. "Your birthday is sometime between April second and April ninth. You're an Aries—and you act like one, too. And for the past few months, ever since your eighteenth birthday, you've been dreaming of us: all of us, dancing together around a bonfire, summoning the God of the Earth to set things right. You've dreamed of us, and seen our eyes, and just before you wake you hear a voice telling you to find the vein."

Heather's knees buckled, and she leaned against the door for support. "How do you know?"

"Because we've all had them, too." Luna's voice was soothing, rubbing away at her fear. "Those dreams were messages from the God of the Earth, calling his children home.

"And now you're here!" Luna clapped her hands with childlike delight, her jade eyes sparkling. "And just in time, too: The moon is already waxing. Oh, I know—you probably have a million questions. Let's go upstairs, and I'll tell you everything."

She reached out a hand, urging Heather to take it, to follow her.

"No," Heather whispered. She shrank back, wedging her hands behind her back, not trusting them. "I'm not going anywhere with you. I'm getting out of here. I'm—I'm going to Moab."

Darkness winged briefly across Luna's face. She locked eyes with Heather, and even though she wanted to, Heather couldn't look away—couldn't focus on anything else. It was like the entire world, the galaxy and universe and everything beyond, was concentrated in those eyes.

"You want," Luna said, "to come with us. You want to be here, with your family."

The words wound hypnotically through Heather's brain and spread in a warm blue-tinged haze to her heart. She *did* want to follow Luna, to be part of this strange yet strangely familiar tribe. She wanted it desperately, and she understood that part of her had wanted it her whole life. She knew without having to be told that the darkness she'd felt back in Oneonta, the loneliness that plagued her heart even when she was around family and friends, would turn to light once she surrendered to Luna and accepted her place with the Children of the Earth. She knew that this was her true family, where she'd always belonged.

With Luna's voice singing in her head and Luna's words flowing through her veins, it didn't matter that she was supposed to go to Moab, to Tucson, to the University of Arizona and her sunny new life. That was all meaningless, a shadow world to distract her from the truth. Nothing mattered but Luna.

Slowly, somnambulantly, she brought her hand from behind her back and stretched her fingers toward the wild-haired girl standing before her. She felt the cool, dry pressure of Luna's hand in hers and let herself be led through the red-lit room, eyes fixed on the tattoo of a gnarled, wizened tree that covered Luna's back and sent twisted branches across her shoulders and down her arms.

The rest of the Children of the Earth followed silently as Luna opened a hidden door by the bar and started up a rickety wooden staircase, her hand still wrapped around Heather's, the charms in her dreadlocks lightly jingling.

The stairs brought them to a large, open attic with a steeply peaked ceiling that sloped almost to the floor. Starlight filtered in through the many skylights, illuminating what looked like a gypsy camp: Mattresses covered in patchwork quilts and tie-dyed pillows littered the floor, clothes hung from mismatched wall hooks and peeked out of beaten dressers, half-burnt candles sat in hard puddles of wax, and scarves had been thumbtacked to every surface to create colorful clouds of silk, batik, and velvet.

"This is where we live," Luna said. "All together, just like when we were kids at the commune. Now let's make a circle! Everyone grab a cushion. There's so much we need to discuss."

Someone handed Heather a red-and-gold pillow embroidered with an Indian elephant, and she found herself settling into it, wordlessly taking her place on the floor. There was something so familiar, so comforting about being in a circle with these people, her Earth Siblings with the matching eyes. It was like they'd done this before, many times, back when she was too young to remember. Her mind couldn't recall those days, but to her body, her heavy obedient limbs, it felt right.

Luna lit candles and incense, filling the room with a thick, sleepy scent. The firelight danced on her face as she took the lotus position on a purple velvet cushion, her back straight and proud.

"Ommmmm," she chanted, her voice low and husky in her throat.

"Ommmmm," the Children of the Earth echoed.

To the old Heather, the Heather who was captain of her soccer team and secretary of the student council, it would have felt silly to sit in a circle and chant. She'd never gone in for new age-y stuff, couldn't even sit through a yoga class, but the new Heather, the moody shadow-Heather plagued by nightmares, let the vibrations echo in her chest and mingle with the voices of the others. To shadow-Heather, their chant had the power of a mountain rising from flat land, strong and rare and magical. It stirred her blood and buzzed wildly in her mind.

The chant came to a slow close.

"Children of the Earth," Luna's voice resonated through the loft, "we were called here for a reason. The earth is in trouble—grave trouble. In their material greed and lust for power, humans have destroyed the planet we call home, clear-cutting forests, polluting the air and oceans, killing our sacred animals. Right here in Carbon County, an oil rig is scarring the land and bleeding this planet of its life force. And only we can stop it."

Around the circle, the Children of the Earth nodded, eyes serious.

"The God of the Earth called us here to save this beautiful planet and save humanity from itself," Luna continued. "But we can't do it by marching and carrying signs or writing letters to our congressmen. Those things have been tried, and they've failed. They are powerless against the greed machine."

"Yeah!" Across the circle, a slight boy with a black Mohawk pumped his fist in agreement. Layers of black clothing drowned his body, and a fist-sized anarchy tattoo dominated his neck.

Luna fixed him with a fleeting smile. "Instead, we're going to harness the power of the elements, and our power as Children of the Earth, to bring about real change. Because we *are* powerful, even if we've spent our whole lives trying to hide from it. Our abilities are our birthright, passed down from our all-powerful father, the God of the Earth."

Although the attic was warm, Heather felt herself shiver. Luna's words forced her to face truths about herself that she'd never allowed into the light, that had always lingered in the dark corners of her dreams.

Luna peered around the circle, her eyes resting on each of them in turn. "What *is* your power?" she asked. "Some of you already know. Like Ciaran." She indicated a boy to her left with toasted-almond skin and honeyed hair. "His power is intuition. He can tell what people are feeling, even if they don't say a word."

Ciaran lowered his eyes and smiled an elfin, enigmatic smile.

"Kimo's power is location." Luna nodded at the boy with the Mohawk and anarchy tattoo. "He's like a human GPS. He can sense where people are just by concentrating on vibrations in the air."

"Like a bloodhound," Kimo agreed.

"And Abilene." A girl with round cheeks and skin like polished mahogany fluttered her lashes. "When she sings, no matter what you're doing, you'll stop in your tracks and join. Even if you've never heard the song before."

"Even if you can't sing on key with a gun to your head," Kimo added.

Abilene rested her hands on her purple broomstick skirt and cast her eyes downward, a humble smile on her plump lips.

Luna placed her hands palm-up on her knees, thumb and fingers making a circle. "Let's all meditate for a moment on our power, whatever it may be." She closed her eyes, and the Children of the Earth followed suit.

In the pinkish darkness behind her eyelids, Heather saw nothing. She was just an ordinary kid from an ordinary family in an ordinary town: kind to children and small animals, decent at soccer, a declared geology major who, she was starting to realize, might never start her freshman year.

She thought of Arizona, which now seemed light years instead of a couple of states away. She thought of her geology major, the way rocks felt in her hands. She'd always loved to be around rocks, ever since she was a little girl—they seemed almost like friends, like if she concentrated hard enough they'd tell the story of where they'd been and what they'd seen. Sometimes it even seemed like they were coming to greet her, like all she had to do was ask nicely and they'd move for her, leaping into her hands.

Her eyes flew open. Could that be her power? What if it *wasn't* just a feeling? She looked around the circle, at the Children of the Earth sitting still as boulders, eyes closed, breath coming in slow, even waves. When her gaze landed on Luna, her Earth Sister opened her eyes and gave her a slow smile.

"Did you picture your power?" she asked the group. There were a few muted yesses, scattered nods.

"Good." Luna uncrossed and recrossed her legs. "We'll need them, and we'll need to stick together no matter what, even if things get uncomfortable or weird. We're not that strong on our own, but when we put our powers together we'll be unstoppable. Don't forget what we're up against: a multibillion-dollar oil business with the government in its pocket, and millions of religious fanatics who believe it's okay to destroy the earth because God is on their side. It's crucial that we use every tool we have—after all, we're just a bunch of hippies trying to save the earth."

Her smile was modest, almost ironic.

"We've already performed the air ritual," Luna went on, looking at Heather and winking. "It's what blew Heather into town. But now that all of us are here, our numbers are stronger and our magic is multiplied."

Next to her, Ciaran shifted on his straw mat. "What about Owen?" he asked.

A cloud drifted across Luna's face. "That's what our next ritual is for," she said smoothly. "But, I have to warn you: These rituals are powerful. They're old magic, not for the faint of heart. If you're not strong enough, they won't work. Do you all think you're strong enough?"

"Yes!" Heather was surprised to find herself piping up along with the others.

"Good." Luna leaned forward, her eyes burning. "Because in order to do these rituals correctly, we have to offer sacrifices. It's the only way to repay the God of the Earth for all the centuries of destruction our species caused. It's not enough just to say sorry. The God of the Earth demands blood."

Blood. The word vibrated through Heather like a gong.

"That's where my special power comes in." Luna glanced intently around the circle, meeting and holding their gazes. "Most of you have already seen it in action. You've seen the way I can tap into people's hidden desires, finding the ones that suit my needs and bringing them to the surface. Haven't you?"

Heather felt a cold wind stir beneath the shroud of warmth that enveloped her. Was it Luna's power of persuasion that had lured her upstairs and kept her there, destroying the pragmatic streak that should have sent her running to her car and away from Carbon County hours ago? She didn't like the idea of someone else controlling her thoughts. But at the same time she felt happier and more at home with the Children of the Earth than she'd ever felt in her life. She knew that if she tried to go, the nightmares would just come for her again.

"One of the greatest universal desires, deep in the darkest recesses of the soul, is a curiosity about death," Luna continued. "Everyone wants to know what it's like on the other side. And in order to honor the God of the Earth and consecrate these rituals, I'll need to use my power to help people overcome their fear of death, so that they'll willingly offer their blood to the God of the Earth as a sacrifice."

Even wrapped in the hypnotizing cloak of Luna's voice, Heather felt pinpricks of cold sweat prickle her skin. "You mean we're *killing* people?" she broke in.

"Not at all," Luna said serenely. "It's wrong to take another life—we don't even eat meat. We're simply activating the latent desire for death, helping our sacrifices transition from this world into the next. It's what the Earth God wants. It's what he *needs*."

Her eyes blazed, and Heather felt her jaw clench shut and her head bob up and down. Of course, what Luna said made sense. Everything Luna said made sense. Her question, examined under the bare bulb of Luna's gaze, seemed trivial, a senseless detail. She hoped her brothers and sisters didn't think less of her for asking it.

"The next ritual will be in three days, at the quarter moon." Luna's voice filled the room. "We have to act when the moon is waxing, indicating growth and potential. And when the full moon is here, we'll perform our final ritual and summon our true father, the God of the Earth, to make people stop destroying the planet once and for all. Are there any questions?"

The Children of the Earth sat silent, shaking their heads. Heather felt like she *should* have questions—fragments of thoughts drifted through her head, fleeting and iridescent like dragonflies. But before she could close a net around any of them, they were gone.

"Good." Luna stood and brushed imaginary dirt from her bell-bottoms. "Now let's find Heather a place to sleep and help her unpack her things. After all, she's one of us now."

7

"YOUR PROPHET HAS SPOKEN!"

Pastor Ted paced back and forth on the stage. His voice echoed off the walls of the packed Carbon County First Church of God and crackled through a series of hastily erected speakers outside, where a swelling crowd jostled each other to peer through the windows at the Sunday sermon.

Sweat swam down Daphne's back. She had just finished describing her vision to the congregation, and now she felt exhausted from the effort and desperate to escape the hundreds of eyes staring up at her. She'd told them about the dark shadow with shoulders wide as mountains, about the way he coaxed fire down from the mountains to engulf the rig.

She'd only omitted one detail: that the dark figure had been Owen. That still felt too private—and too dangerous—to share.

"Now, folks, we don't need to be rocket scientists to figure this one out." Pastor Ted clutched the microphone and leapt into a feral crouch at the edge of the stage. "Fire. Fear. A dark shadow emanating evil. There's only one thing this can mean, this vision from a prophet of God. We all know who and what that shadow is, don't we?"

Heads were already starting to nod.

"It's Satan himself!" Flecks of spittle flew from Pastor Ted's mouth and glinted in the light. "Lurking right here in Carbon County, trying to claw his way up from Hell to steal our souls. Do you believe?"

"I believe!" The crowd's fury was a dull roar in Daphne's ears.

"We know what this means." Pastor Ted resumed his pacing, passion painting his cheeks scarlet. "That the End Times are almost upon us, and Satan is waiting in the wings, ready to destroy. Will we let him?"

"No!" the crowd cried. Daphne gripped the sides of the pulpit, dying to sit down. It was hot at the front of the church, with all of the lights beating down on her, and her dress clung to the small of her back with sweat.

"Folks," the pastor continued, "each and every one of us has a choice, and that choice is clear. We can choose God, or we can choose Satan. If we choose Satan, come Judgment Day we'll burn alongside him in the eternal flames of Hell. If we choose God, we'll experience a Rapture unlike any other, knowing perfect peace and perfect light forever. Sounds like an easy choice, right?"

Daphne watched the sea of heads bob up and down. "Let me tell you: It is *not* an easy choice." Pastor Ted's piercing stare swept over the congregation. "To choose God, we have to rid our lives of sin. Living a righteous life isn't easy. It means sacrifice, and patience, and virtue. It means saying no to that cold beer after a long day's work, turning off the radio when the devil's music comes on, taking those hard-earned funds you saved up for that nice Caribbean vacation and donating to the church instead." He spun suddenly, facing Daphne head-on. "It means resisting the temptations of the flesh."

His laser-blue eyes bored into hers until she had to look away. She felt color creep into her cheeks as she stared down at her shoes and took a deep breath, trying to slow her pounding heart.

Could Pastor Ted know somehow? Could he know about her love for Owen, about the relationship she tried so hard to hide from her disapproving community? Did he suspect her of hiding part of her vision as well? Or was she just being paranoid?

She wished, once again, that everyone could just forget about Owen's role in Trey's and baby Jeremiah's deaths. He'd been there for both, yes, but that was coincidence, and neither was his fault. Pastor Ted spoke so often of forgiveness and redemption, but for some reason he refused to apply those values to Owen. All of them did.

Pastor Ted finished his sermon to a round of wild applause, but Daphne could barely focus on his words. Owen dominated her thoughts, crowding everything else from her mind. Her life in

Carbon County would be so much easier without him—but without him, she may as well not bother living at all.

↔

Hilary found her at the potluck after the service, sitting at one of the packed picnic tables outside. Across the street the skeleton of the new mega-church towered above them, its expansive parking lot littered with lengths of lumber and fat, pink rolls of insulation. It was Floyd Peyton's gift to the Carbon County First Church of God, and Daphne knew from his blueprints that it would be large enough to finally accommodate Pastor Ted's hundreds of new devotees. Even though construction was moving along rapidly, with winter on the horizon and more people joining the congregation every week it felt like the new church couldn't go up fast enough.

"Great job on the pulpit." Hilary gave her a hug that was all bouncing curls and smiles. "I'd seriously throw up if I had to get up and speak in front of everyone like that."

Daphne couldn't help laughing. "I almost did."

Hilary giggled, but her expression turned serious as she finished her lemonade. "Hey, have you seen Janie at all today?"

"No." Daphne frowned. "She hasn't been to church in ages."

"Damn it—I mean, sorry, *darn* it." Hilary shook her head. "I went up to see her this week, and she promised me she'd come."

Guilt soured in Daphne's stomach as she recalled the last time she'd seen Janie, and her cousin's accusatory words. *She* hadn't been up to the Varley house to see Janie. She'd been too busy with work and too preoccupied with Owen and the disturbing contents of her vision to make the time.

"How did she seem to you?" Daphne asked cautiously.

"Honestly?" Hilary lowered her voice and looked around, making sure the Peytons were out of earshot. "Not good. She was drinking vodka straight out of the bottle, and she looked like hell—I mean, she looked like heck. Is that even an expression? Anyway, I'm worried about her."

"Me too." Daphne pushed her plate away, her appetite gone.

"Poor Janie." Hilary shook her head sadly. "Next week I'll just go pick her up and *make* her go to church. I kind of feel like if she comes back, she'll find her faith again. Want to come with?"

"Uh . . ." Daphne shifted, the wood of the picnic bench suddenly too hard beneath her. "I don't know if I should. I'm not exactly her favorite person right now."

"Really?" Hilary cocked her head. "But she's always been crazy about you. You'd think now, with you being a prophet and all . . ."

She trailed off, leaving Daphne to shrug into the gaping silence. "I don't think she believes I'm a prophet," she said finally. "She said she thinks I'm faking it."

"Oh, well, that's just stupid." Hilary tucked a curl behind her ear. "She's going through a hard time, so she's probably lashing out. You just need to turn the other cheek, like Jesus says. You didn't take it personally, did you?"

Daphne sighed. "Maybe a little," she confessed.

"You shouldn't," Hilary insisted. "There's a whole mess of people who believe in you, people who came here from a long way off just to be near you."

Daphne shook her head. She knew that the church was growing, that people were coming to Carbon County from all over the country just to join, but that was because of Pastor Ted's new TV show, his charismatic personality, and his predictions that Carbon County would be the epicenter of the Rapture. Not because of her.

"It's true." Hilary nodded emphatically, her curls shivering. "Actually, I don't know if you know this but I started a youth group in the church. We're helping out with the new building, and we're starting a community outreach program and teen center and all sorts of stuff. *Anyway*, the kids in it are crazy about you, and they're *dying* to meet you. If, you know, you have a minute."

"You mean, now?" Daphne asked. "Are they here?"

"No, the Christian youth group decided to skip church this Sunday." A sly smile started to spread across Hilary's face, but she stopped it with a quick smack to the forehead. "Crap, I'm trying to stop being sarcastic, too. Pastor Ted says sarcasm is like a veil that hides your soul from God. But anyway, yeah, they're here, and they would *love* to meet you. They talk about you all the time. You're like a celebrity to them."

Daphne swallowed the urge to turn and run. She'd been enough of a celebrity in Detroit, when her unsmiling mug shot appeared in the paper with headlines like *Teen Killer Says, 'Not My Fault,'* to know that life in the spotlight definitely wasn't for her. She reminded herself that she had a responsibility to her church and her community, whether she'd asked for it or not. "Okay," she finally said.

"Great!" Hilary bounced to her feet and led Daphne through the crowd of picnickers to a group of teens occupying a series of overlapping blankets on the edge of the lawn.

"Guys, I want you to meet someone really special." They stopped talking at the sound of Hilary's voice. "This is Daphne Peyton, aka Carbon County's hometown prophet."

A collective gasp spread through the group. In moments they were on their feet, plates of food forgotten as they fixed her with wide smiles.

"Hi, everyone." Daphne forced a grin, raising her hand in a limp wave.

"Wow, Daphne Peyton!" The guy closest to her extended a flannel-clad arm, offering a firm handshake. His face was square and friendly, with twin dimples framing a sculpted chin. "It sure is a pleasure to meet you. I'm Mark, from Cincinnati. I can't tell you—I mean, wow, this is such an honor." Thick blond hair gleamed in the sun as he shook his head, the broad smile never leaving his face.

"You've inspired all of us." The girl next to him beamed. She wore a vintage '50s housedress printed with cherries and had braided her hair into a complicated crown that circled her head. "The relationship you have with God—it's just amazing. It makes us all want to lead better lives."

One by one, they approached her with hearty handshakes and words of praise, words that sounded like they ought to be about someone else, someone who wasn't anything like the person she felt like inside. Their Daphne was strong and brave, devout and righteous and special. She was a guiding light who brought out the goodness in others, inspiring them to follow their beliefs across the country and start organizations to help those in need. She was anything but the real Daphne, who lived on a diet of guilt and fear and looked over her shoulder with every step. Honestly, she liked their Daphne a lot better. She wished there was a way for her to actually *be* that person instead of just coming across that way.

The youth group invited her to sit, ran to fetch her lemonade, and passed her a plate of chocolate butterscotch blondies. "They're my grandma's secret recipe," giggled Monica, the girl in the vintage dress. "I put most of them out for the potluck, but they always go quick, so I kept a secret stash just in case . . ." She smiled and glanced at her knees, then back at Daphne.

"They're delicious," Daphne said honestly. She let the sugar and the youth group's chatter lull her into a comfortable haze, watched their faces animate as they volleyed around ideas for the teen center.

"We should raise money for a ping-pong table," said a Hispanic guy with sparkling brown eyes. "And have tournaments!"

"We can host dances every month, with cool themes like the Roaring Twenties and Ski Lodge Chic," Monica suggested.

"And we can do an antidrug series, but not like one of those cheesy after-school-special ones that just make everyone want to try them more," Mark added.

Monica took out an iPad and started jotting down everyone's ideas, "so we don't miss any of the awesome," she said, beaming at Daphne.

"This is what all our meetings are like," Hilary whispered in Daphne's ear. "Don't tell me you don't want in."

Daphne nodded. She could feel the positive energy in the group, and she longed to let it sweep her away. But the more they talked, the more she felt herself retreating into the emptiness inside of her, succumbing to the doubt that thrummed like a plucked guitar string through her days. She would have given anything to be like the youth group: strong and solid in their convictions, always sure that what they were doing was right.

But how could she be sure of anything? God told her one thing, but her heart said another—and the more at odds they were, the less she knew what to believe.

HIS DAD'S BUICK STILL SMELLED like dead cow and old people's breath, but Doug didn't care as long as it was driving him away from the mansion on the hill and Janie's impenetrable sadness. He pushed the passenger seat back as far as it would go and stretched out his legs, grunting with satisfaction as his toes cracked inside his Nikes.

His dad gave him the side-eye but kept his mouth shut. They'd never really seen eye to eye, but the old fart had actually started being decent to him since the wedding. All of a sudden it was like they had something in common: both tethered to Carbon County by an unwanted ball and chain, both itching to get to the world beyond those mountains but not even sure where they'd go if they did.

It didn't really surprise him when Vince Varley knocked on the door to the den earlier that evening, interrupting the game Doug was half-watching.

"Son, let's take a ride," Vince said. His frame blocked out the light filtering in from the hall, a dark silhouette in jeans and a cowboy hat.

Doug didn't argue. He just stood and left, the TV casting flickering lights across Janie's face as she snoozed on the far end of the couch, an open-mouthed lump inside her grimy sleeping bag.

Getting away from her felt good. She wasn't the Janie he'd married, the girl whose Victoria's Secret Pink panties he'd been obsessed with getting into in high school. That Janie was blond and pretty. She had big boobs, wore sexy clothes, and knew how to laugh and have a good time. This Janie was a zombie, gray skinned and foul breathed. She never laughed. She never did *anything* except give Doug a royal sense of the creeps.

If there was something he could say or do to bring the old Janie back, he would. He'd take being tethered to that chubby-cheeked Jesus freak over ghost-town Janie any day. But everything he said or did slid right down those placid cheeks like rain on a windowpane. And so he'd stopped trying, started spending more time away from the house, in bars like the Vein, where there was music and excitement, cold beer and loud laughter and the thrum of life.

"Son, open up that glove box and pull out the map." Vince's gruff command snapped him back to the Buick's leathery interior and the swirling fog outside the window.

"Dude, we're not lost." Doug made no move to follow his dad's instructions. "You've driven this road a million times."

"Not for directions." Vince's hands tightened on the wheel. "I want to show you something."

"Fine." Doug fumbled with the fancy fake-gold latch. A bulb went on inside the glove box, illuminating a single, folded county map. He took it out and spread it across his knees. "It's Carbon County. So what?"

Vince cut his eyes from the road. "Take a look right there." He tapped the map, making the paper crackle on Doug's knees. "See that spot?"

Doug squinted. Dusk was closing in outside, the sunset obscured by a heavy blanket of fog. "It's the Peyton land. I know, Dad—you want it back. That's why you started that lawsuit."

"*Screw* the lawsuit!" Vince slammed his fist hard on the wheel. "That damn lawyer's taking too long—and charging by the hour at that. That's not how the Varleys do things. We're men, Wyoming men. We take action."

"Okay, Dad." Doug rolled his eyes, but he secretly liked the way his dad said *Varley men,* his voice swollen with pride. It made Doug feel like they still meant something, he and his dad, even if the rest of the town didn't realize it. "So what's the plan this time?"

"That spot." Vince jabbed a thick finger into the map. "See where the western border falls?"

"Uh." Doug scratched at his perpetual stubble. "That's in the scrubland, like, at the base of the mountains. Right?"

"Mm-hmmm." Vince nodded. "And guess who owns the land just over that border?"

"I dunno." Doug squinted at the thin red line. "The Forest Service?"

"No, son." Vince hit the turn signal, maneuvering the Buick onto a narrow dirt road. "We do."

"Huh." Doug looked from the map to his father and then back again. "So?"

"So, that land is right next to where those damn Peytons struck oil. It was *all* ours, until my great-granddad turned around and sold that parcel to the Peytons for a dollar, like a fool."

"So you think there might be oil on our land after all?" Doug asked hopefully. Striking oil would solve all their problems. They could finish the house, and his mom would stop hounding him about getting a job, and he could finally send Janie to a shrink or something, get her the help she obviously needed.

"No, son." Vince sighed heavily. "You know the only oil in town is below Floyd's land—and don't think half this town isn't looking. But the reserves on the Peyton land: Now those are deep. Way deeper than they've drilled for."

"Huh." Doug squinted out the windshield. He didn't know what his dad was getting at, but he bet Vince would give it up soon.

"So you see," Vince continued, "if we open up our own rig on this land here, on *our* land"—he jabbed at the map again, his finger poking into Doug's thigh—"if we do that, we can run a pipeline down to *below* Floyd's well. We'll pump it out of a rig on our land, call it Varley oil, and make a mint." He laughed gruffly. "Oh, it'll be beautiful, all right. We'll drink from Floyd Peyton's milkshake, and justice will be restored."

"Hey." Doug sat back against the leather seat. "That's not a bad plan, Dad. That's actually pretty fucking genius."

"Language!" Vince snapped automatically. But he was grinning, the thrill of a newly hatched plan glowing in his eyes.

He brought the Buick to a slow stop below the old motocross track parking lot, cutting the motor and letting the car tick into silence.

"So, uh, what're we doing here?" Doug asked. The motocross track still gave him the creeps. Sure, it sucked to see his brand-new dirt bike, the one he'd only ridden once, gathering dust in the garage. But it was worth it to never have to go back to the track. There were too many bad memories there: his best buddy, Trey, dying in the race against Owen that Doug should have run himself, his wife thrashing and writhing in the firelight, about to give birth to a hideous dead thing that should have been his son. Thinking about that night made something small and hard clench inside of him. He'd run away from her that night, powerless in the face of birth, absent in the moment of death. And even though he'd never admit it, he wasn't proud of the way he'd acted. Being at the track brought it all rushing back in bright, painful flashes.

"C'mon, son." Vince was already out of the Buick and striding up the dark slope toward the parking lot. "Now's not the time to get chicken—we got business to take care of."

Doug fumbled with his seatbelt and stepped out into the cooling night. The wind picked up whispers of smoke and the cloying scent of generator fuel, night mutters and bawdy laughter from the drifters.

"Why are we here again?" Doug heard a whine creep into his voice and hoped his dad didn't notice.

"I told you." Vince didn't break stride. "Taking care of business."

Doug was a big guy and prided himself on walking like a man, fast and with purpose, but he still had to practically scamper to catch up to his dad. A low haze of light hung over the parking lot as they approached, the sickly gleam of gas lanterns throwing shadows on the earth, and bare, strung-up bulbs scattering beams into the sky. A feeling of unease gnawed at Doug's stomach, fueled by the stench from a pair of beat-up porta-potties set flush with the edge of the woods. He'd heard rumors about this place from his friends at the Vein, rumors that the guys here packed heat and didn't appreciate nonsense, rumors that knife fights were as common here as money was scarce. Heck, even stuck-up Daphne Peyton had gotten attacked here. But Vince didn't flinch as he approached a group of stringy-haired, unshaven men huddled in camp chairs around a fire that was more smoke than flame.

"Gentlemen?" Vince went right up to their circle and tipped his cowboy hat. One of the drifters, a lanky guy with a weathered face and hooknose, guffawed.

"Gentlemen? Hardly."

Vince placed his hat back on his head, undeterred. "Whatever you want to call yourselves—who here's looking for work?"

The chatter around the campfire died as a dozen pairs of eyes turned hungrily toward them. Vince had their attention now, and Doug felt his chest puff out with pride. The Varleys may not have had much, but they had something the drifters wanted.

"That's what I thought." Vince surveyed the circle with approval. "I've got a deal for you fellas—a good one. I had a little luck on a piece of land I happen to own down by the Global Oil rig. I've got a foreman and an investor, now all I need is folks to work. The first twenty able-bodied men who show up at eight A.M. tomorrow are guaranteed jobs. And just to sweeten the deal, I'll pay twenty percent more than those suckers on Floyd Peyton's rig make."

There was silence around the circle as Vince fingered his belt buckle, a self-satisfied smirk on his face. Then the drifters exploded with questions: "Where do we show up?" "How soon do we get paid?" "Is this even for real?"

"Hey." Vince held up his hands, quieting them. "It's *my* rig, and I ask the questions. Got it? I got equipment coming into the train yard outside of town. Be there at eight A.M. And have a valid driver's license, okay? I don't need the law on my back."

He turned so quickly a spume of dust spun in his wake, then he started briskly away from the camp. Doug watched him, realizing a smile had settled onto his own face as well, the first in what felt like months. He quickly wiped it clean, not wanting the drifters to think he was the type to get swept away by emotion. He'd be their boss soon, he reckoned. It was time to toughen up his game.

"See you tomorrow, boys," he said authoritatively. Then he turned and followed in his father's footsteps, back down the dark road that no longer seemed scary and ominous, to the car gleaming like a soft beacon of hope in the night. The Varleys would be on top again in no time—and boy, would it feel good to be back.

"WANT TO HIT THE CANTEEN?" Daphne loped across the hard-packed dirt toward Owen, hardhat in hand. Her hair was matted to her forehead and her black T-shirt clung to her sleek, hard curves. The rig pumped away behind her, dipping into the yielding earth and bringing up gallons of oil.

Owen's appetite surged at the sight of her—but he wasn't hungry for food.

"My truck." His voice was gruff. "Now."

Daphne looked him up and down. He'd been hauling sacks of drilling mud all morning, and his muscles were tight and hard under his thin shirt as his heart thudded from the morning's work and his sudden, all-consuming desire. He saw her take in the look in his eyes, the need for her so overwhelming it made him dizzy. Her eyes widened, and her mouth parted in soft surprise.

"We don't have much time," she said as they started toward the parking lot.

"We have enough." His voice was a low growl, and it took every fiber of his self-control not to grab her right there in front of the rig, to kiss her with all their coworkers watching.

They couldn't get into his truck fast enough. He fumbled with the keys, could barely see straight as he turned them in the ignition, hands shaking while the motor rumbled to life.

"Drive," she begged.

He peeled out, scattering gravel, and careened onto the service road that ran the perimeter of the rig's property. Five minutes later they were tucked safely into a scrubby grove of trees at the base of the mountains, soft pine needles brushing the windshield.

The motor was still dying as he reached for her, plunging his lips onto hers. He drank from her, tasting the metallic tang of sweat above her lip, running his hands over the contours of her body and up under her shirt, feeling the heat come off of her in waves as she pressed into him, moaning. He submerged himself in their kiss, the ache in his muscles melting as their bodies pressed together until there were no thoughts or feelings, no pain or memories, no nightmares or prophetic tablets or Children of the Earth—just the two of them, sealed inside his car, far away from the rest of the world.

"Hey, there are people in here!"

Owen and Daphne leapt apart, struggling to straighten their clothes. Owen turned to the window, where a face loomed like a pale moon pitted with acne scars, surrounded by choppy layers of dusty blond hair.

“Who are you?” Owen’s arm was somehow tangled in his shirt.

“I could ask you the same thing.” The man took in Owen’s skewed clothes and the way Daphne’s cheeks blazed as she adjusted the waistband of her cargo pants. He looked to be in his midtwenties, rugged in an unseasoned way, a clipboard pressed to his brown Carhartt jacket.

Owen introduced himself, coolly extending his hand.

“Dwayne.” The man gave it a hearty shake. “Are you on my list?”

He examined the clipboard, squinting, and clicked his tongue softly against his teeth. “Hmm . . . I don’t see an Owen here.”

“What is this?” Owen started to ask again. But a rumbling phalanx of construction vehicles interrupted him, roaring into the clearing carrying bags of concrete, lengths of pipe, and spidery pieces of rigging. “You guys aren’t drilling over here, are you?”

Dwayne grinned. “Sure are.”

“But,” Daphne looked up, confused, “Floyd’s not planning to expand. I just talked to him the other day.”

Dwayne shrugged. “This ain’t Floyd Peyton’s land.”

“Then who’s drilling?” Owen asked.

Daphne put a hand on his arm. “I think I know,” she said darkly. “C’mon. We have to get out of here. Break’s almost over.”

“Right.” Owen checked the time on the dashboard. “Crap. Dale’s gonna be on my ass if we’re late.” His rig’s foreman had started giving him a hard time recently, most likely influenced by Floyd’s mistrustful glances whenever he was around.

Owen turned the keys in the ignition, and the truck roared to life. "So who do you think is behind this?" he asked Daphne as he peeled away, leaving a fountain of dust in his wake.

Daphne bit her lip. "I'd bet money it's Vince Varley. This is his family's land."

"That guy?" Owen shook his head. "He'd have to be crazy. A million prospectors have been by here, and nobody found a thing."

Daphne sighed. "I don't know what he's thinking. But if I know that guy, he's got something up his sleeve."

They pulled into the parking lot, and she turned to him, her eyes dark with anger, mouth still swollen and red from their all-too-brief encounter in the scrub grove. Owen couldn't help it—he leaned forward and kissed her, his lips lingering on hers. For one sweet moment he felt her acquiesce before she tensed up and pushed him away.

"Owen, we can't." Her voice was steel, but he could hear the longing underneath. "You know how Dale is about relationships on the crew."

"I know," Owen muttered. He knew all too well. He tried to cool the fire in his blood as they walked back to the rig side by side, getting there just in time to punch back in and start a grueling afternoon of work.

Owen was on valve detail, in charge of checking pressure up and down the complex web of pipes in the rig's bowels. It was work he'd done a million times before, and he went about the task mechanically, his hands flying over the warm steel connectors, his eyes automatically scanning and recording numbers on the pressure meters.

Usually work soothed him, made him forget that he was stuck in what felt like a dead-end limbo in a one-trick town, denied the release of motocross or the relief of following the voice in his dreams, the one nudging him ever closer to the other side of town and the Children of the Earth. But with news of the latest, competing oil rig banging around his brain and Daphne's caresses a stinging, unfulfilled memory beneath his skin, even the easy repetition of hard work couldn't quiet his mind. He thought of Daphne's body, the iron of her muscles softening beneath his touch. He thought of his mother and sister and stepdad, back home in Kansas, missing him. He thought of his dream the night before, in which he'd finally seen all twelve faces of his earth siblings. He believed that meant the last one had arrived in Carbon County, and soon he'd need to figure out a way to let Daphne know.

And as much as he tried to push away the image, he thought of his sister Luna, her green eyes brimming with tears as she packed up her things to move out of the small apartment they'd shared when they first moved to town.

"Come with me, Earth Brother," she'd begged, her eyes the color of a rainforest after a storm, tears streaming down her face. "It's your destiny—*our* destiny. Once we open the Vein, all our brothers and sisters will come."

"No." He'd shaken his head, trying not to look at her, yet drawn in by the magnetic force that kept him loyal to her even as she became more and more unhinged, a force that felt stronger than loyalty and ran deeper than blood.

"Owen, please!" Luna sank to her knees then, taking both his hands in hers. "We'll finally be a family again, and we can do what we have to do to make things right."

He wanted to follow her like he wanted to win at the motocross track, like he wanted to succumb to the voice in his dreams. But he held himself back, yanking his hands from her grasp.

"I *am* making things right." He gritted his teeth against the siren song of her sobs. "I'm keeping my job at the oil rig and staying with Daphne. There's nothing you can say to stop me, so don't even try."

"Daphne!" Luna spat the name like it was poison. "That false prophet. And the oil rig! How could you? How could you go against your nature like that?" She looked up at him from beneath a colorful veil of dreadlocks. "That oil is the blood of our father. It's the blood of the earth."

The blood of the earth. The phrase echoed in Owen's mind as he balanced on the rig's scaffolding high above the ground, reaching to turn the metal wheel that would tighten one of the valves.

The wheel broke off at his touch, tumbling from the pipe like a ripe apple falling from a tree.

"Heads up!" Owen screamed to the workers below. He dimly heard the echoing ping as it bounced over metal beams, but in seconds a rumbling roar overshadowed it. Owen turned back to the valve. With a sinking feeling, he realized it was trembling, shaking from the pressure of oil building up in the pipe behind it.

Without a wheel there was no way to adjust the pressure. The trembling grew in force as he fumbled in his tool belt for a wrench, bucking and shaking as if the rig's metal scaffolding wanted to throw him to the ground.

He had just wrapped his hand around the wrench when the valve burst, sending geysers of thick, warm oil spewing into the air.

For a moment he was blind. The oil was in his eyes, turning his vision scarlet, filling his nostrils with a warm, spicy scent. *Oil is the blood of the earth,* his brain whispered as he swiped it away, smearing it across his cheeks, his vision still blurred. He forced the idea to the back of his mind and tried to stop the leak with his hand, watching in horror as oil seeped out between his fingers.

There was something wrong with it, something deeply wrong. The oil wasn't black and tarry, like it should have been. It didn't have the telltale smell of crude, a moldering organic scent that made him think of dinosaurs slowly fossilizing in the earth. It was thick and red, and its scent was metallic.

Oil is the blood of the earth.

There was no time to analyze. The pressure under his hand was building, pulsing against his palm. It would only be a matter of seconds before he couldn't hold it off on his own anymore.

Ordinarily he would have reached for the wheel, twisting it until the valve closed and the flow went back to normal. But with the crucial piece a dozen stories below, he'd have to improvise. He struggled to close the wrench over one of the bolts where the wheel had been attached, but the oil made everything slippery, impossible to grip. After several attempts he tore off his T-shirt, the seams screaming as they ripped. Bunching it up in his hand, he used the soaked cloth to wipe down the valve, rushing to clamp the wrench in place before the next gush could soak it in thick, slippery oil.

Biceps straining, he yanked on the wrench's handle, hoping the leverage would compensate for the missing wheel. He felt a muscle in his shoulder flicker as the valve refused to budge, and pain spilled through him. He kept pulling through it, trying to coax the valve with his mind as well as his aching arms.

"C'mon, I know you want to move," he muttered at it.

He visualized the valve spinning slowly shut even as the pain in his shoulder grew to a roar. He was about to give up and radio for help when he felt something start to yield beneath his grip.

"You want to move." The words were clearer now, crowding everything else from his mind. The pain in his shoulder and the pounding in his heart and the clanging, screaming commotion below him faded away, and it was just him and the broken valve, a battle between his mind and the metal before him.

"You want to move," he said again, out loud, and as the bolt began to budge he knew with a searing, tingling certainty that he was going to win.

Shaking and straining, the veins in his arms popping with effort, he managed to bring the wrench in a full circle, shutting the valve. The last spurt of oil sputtered out around the opening, and he found himself standing limp and exhausted at the top of the derrick, the machinery around him drenched in thick, viscous liquid.

"Hey, what the hell happened up there?" Dale was below him, hands cupped to his mouth as he called up to Owen. "You wanna get down here and explain?"

Owen's blood felt thick and electric as he climbed down the side of the derrick. He knew this feeling: It was the same sensation he'd gotten when he'd freed himself from Daphne's seizure grip. Maybe it was adrenaline—but he'd felt adrenaline before, plenty of times on the motocross track. This was something else, something more powerful.

He was less than a story from the ground when he saw that a crowd had gathered around Dale, and the closer he got to them, the more their faces twisted in horror.

"What?" Owen knew he was dirty and sweaty, shirtless and covered head to toe in oil, his arm moving a little slow from the pain in his shoulder. But that was nothing new. Minor injuries were common on the rig, and every single one of them left work each day smeared in crude.

He started toward his crew, but they all stepped back, terror etched across their faces. Only Dale stood his ground, something between fear and resolve flashing in his sun-faded blue eyes.

"What's going on?" Owen asked again. He looked down at himself, expecting to see oil snaking in trails across his chest and puddling in the dents between his muscles.

Instead, he saw blood.

"Oh." The sound escaped in a slow puff of breath. He held out his hands and saw that they, too, were soaked in scarlet, the blood already coagulating between his fingers. His jeans, his shoes, all of it . . . covered in blood.

"Everyone back to work!" Dale hollered. The crew scattered, leaving him alone with the foreman in front of the rig.

Owen ran a hand down his chest, searching for a cut. But there was no cut. *The oil is the blood of the earth,* he thought, chilling the sweat on the back of his neck.

"You find where that blood's coming from?" Dale's voice was thick with suspicion.

"Not yet," Owen admitted.

Dale's eyes narrowed. "Well, there sure is a lot of it. Want to tell me what happened up there?"

"I was just checking the valves," Owen began, "and I guess my mind was wandering a little, and I thought . . ." He trailed off mid-sentence. He'd thought *the oil is the blood of the earth,* and now he was covered in blood, blood that had gushed from an oil pipeline, blood that should have been oil.

He'd thought: *You know you want to move,* and the bolt had moved.

Something was happening to him, something he didn't know how to control and couldn't understand. The dull roar of fear pounded in his ears, almost drowning out Dale's next words.

"Your mind's been wandering a lot lately." Dale's tone was flinty. "You think I don't see what's going on with you and Daphne, but I do, and I don't like it. Floyd wouldn't like it either, if he knew, and he's the one I answer to."

Owen looked down at his boots, where blood was drying to a rusty stain on the toes. "I know, Dale. I'm sorry. I'll keep it off the rig from now on, I promise."

"Yeah." Dale shoved his hands deep into his pockets, refusing to meet Owen's eyes. "It's not just that. I *wish* it were just that. But this . . ." He gestured at Owen's blood-soaked clothes and heaved a deep sigh. "People are saying things about you: that you're not an ordinary guy, that you're touched by the devil. There's a lot of talk in this town, and I don't like to listen, but all this blood and no cut: I gotta say, that gives me the creeps."

"So what are you saying?" The electricity in Owen's limbs had relocated to his brain, buzzing so loud he could barely process Dale's words. All he knew was that they weren't good.

Dale looked up finally, regret in his eyes. "I'm going to have to let you go, Owen. I'm a fair guy, so I'll let you go with an extra week's wages, but that's the best I can do. I'm sorry."

Owen felt a storm building in his chest, anger clouding his vision.

"You mean, I'm fired?" he shot back. "Just like that? After being one of the best roughnecks you've had since this thing opened?"

"I wouldn't call it being fired." Dale struggled to keep his voice even. "Think of it as a leave of absence. Once this all blows over, you're welcome back."

"Whatever." Owen kicked at the ground, feeling the electricity build and throb in his veins. "I know how to call a spade a spade. I'm so glad I just practically killed myself trying to keep your rig from exploding."

He turned and stalked off, the storm inside him gaining power, threatening to spill out into the world. Dale called after him, but he refused to turn around, afraid that if he did it would be his fists instead of his mouth doing the talking. He had to get out of there. The currents zinging through his body thrummed with rage as he ran for the parking lot, blood squelching in his boots.

His breath came in jagged gasps as he jumped in his truck and slammed the door. In the corner of his rearview mirror he saw

Daphne running after him, calling his name, but he couldn't stop even for her, not then. He needed to be alone with his thoughts and his rage, to put as much distance between himself and the oil rig and Carbon County as possible before the surging, strangely addictive power took over and turned him into something he didn't recognize. Something strange and dangerous. Something he'd sworn to himself he would never become.

↔

Daphne stopped running, tasting the dust from Owen's tires and feeling his sudden absence like a cavity in her heart. She knew something had happened, something bad, and she'd wanted to comfort him ever since the rumor that something had happened to him started zinging through the rig.

But something in his eyes had stopped her when he strode past, something monstrous. It was more than anger—it was molten rage, rage that could tremble mountains, the same evil glare she'd seen in her vision. It was only when his back was turned and he was walking away from her that she'd regained the will to run after him, but by then it was too late. She saw his eyes meet hers in the rearview mirror, but then he was gone, the truck accelerating out of the parking lot and racing away down the road.

“Owen.” She whispered his name, small and hopeless within the vast ring of mountains. Fear and pain dug into her flesh like nails, making her choke on her breath and clutch at her arms. It felt like her skin was tearing open and her guts were spilling out into the dust, and as she opened her mouth to scream, her eyes rolled back in her head and, for the second time that week, her vision went black.

Vision of the Great Divide

And yea, the ground shall rumble and trees shall fall

And a great fissure will open in the earth.

On one side, the Children of God raise

Weapons of justice, defending the divine;

On the other, the Children of the Earth

Chant to their demon god,

Raising Beelzebub from the pits of Hell

To destroy the righteous.

The earth shall tremble

And the fissure shall grow,

Releasing fire and demons

Brought unto us by the Children of the Earth.

And yea, my child, my prophet,

When the fissure opens and the earth divides

You shall find yourself on the side of evil,

Separated from the righteous by a crack in the land.

You shall tremble,

As the demon children reach for you

With scaly claws

And green hellfire in their eyes.

In this moment of truth

Your heart shall divide

Like the crack in the earth

And in this moment you must choose

Heaven or hell?

Good or evil?

The holy light of the divine

Or the stain of Satan upon your soul?

10

MANAGING A BAR WAS LIKE having a permanent ear to the pipeline of Carbon County gossip. Booze loosened lips, and as the taps flowed and the night wore on, the patrons of the Vein spilled more secrets than drinks. Even without their collected powers, the Children of the Earth knew exactly how many gallons of crude oil the Peyton rig pumped each day, who was prospecting where and how little success they'd had, which of the drifters had been fighting up at the old motocross track and who had won. They knew every item on the police blotters, every new face that rolled through Elmer's Gas 'n' Grocery, every starry-eyed born-again who joined Pastor Ted's flock. They even knew who occupied beds in the county hospital and what (or who) had put them there.

Luna had planned to use Kimo's powers of location to find her missing contractor, the one with one gray eye and one brown, but the rumor mill whispered everything she needed to know. She caught snippets of conversations: "beat up by a girl" . . . "that chick who works the Peyton rig, the one they call a prophet" . . . "strangled him with her own two hands, put 'im in a coma" . . . "they say she was having a seizure, that her strength came from God" . . . "in the county hospital, not sure if he'll pull through" . . . "good riddance if he doesn't, attacking a woman like that."

It was enough. In the blustery cold of an autumn afternoon she wrapped herself in her moss-colored cloak and borrowed Ciaran's rusty Honda, soothing herself with old Grateful Dead tunes as she drove to the hospital, humming dreamily along.

In a sterile white room she found her contractor unconscious, his neck covered in bruises: purple where Daphne's fingers had pressed into his flesh, yellow around the edges where the blood had ceased to flow. The hospital had washed his hair, so that the thin strands fanned gently behind him on the pillow, fluttering with the even push and pull of an oxygen tube that fit over his nose and mouth. Even with his eyes closed, it was obviously him: the nobody who had drifted into the Vein one night and promised to do anything she asked of him, anything at all.

Now he'd left her with an even bigger mess than before. There was no telling what he'd remember or where his loyalties would lie when he came out of the coma, and if Luna's name was on his lips, she'd have a lot of explaining to do.

She sighed, taking one of his limp hands in hers, flinching as his yellowed nails brushed her palm. It was hard to control someone unconscious, their will buried beneath layers of beta waves thick as winter quilts. But with her Earth Brothers and Sisters around her at last, her power was growing. She drew energy through her throat chakra, the center of communication, and felt it vibrate within her body and flow through her fingers. Blue was the color of communication—a bright, clear blue that pulsed with clarity and intention—and so it was a blue light that started in her throat chakra and flooded her senses, eventually spilling out into the hospital room and bathing the unconscious man lying below her in its glow. As waves of power surged between them, she located his will, withered to the size of a pea, weakened almost to extinction.

She spoke to him silently through the pulsing blue light, sending him a message of surrender, telling him that it was okay to let go, that only machines stood between him and eternal peace.

Like iron being smelt in a furnace, she felt the shell of his will bend to her message. His hand went cold in hers, and the blips on the heart rate monitor above his bed slowed, then flatlined, filling the room with a loud, dull, endless tone. Her work was done: The contractor had slipped from this world into the next, taking with him a story that would never see the light of day.

An alarm sounded, and a flashing red light blinked to life over the door, illuminating the room in a candy-cane glare. A cry of "Code blue!" keened from the nurse's station, and Luna ducked out of the room and walked quickly down the hall, her boots flowing silently over the white tile floor.

Working her magic always left her feeling a little spacey and light-headed afterward, like the air around her was made of feathers. She almost collided with a team of nurses and doctors thundering down the hall.

"Excuse me," she murmured, shrinking out of the way. She thought gratefully of the warm, cozy loft above the Vein, of the strength she'd find in her family. Soon she'd be home, and the necessary business with the contractor would be nothing more than a vaguely unpleasant memory, one more tiny battle in her war to save the earth.

A fat-fingered hand closed tightly on her shoulder, and she jerked her head up, emitting a small gasp. She found herself looking into a piggish pair of eyes, shadowed by the brim of a policeman's cap.

"Where do you think *you're* going, little missy?" the sheriff sneered.

Luna stood tall, resisting the urge to sink her fingernails into the fleshy back of his hand. "Home," she said simply.

"And just what were you doing here in the first place?"

"Visiting a friend."

"Who?" The sheriff's breath smelled of halitosis and lard.

Luna had been to enough protests to know her rights. "May I ask why I'm being detained?" she asked politely.

The sheriff's face went from the sickly color of pizza dough to a furious purple. "Listen, you don't ask the questions around here. *I* do. Got that? Now you're coming with me, and you'll keep your mouth shut until I tell you to talk, and when I tell you to talk you'll tell me the truth, the whole truth, and nuthin' but the truth. You got all that?"

Before she could answer he grasped her arm roughly and yanked her into an empty hospital room, slamming the door behind them. He tossed her across the room so that she half-flew, half-stumbled against the bed, her hip slamming into the steel railing. Vines of pain blossomed down her leg as she looked up to find him blocking the door, an ugly sneer spreading above the collar of his uniform.

Luna found her balance and leaned back against the bed, letting her cloak fall open. Underneath it she wore a midriff-baring halter top and a long, flowing skirt that rode low on her hips, her legs clearly visible through the sheer fabric. The sheriff's mouth dropped, and she watched his Adam's apple bob as he swallowed a long, deep gulp.

It was almost pathetic how easy it was to control men. Half the time she didn't even need to use her powers—just flash a little skin, bat a few eyelashes, and they were eating out of her palm.

"Now what did you want to ask me, officer?" she purred, sliding her body against the hospital bed in a way that made sweat glisten on the cop's forehead.

"Uh . . ." The sheriff struggled to regain control. "Well, it's awful suspicious that you're here, see. Cause there are only two people in the ICU you could be visiting right now, and one of 'em's just a baby with a high fever. I think you're here for that guy, the one in a coma."

"And what if I am?" Luna tossed her head.

"Well." The sheriff's eyes roamed up and down her body as he struggled to formulate a reply. "He's in here 'cause he attacked a girl, see? And if you're his friend, you might know something about it."

"How do you know he attacked her?" Her throat chakra was exhausted, but she breathed into it nonetheless, feeling the blue aura of persuasion turn the air around her cool and vibrant. It sensed the sheriff's desire and lapped at it greedily, drawing it out like a leech suckling blood.

"Well . . . 'cause she says so, that's how." The sheriff took a step forward as she undulated against the bed, sending blue tendrils of light deep into his mind. She cocked an eyebrow, daring him to go on, and laughed on the inside as he struggled to catch his train of thought. "She says it, and she's got witnesses," he finished lamely.

"Did they witness an attack? From start to finish?"

"Well, no, not exactly. The guy I questioned said he came in when the two of them were on the ground and she had her hands around his neck. There was a knife there that I guess he was going to use on her."

Luna's breath was a silk thread pulling the sheriff toward her. The suspicion had vanished from his eyes, replaced with an eager, blazing need, and she visualized his opinion changing, curving in the direction of hers until they were train tracks running parallel into the distance.

"You know about Daphne Peyton, though, don't you?" She tilted her head, engulfing him in the cool jade of her gaze. "This isn't the first time she's tried to kill a man and call it self-defense."

"I—I guess I did know that," the sheriff stuttered.

"She may look innocent," Luna continued, "but she's murdered before. And if you don't keep a close eye on her, she might do it again."

The sheriff was inches from her face now, eyes popping as he tried to take all of her in: her body, her eyes, her story. He didn't notice the blue light radiating from her in waves and giving the room an underwater glow, entering his mouth and ears and nostrils and locating his centers of desire, pulling them from him on invisible currents.

"I guess I never thought of it that way." His voice was wooden. "I—I'm really sorry, miss. I shouldn't have detained you like that. You—you'll let me know if there's any way I can make it up to you."

She could have let him go then, her mission complete. She could have gone home to the warmth and safety of the loft above the Vein, to the open and adoring arms of her family. But the blue light had found something else in him, something unexpected: a desire that cut deeper than lust or power, a desire stronger and more powerful than them all.

"Actually," she whispered, wrapping the shriveled remnant of his soul in an indigo web, "there *is* something you can do for me."

"What?" His mouth barely moved.

"Go back to the station and file all of this in a report. Then meet me at Hatchett Lake tomorrow at sunset."

Luna waited until he nodded his understanding. Then she brushed by him and glided out the door, leaving the sheriff frozen and open-mouthed, staring at an empty hospital bed.

11

THE NEEDLE ON HIS GAS gauge was pushing toward empty when Owen finally returned to Carbon County. He'd lost count of the time spent barreling down highways and climbing abandoned back roads, the blood caking dry on his clothes and his knuckles white on the steering wheel, every mile unleashing a new torrent of questions.

He'd been going well over the speed limit, but his truck still couldn't go fast enough to staunch the waves of anger and fear broiling in his blood. Even with the windows rolled down and the wind whipping against his cheek, he felt like a lobster boiling in a pot. There was only one true release when life got this tangled, and it was a release he'd denied himself for too long.

Not bothering to change clothes or shower off the blood, he grabbed his old leather jacket and wheeled his vintage Husqvarna out of the garage. Even after months of neglect, the chrome accents winked at him in the pale beam of his porch light, an old friend welcoming him back. The bike felt warm and pliant under him as he settled into the saddle and kicked it to life, its metal frame yielding in a way that even Daphne never could, a way that whispered of being at his mercy, a minion of his will and his alone.

The cool autumn afternoon embraced him as he flew over back roads, dipping and leaping to avoid potholes. The wind tousled his hair and crackled the changing leaves, filling him with elation he hadn't known since the town had shut down the track and he'd had to relegate his bike to the garage. As the Husqvarna gathered speed, he felt his thoughts begin to slow and untangle, the adrenaline working its way into the steady focus that had won him first place at countless races across America before Carbon County and Daphne had claimed his soul.

Within minutes he was at the drifters' camp, maneuvering the bike around weather-beaten tents and trailers, immune to the dirty looks and dirtier words the prospectors flung his way. The gate to the track loomed before him, the rusted eye of the padlock glowering a dare.

Revving his engine, he sped toward the gate, gripping the bike between his knees. He nosed the wheels off the ground, and a moment later he was airborne, the gate's metal arm receding beneath him as he lunged toward the stars. *I wish I could stay this way forever*, he thought in the middle of the jump: suspended in the air, in that moment when speed overtakes gravity and time slows, when everything seems to stop.

He braced himself to land, but instead of coming down on the other side of the gate his bike rose higher into the air, past the point where gravity ought to have caught and landed it.

The earth rushed away, the pitted and unkempt motocross track smoothing to a dark ribbon below him. Thin, cold air rubbed his cheeks raw and froze his breath. The ground was so far away it looked like a map crinkled by mountains, and still he continued to rise.

I wish I could stay this way forever. The words, his thoughts from just moments before, pounded in his brain.

"Get down!" he croaked, the wind coating his tongue with dust and swallowing his voice.

He pressed on the handlebars with his full weight, trying to force the bike to land. "Please," he whispered. "Get down now."

The bike gave a rambunctious buck. Its front wheel lowered, plunging him into free fall, the backdraft biting Owen's cheeks as the motocross track came screaming up at him.

"No!" he cried, desperately trying to reorganize his thoughts.

He closed his eyes and tried not to think of his bike crashing and burning on the ground, his body breaking into pieces along with it. His only chance at survival was a soft landing.

"Get down *gently*!" he screamed. He pictured a parachute opening above him, dragging at the air. He imagined the needle on his speedometer plunging out of the red, his wheels dropping soft as a rabbit in the dirt, and as the image took hold and dug into the recesses of his brain he could swear he felt his velocity slacken and the rush of air slow against his face.

It was only with the soft bump of his wheels hitting the ground that he dared open his eyes. His heartbeat, suspended by fear until that moment, crashed against his rib cage and thudded in his ears, drowning out the buzz of his motor as he careened toward the track's sharpest hairpin turn.

Reflexes and adrenaline took over, and he swooped the bike around the curve, his shoulder nearly brushing the ground. As he settled into the rhythm of the track, guiding the Husqvarna by instinct over the jumps and berms, he tried to make sense of what had just happened.

His thoughts had power: That much was clear. At first he'd thought it was coincidence, or adrenaline—something that could be explained by biology or physics if only he looked hard enough for an answer. But it had happened too many times to be coincidence, and there were too many patterns. His mind skimmed over the time he'd unwrapped Daphne's hands from his neck in the throes of her seizure, and the scary few moments after Trey's death when Doug had attacked him and Owen threw Doug high into the air, seemingly by will alone.

He'd imagined oil as blood, and blood had gushed from the oil rig. He'd pictured the bolt turning under his hand, and it had.

A fleeting wish to stay in a jump forever had loosened the grip of gravity and sent him skyward. And when he decided he wanted to come down, he plummeted back to the ground.

Each time, it started with a simple thought: a thought that stuck like a song in his brain and unfurled in rich detail before coming true before his eyes. Was he—could he be—somehow controlling the world around him with his mind?

The idea rippled goose bumps down his arms as he sped around the track, the bike swooping through turns like a bird of prey looking for its next meal. Things were weird enough in Carbon County without him discovering unwanted superpowers. And yet . . . he wanted more. Under his skin he sizzled with the need to experiment, to see just how much he could really do.

He had to know.

He was coming up on the old berms, deliberately sculpted mounds that had washed away when the track fell into disrepair and were now filled with rainwater several inches deep. Squinting at the puddles, he wondered if he could turn water solid, if he could give himself a smooth ride across simply by picturing the puddles turning to dirt.

Turn to dirt. The words took shape in his mind as he focused on the puddles, and he began to feel energy gather in his skull. The water shimmered, its molecules buzzing confused circles as his bike bore down. His front wheel nosed into the berms and he braced himself, waiting for a splash.

But none came. He sped through, and only dust swirled in his wake.

Owen yanked the bike to a hard stop and turned to stare at the place where the puddle had been. Dirt gazed back at him, marred only by a thin strip of tread-mark from his tires.

It wasn't a coincidence or an illusion: He really could control matter with his mind.

All he had to do was learn to harness his skill, to control it instead of letting it control him, and there was no telling how far it could go. He could be something more than just Owen, a confused nineteen-year-old who had just lost his job. He could be more than just the boyfriend of Daphne the Prophet, more than someone who used to win a motocross race every now and then. He could be more than human. He could be a god.

He felt strong, pumped, like he was made of stars. He laughed, and it rang out clear and high through the valley.

And then, just to see what would happen, he slowed his breath and imagined the atoms on the ground shivering back into liquid. Seconds later, a wavering reflection of his face stared up at him from the spot where the puddle had reappeared.

Owen's laugh died in his throat. The face that stared back at him was twisted into a demonic grin. His skin was an otherworldly white, glowing moon-pale, and dark circles lurked beneath his eyes. But it was his eyes themselves that made him gasp, his eyes that made bile rise from his gut and coat the back of his throat. They were neon green and lit up like laser beams, piercing the air and illuminating everything around him in a sickly glare that hinted at other, eviler worlds: worlds beneath the earth, and under his skin.

He staggered back, away from the puddle he'd called into existence with his mind. Moaning, clutching at his face and covering his eyes, he sank to his knees on the cold dirt track.

↔

Daphne's eyes snapped open. The images from her vision—a great divide in the earth, separating the Children of God from the Children of the Earth; chanting and fire and demons and weapons and her on the wrong side, forced to choose—faded against the skim-milk gray of the afternoon sky, making her squint in the sudden light.

She tasted dust in her mouth and looked around. She must have fallen by the side of the road when the vision overtook her; in the background she could hear the rig clanging and the voices of her coworkers calling to one another as they went about their afternoon. Likely, nobody had been around to witness her fall or see her seizing, and she was glad for that. She didn't want their concern right then—or, worse, another trip to the hospital. She'd been on a mission to talk to Owen after he stormed off the rig covered in blood. She had to find him and make sure he was okay.

Her head spun as she stood, trying to ignore the black spots dancing in her eyes and the dark, terrible images from her vision still raking at the corners of her mind. They clawed at her while she walked unsteadily to her car, her legs shaky beneath her, and sank into the driver's seat.

Why were these visions stalking her, and what did they mean? She knew what Pastor Ted would say: that it was because she was a prophet, blessed with messages from God. But the visions didn't *feel* like a blessing: They felt like a puzzle made of pieces that didn't fit together or were missing entirely, a puzzle that she'd never be able to finish or that would be too awful to look at if she did.

Yet she couldn't let it go. Her latest vision consumed her as she drove through town, searching for answers as she scanned the streets for Owen's truck. She had seen a crack in the earth, with Pastor Ted's congregation, the Children of God, brandishing weapons on one side and the Children of the Earth dancing and chanting on the other. Was this the Great Divide that had been predicted in the tablet, the one it claimed would herald a great battle between good and evil that would ultimately determine the fate of the world? It seemed so far-fetched, so improbable. She would have dismissed it entirely as delusions brought on by her seizure . . . if everything else predicted by the tablet hadn't already come true.

The Great Battle, the Great Divide: These were the events the tablet warned of. Now it seemed like her visions were synching up.

But she thought that she was one of the Children of God, that she was supposed to lead them through the great battle. So why, in her vision, was she on the wrong side?

She turned, finally, into the one place in Carbon County where she least wanted to go, a place that made the hair on the back of her neck stand up and her stomach clench in nervous knots. She hadn't been back to the old motocross track since she'd been attacked there, triggering her first seizure and, with it, her first vision. Still, she knew it was where Owen would have gone—where she should have been looking for him all along. She knew that he needed her then, even if he was too tough to admit it. And, in the wake of her vision, she needed him, too.

Sure enough, she could hear the keening whine of his dirt bike over the prospectors' gas generators and campfires. She knew better than to cut through their camp again, so instead she took a little-used path through the woods, her feet crunching on dry branches and her heartbeat echoing in her ears.

She broke, panting, through the barrier of trees and paused on the rusting bleachers as Owen's bike tore around a bend.

He was helmet-less, still covered in blood, his body tensed with concentration. Crows' wings of hair flapped in his wake. Even if she'd waved and shouted, she knew he wouldn't have noticed her. His eyes blazed. Maybe it was just a trick of the light, but for a moment it seemed like there were flames dancing in his pupils.

His bike seemed to paw at the ground as he bore down on a puddle, his eyes green pinpricks of light. She winced, anticipating a splash—but it never came. Milliseconds before his wheels hit the puddle, the water transformed to solid dirt.

Daphne sat down, hard, on the bleachers.

She must be seeing things. Maybe the vision earlier had messed with her mind.

She hugged her thin shirt around her shoulders as Owen stopped the bike and dismounted. She watched him approach the depression where the puddle had been, the light from his eyes bathing the track before him in a sickly underwater green that made her stomach twist and clench. He seemed to grow taller as he regarded the dirt by his feet, his shoulders widening until it looked like he'd swallowed all the space on the track.

Daphne flashed back to her first vision, of Owen larger than life by the oil rig, holding up his hands to draw a raging fire down from the mountains. The Owen standing below her now was the same Owen she'd seen then, in those dark, terrifying moments when her eyes rolled back in her head and she hovered between two worlds. He was wholly different from the Owen she'd fallen in love with, who was kind and caring underneath his leather jacket and grim half smile. It wasn't just that figure below her, and the one in her vision, didn't look like Owen—he didn't even look *human.*

He stared down at the place where the puddle had been, and a twisted grin split his face, a carnival distortion of his usual smile. He laughed: a metallic, staccato sound that filled the track and made Daphne want to throw her hands over her ears. Then the light from his eyes focused into laser beams, boring into the dirt by his feet. The earth there shimmered, rearranging itself—and suddenly, the puddle was filled with water again.

Daphne and Owen gasped at the same time as his reflection stared up at him. She watched as the smile vanished from his face and the neon light faded from his eyes. He stumbled back, falling to his knees and covering his face with his hands. So he had seen it, too. It wasn't just her imagination, wasn't leftover hallucinations from her vision earlier that day. Owen knew as well as she did that something was wrong.

She called to him, and he jerked to attention, scanning the bleachers. The eyes that found her were his regular eyes, that clear emerald green she'd grown to love even though she knew it marked him as a Child of the Earth.

"Daphne." Relief and fear flooded his voice, and they stood at the same time, rushing to each other, her feet scrambling and slipping on the steep slope down to the track. She half-fell into him when she reached the bottom, and as his arms closed around her she couldn't tell where her trembling stopped and his began, which of the two heartbeats thudding violently between them was hers and which was his.

"Are you okay?" His voice was tight.

"I don't know." She raised her eyes to his, half-terrified that she'd find the beast from her vision again. But it was just Owen, *her* Owen, looking down at her, his lips a thin, worried line. "What *was* that? That thing with the puddle, and the dirt, and your eyes?"

"I wish I knew." Owen's weight sagged against her, and Daphne realized suddenly just how rough he looked: His eyes were dark and sunken, surrounded by bruise-colored circles, and dried blood still coated his jeans. "It's so messed up. *Everything's* so messed up."

She held him tight, smelling the fear burning off of him and wanting to make it right. But her own fear got in the way, tangled up in images of his neon-blazing eyes and a fire by the rig and a great divide separating the Children of God from the Children of the Earth, images from real life and her visions mingling until she could barely tell what was real and what had happened in the darkness behind her rolled-back eyes.

"That thing you did, turning the water to dirt and then back again," she started. "Was that . . . did you ever do anything like that before?"

"Not on purpose." Owen spoke into her neck, muffling his voice. "I don't know what's happening to me. It's like, I think these things and then they happen. I just wanted to see if I could control it, just that one time. And I guess the scary thing is, I could."

Daphne stepped back, away from him, pulling her shirt tighter around her shoulders. Flaming reminders of her first vision licked at the edges of her mind: Owen controlling a raging fire without touching it, bringing it closer to the rig. Now, with this new revelation, her vision was one step closer to coming true.

"Do you think you could control fire?" She sounded weak, almost pleading. She couldn't tell him how much she wanted the answer to be no.

Owen shook his head sadly. "I kind of have this feeling like I could control *anything* if I concentrate hard enough."

"This can't be happening." Her words were a low moan. He drew back, hurt percolating in his eyes.

"It's just that"—she forced a hint of gentleness into her tone—"there's this thing, something I didn't tell you before." She reached for his hand, tracing the course of his calluses, the damp flesh in the apple of his palm. It was only then, with his hand safe in hers, that she told him the whole truth about her first vision: about how the shadow hadn't been just any shadow. It was him.

He paled as she spoke, and his hand grew slack in hers.

"I'm worried about what you could become," she finished.

"Me too." His whisper wasn't much more than a vibration against her cheek. "It's bad because it feels good. Because it feels like I'm being true to myself somehow," he continued. "Like this is who I'm really supposed to be."

The words buckled her knees, making her sit down hard on

the packed dirt of the track. "Because of where you were born," she prompted. "Because of the Children of the Earth."

Guilt flashed in Owen's eyes as he joined her on the ground.

"Is there something you need to tell me?" she asked. His silence stretched across the valley. "Something about the Children of the Earth?"

Owen's shoulders slumped. "I guess we've both been keeping secrets to protect each other."

"Tell me." Daphne gave his hand a squeeze.

He let out a ragged breath. "The Children of the Earth are here. All of them. They work with Luna up at the Vein. I've seen them around town, but also in my dreams. It's how I know they're so close."

Daphne paled. "All of them?"

He nodded miserably.

"How long have they been here?"

"The last one showed up a few days ago."

She snatched her hand away. "Why didn't you tell me?"

Owen dug his elbows into his knees, resting his head in his hands. "I didn't want you to have to choose," he said finally. "Between staying with me and . . . I didn't want to put you in that position. I guess—I was afraid that you wouldn't choose me."

She looked at Owen, at the sad curve of his back, and even through her frustration she felt love for him run warm in her blood. "Maybe I don't have to choose," she said softly, wishing she could fully believe her own words. "I just wish I knew how dangerous they really are. What if they can do what you do?"

Owen leaned forward and tucked a strand of hair behind her ear. "There is a way to find out."

"You want to go there?" The thought of meeting the Children of the Earth made something dark and foreboding churn in her gut, but maybe if she knew what she was really up against she'd be able to figure out what to do. If they were gearing up for a showdown like the tablet suggested and Pastor Ted seemed to believe, then maybe she'd still have time to warn the congregation, so that they could protect themselves. Maybe, with Owen's help, they could put a stop to all of this before it even began.

Owen's jaw set in determination. "I think I should."

"*We* should," Daphne corrected him.

"No." Owen shook his head. "They'll trust me if I go alone. You know Luna keeps begging me to work there. And now that I got laid off at the rig, I'll have an excuse."

Doubt tugged at Daphne's stomach. She didn't like the idea of Owen going to the Vein alone; she'd seen how vulnerable he could be around Luna, how torn he still seemed about abandoning his sister.

"I'll just go up for an afternoon," he assured her. "Pretend I'm interested in a job, ask a few casual questions, and report everything back to you. Like your own personal private eye."

He flashed a tentative smile, relaxing something small and hard that had been growing inside of her ever since her first vision. He was doing this for her—for both of them. If she didn't trust him, who *could* she trust?

"I'll go tomorrow," he said. It looked like the color was starting to return to his cheeks, but maybe it was just the bite of the wind.

"Okay." She traced the line of his jaw, the first whisper of the next day's beard scratchy beneath her fingers. "Just don't forget who you're working for."

A familiar look of desire flashed across his face. "Impossible," he said.

She reached for him, and he was there, strong and solid, holding her, kissing her, letting her heart pound and clash against his.

12

AS OWEN AND DAPHNE SANK into their kiss at the abandoned motocross track, Heather Anderson found herself in a cargo van jouncing along a high mountain road, the Children of the Earth stuffed in close around her. Aura drove, with Luna in the passenger seat, staring out the window and nearly vibrating with anticipation.

From atop a spare tire, bracing herself against the van's paneled side, Abilene led them in an old folk song. Her voice was throaty and grainy and thick, and even though Heather had never been much of a singer, she gladly joined the tangle of voices.

She'd been with the Children of the Earth for five days, but it may as well have been five years. She'd fallen effortlessly into the routine of cocktail waitressing at the Vein each night and sinking onto a mattress beside her brothers and sisters after the bar closed, their breath mingling in a tender lullaby. Each morning Luna woke them up early: There was cooking and laundry to do, the bar had to be restocked and the dishes washed. In the afternoon they took long walks together outside, breathing in all of nature's beauty as Luna swept her arms across the wild mountain panoramas to remind them that this was what was at stake, this was the world they would lose if their father, the God of the Earth, was defeated.

There was so much lost time to catch up on, so much to learn. Heather drank in stories of her childhood on the commune with a dizzy thirst, sat motionless for hours as Luna taught her meditations to clean and purify her mind. She was dimly aware that she ought to have completed freshman orientation, should have been all moved into her dorm and registered for classes. But college seemed far away and irrelevant, a hazy memory from another lifetime.

It was only in the chilly hours before dawn, with the bar's noise and activity still buzzing in her head and her siblings crashed soundly beneath their patchwork quilts all around her, that it occurred to Heather to wonder what had happened to her. Thoughts of her parents, anxious at not hearing from her, scratched at her mind, and doubts about the Children of the Earth and her place among them made her toss and turn until she fell finally into an exhausted sleep no longer tainted with terrifying dreams. Those had stopped the moment she reached Carbon County, as soon as she found herself among the people she knew to be her true family.

"We're here," Luna announced. The Children of the Earth braced themselves as the van turned sharply and came to a halt, pebbles plinking against its underside. They tumbled out of the rear doors, and the scent of pine engulfed them, its freshness a welcome relief after the gasoline-smelling closeness of the cargo hold.

Hatchett Lake glittered before them, surrounded by mountains that cupped it like a woman's hands gathering water to drink. The silent sunset and feathery tops of evergreen trees wavered on its glassy surface, marred only by the occasional ripple of a heron swooping in for its last meal of the day.

"Isn't it perfect?" Abilene said close to her ear. "The energy here is amazing."

Heather nodded. She had never attended a ritual before, but according to her brothers and sisters they were the culmination of all their prayers and meditation, a celebration of their power. Plus, the rituals had a way of making things happen: things like drawing her to the Vein, where she'd found her family at long last.

She tried to stay out of the way as the Children of the Earth prepared for the ritual, bees bustling around the rusted hive of the van. Orion struggled under the weight of two enormous, skin-covered conga drums while Freya and Abilene carefully dragged their heels along the ground, casting a circle in the bed of pine needles.

Kimo lit incense that sent rich-scented smoke spiraling along the currents of the early evening breeze, and Luna carefully polished a small, sharp dagger on the edge of her moss-colored cloak before sheathing it in a holster strapped to her thigh.

From the depths of the van, Ciaran brought out a stack of hammered-copper bowls.

"Now," Luna commanded, "each of us will fill a bowl with water from the lake. Don't let your minds wander; in order for this to work, it must be done with full intention."

Heather accepted her bowl wordlessly, her fingertips falling easily into the metal depressions. She trained her mind the way Luna had taught them in meditation, focusing fully on her task as she walked slowly toward the lake's shore and knelt where its rippling edges lapped at the land.

Frigid water cascaded over her fingers, but she forced herself not to flinch or even shiver. Luna had given her instructions, and she was determined to fulfill them to the letter. That was her purpose now, her reason for being: to learn from Luna and to do as she said.

"Now place your bowls before you and stand in the circle." Luna's voice was smooth, hypnotic. Heather found a spot facing the lake, where she could see the last golden wisps of sunset reflected in its ripples.

"In our last ritual, we called on the Gods of Air to bring our Earth Sister Heather to Carbon County." Luna gave Heather a smile that spread like warm tea through her chest. "This ritual is for our Earth Brother Owen. He may be right here in Carbon County, but powerful forces are keeping him from us. Tonight, we turn to the west, where the Gods of Water reside. We humbly ask the Gods of Water to freeze the air, bringing us an early winter. When the snow falls, Owen will return to our hearth. He'll come home."

As Heather nodded along with the rest of the Children of the Earth, the sound of a car engine rumbled down the road. She tensed, wondering what kind of stranger would come to a deserted mountain lake at sunset—a lone fisherman, maybe, or a couple packing a romantic picnic? The ritual had to be that night, the evening of the perfect quarter moon. If they ruined it, what would Luna do?

"Oh, crap," Kimo muttered as the car swung into view. It was a boxy four-door sedan, white with a thick blue stripe down the side. "It's the cops. We better run."

He shivered under his black hoodie, making the anarchy tattoo on his neck contract and expand. A scrawny former gutter punk who'd been arrested for everything from dumpster diving to possession, he was no stranger to run-ins with the law.

"It's okay." Luna glided to Kimo and put a comforting hand on his shoulder, instantly relaxing him. "We're not getting busted. Tonight, the sheriff is our guest."

The car door opened, and the sheriff emerged, his doughy head peeking out from the driver's-side door. He wore civilian clothes, a plaid button-down shirt and new-looking chinos that stretched over his sagging belly, and he carried a bouquet of drugstore carnations. Freya and Abilene exchanged knowing glances, laughter dancing in their eyes. It was obvious that the sheriff was dressed for a date.

"So glad you could join us." Luna glided to greet him. His eyes lit up, drinking her in, and he held out the flowers almost shyly. A smile frolicked across her face. "We've been waiting for you."

"We?" The sheriff glanced past her and saw her assembled brothers and sisters. The softness in his face hardened, and he dropped the flowers on the hood of his car.

"I thought . . ." he began uncertainly.

"Shhhh." Luna placed a finger on his lips. "This will be even better than what you thought. Come with me."

She took his hand and led him to the lake's shore. His eyes shifted suspiciously over the Children of the Earth silently apprais-ing him from the circle drawn in pine needles, copper bowls of lake water at their feet. Heather wondered how they must look to him, with their earth-toned clothes and long, messy hair, their backs straight and tall as Luna had said they must always be when summoning the elemental gods, in order to keep all seven chakras open and aligned.

Luna and the sheriff reached the center of the circle. "Sit," Luna commanded softly. But the sheriff shook his head.

"Listen, lady, I don't know about all of this. I—"

Luna wrapped him in an emerald stare, her eyes glowing brighter until they flared neon green. Heather could almost see the power rising through her spine and shooting from her eyes, the indigo glow of Luna's mind entering the sheriff's and stopping his thoughts in their tracks.

"Sit," Luna said again.

The sheriff's eyes glazed over, and his mouth clapped shut. He crossed his legs and dropped clumsily to the ground, staring up at Luna like a trusting child.

Luna knelt in front of him, the edges of her cloak brushing the earth. The sunset's persimmon glare glanced off her brow, illuminating flecks of glitter leftover from her go-go dancing makeup the night before.

"Tonight, we make magic," she crooned, her nose inches from his. "Tonight, your dearest wish in the world comes true."

The sheriff's head bobbed like a marionette's, making Luna laugh an icy laugh. She kissed him lightly on the cheek and twirled around, eyes shining.

"Now the ritual begins!" she cried. "Join hands so we can activate the power of the circle. Hurry—the moon is rising."

Heather glanced up and saw a pale quarter moon floating like a slice of lemon in the sky. Kimo's bony fingers slipped into her right hand while Aura's warm, padded palm grasped her left.

"We feel the energy of the earth beneath us," Luna chanted, "feel it rise through the soles of our feet into our legs, through our bodies and into our arms. Our veins drink it in, and our heart chakras fill, and we join our power with the energy of the earth until it's too great for our bodies to contain. Now we pass this energy through the circle, sanctifying this space and our bond."

A jolt pulsed like an electric shock through Heather's arms. She stifled a yelp and forced herself to hang on to Kimo's and Aura's hands, even as aftershocks sparked through their fingers. The energy ballooned inside of her, making her feel like she was about to burst, and then the jolt flowed through her arms and out her fingers. Next to her, Kimo and Aura winced. Their eyes narrowed with pain, but they held on, and a moment later Heather saw it ripple back around the circle, ebbing and flowing through the group's clasped hands and settling evenly into their bodies.

Her eyeballs felt hot. She looked around the circle and saw that all of their eyes were glowing, illuminating the darkened grove next to the lake in phosphorescent green.

"The circle is complete!" Luna cried. "Now we'll use sacred rhythm to awaken the Water Gods."

From opposite sides of the circle, Orion and Silas approached the giant drums that flanked the sheriff like sentries. Orion's drum was slender and tall, like him, while Silas's was nearly as wide as his bouncer's shoulders. They positioned the drums between their knees as the sheriff sat slack-jawed and slump-backed in the center of the circle, legs loosely crossed and beefy elbows resting on his knees.

The drummers' palms hit the skins with slow, deliberate precision, beating a solemn rhythm that echoed across the lake and bounced off the rock faces of the mountains. Heather felt the beat in her feet and her chest, let it stir the molten light glowing in her eyes and vibrate her bones. As the music coursed through her and the drumbeats grew louder, faster, stronger, Heather felt the rhythm pick her up and carry her around the circle, found herself moving instinctively among the Children of the Earth in a dance that took control of her body and left her brain smothered in dust. She was barely aware of her arms rising to the moon and her feet pounding the dirt, was lost in the web of life and sound connecting her to each of her Earth Siblings.

"A-ya-a-ya-ay!" Abilene's voice soared above them.

"O-ya-o-ya-oh!" The drummers' baritones echoed in her gut, propelling the blood ever faster through her veins.

The moon glowed green, and the Children of the Earth raised their faces as one to greet it. Seafoam-colored light vibrated around it, and Heather realized she was seeing the moon's gravitational pull, the waves of power that dictated tides and controlled oceans. She could feel the presence of the Water Gods among them, their seaweed fingers grasping at her hair, their voices sluicing and babbling in her ears. Sweat, or something more than sweat, coated her body, making her skin slick so that she swam rather than danced through the air, her body bubbly and bouyant.

Luna began a guttural chant, her voice carrying over the lake.

"Gods of Water, hear our cries:

Freeze the water in the skies.

Free the wind, release the snow

So homeward will our brother blow."

The Children of the Earth joined their voices to the chant, lacing it into the drumbeats until it echoed like thunder through the mountains. Heather felt her throat open and heard her voice join in, a voice that was deeper and stronger and more powerful than her own. The moon's green glow was blinding, waves of light and energy pulsing and pounding around it to the rhythm of their voices, the power of their chant.

A crash on the lake's shore jerked Heather's eyes away from the throbbing moon and the faces whirling beside her. A wave spread its white-tipped fingers over the shore before diving headfirst to consume itself in a foam-spewing gulp. Before it could fully recede, another wave rose, turning the lake's once-placid surface into a roiling, serpentine sea.

"They hear us!" Ecstasy trilled in Luna's voice.

Still dancing to the frantic, hypnotic drumbeats, she turned to face the sheriff, her hips churning inches from his face. She lifted his chin until he was staring up at her, his mouth open in awe at the wild-haired, wild-eyed creature laughing before him.

The chant died around them and the drums quieted to a whisper as Luna locked the sheriff's eyes in hers and parted her lips to speak.

"The Water Gods demand a sacrifice." She squatted so that her eyes were level with the sheriff's and placed both hands on his shoulders. "But you must go willingly." The indigo halo returned, a glowing bubble that grew to encompass both of them. "This world hasn't been kind to you. The one beyond is better. Would you like to go there?"

An indigo glaze shadowed the sheriff's eyes. Heather saw his Adam's apple bob in his throat.

"Do you want to look into your wife's eyes again, to touch her hair?" The sheriff leaned into Luna's words. "Do you want to hear her laughter and hold her close all night, every night, forever?"

The sheriff opened his mouth, and Heather felt her breath stop. The Children of the Earth were frozen around her, their entire future—their reason for being together, their reason for being—hanging on the sheriff's answer.

"My son . . ." The sheriff spoke in a cracked husk of a voice. "Charlie."

Luna nodded. She took his hands in hers. "I'll take care of him," she promised. "Charlie will be safe. All you have to do is let go."

Tears glistened in the sheriff's eyes. His lips trembled, and his skin seemed translucent in the greenish moonlight. He looked lost and tiny next to the towering pine trees.

"Are you ready to let go?" Luna whispered.

He nodded.

"Yes."

Luna cupped his cheeks, raising his face to the moonlight. For a moment, the sheriff's eyes blazed with the full force of a million lives, with every precious moment from birth through childhood, from adolescence to first true love to fatherhood to middle age. A smile stretched his lips, and his face filled with happiness so pure it stuck like an ice pick in Heather's heart.

Then his eyes closed, and his body went limp. Luna caught him beneath the shoulders and laid him gently to rest as the drumbeats pattered into silence. She tilted her ear to his mouth and listened for breath. Then she drew the dagger from her thigh holster and raised it to the moon, an icicle cutting the sky.

She knelt at the sheriff's side and slid the dagger across his fingertip, releasing a trickle of blood. In one fluid movement she dipped her finger in the scarlet pool and used it to paint a teardrop on his forehead.

The Children of the Earth joined hands as she rose to her feet and looked out over the lake. Heather felt sick and shaken by what she'd just seen, the power that had bloomed like fire in her chest now a small, lost ship rocking nauseatingly in her stomach.

"Gods of Water." Luna addressed the lake, the moon, the pale and trembling circle of her siblings. "Your sacrifice is complete. We have taken from your oceans and rivers, and now we humbly offer you blood in return. Do with it what you will. All we ask is that you consider our plea: Grant us an early winter so that our brother returns home to us."

Ashy clouds began to gather over the lake, plump with moisture and sinking low in the sky, as a chill wind ripped through the pines. The Children of the Earth shivered in their light jackets. The sweat from their ritual dance cooled to a clammy glaze, and Heather watched goose bumps rise on her arms.

"It's cold." She pulled on the sleeves of her sweater, stretching them over her suddenly freezing palms. "Like, *really* cold."

"Do you know what that means?" Kimo turned to her, his skeletal grin stretched wide.

The frigid air rushed to her head, making her feel dizzy and sick. A man lay dead just a few feet away, a man who had passed away at Luna's command, a man whose death she'd helped orchestrate.

"It means it *worked*!" A great cheer dashed through the circle as he threw his scrawny arms around her, squeezing and lifting and spinning until her feet were off the ground and the lake and trees were a blur. The rest of her brothers and sisters pressed in, hugging and squealing and yelping until the lakeside was a blur of limbs, grappling and tackling, a cacophony of excited chatter even as the temperature dipped lower and the clouds hung dark and pregnant over the lake.

Their energy infected her, pushing away the doubt until it was just a tiny nagging voice in the back of her head, and she finally let her mouth fall into a smile, joining her husky laugh with theirs and hugging her family the way they deserved to be hugged, with all the love she had to give.

The cop wouldn't have gone if he hadn't wanted to go, just like Luna said. All they'd done was give him what he truly desired.

13

JANIE COULD FEEL THE MUSIC from the Vein even before she stepped inside. It pulsed through the rough dirt of the parking lot and pounded up through her high heels, thrumming in her legs and vibrating the denim of her curve-hugging jeans. She weaved between sloppily parked cars, shivering in the sudden, unseasonable cold and ignoring the hungry looks from a knot of men smoking by the front entrance.

"Hey, lady," one of them grunted as she passed. "Want to show me a good time?"

She didn't answer. She might have had a clever remark for them long ago, but the Janie with the snappy comebacks was gone.

"What's a nice girl like you doing in a place like this?" the prospector persisted, blocking her way. His voice grated against her, and his eyes were bloodshot over a foul leer.

"Meeting my husband for a drink," she said through gritted teeth.

"Gal like you's too young to be married." His gaze rested on her low-cut fuchsia top, a throwback from when she dressed to show off her body. From when she cared.

Silently, she flashed her ring in front of his face. He looked like he wanted to put up a fight, but just then the door opened, releasing a blast of thick, heavy bass into the night air.

"He bothering you, miss?" The bouncer looked from Janie to the prospector. His massive shoulders blocked out a panorama of pulsing lights and fog, bodies gyrating to the beat.

"I was just wishing her a good evening." The prospector shrank back against the wall.

"That better be all you were doing." The bouncer shot him a look that made the prospector wilt, before stepping aside and ushering Janie through the door. "You let me know if he gives you any more trouble," he whispered as she passed.

"Thanks." She was barely inside when the music assaulted her, an army of sound. Lights flashed between tightly packed bodies, casting shadows in the swirling fog. The club-goers didn't dance so much as ride the beat like surfers dipping and cresting on an endless wave. Liquid sloshed from their drinks and trickled in tiny waterfalls to the floor, where they left a sticky film that sucked at the bottoms of her shoes.

She squinted, trying to pick out Doug's big, square head. She hadn't exactly been lying when she told the prospector she was meeting her husband for a drink. She'd just left out the part where Doug didn't know about it.

She still didn't understand what she was doing at the Vein, not really. She'd been silent as Doug pulled on his sneakers and stomped down the stairs earlier that evening, his truck making a mean squealing noise as he careened down the long, twisting driveway. Yet something had been different that night, not in Doug's behavior but inside of her. Before, she'd been able to tolerate the silence and loneliness, even to welcome it. But that night it tore at her, a screaming pain in her chest. She couldn't bear to spend another night alone with Bella and the Teen Moms, waiting for the vodka to warm away the pain.

And so, without taking too much time to think, she'd dug through the plastic trash bags of clothes still unpacked from her former life, looking for something as bright and fun as the old Janie had been. She'd combed her hair and applied thick, heavy mascara, rimming her eyes with liner until they sat like smoldering jewels in her face. She'd fortified herself with a few slugs of cherry vodka, "borrowed" the keys to Vince Varley's Buick, and navigated the cold, dark roads to the Vein, knowing she was drunk driving and that was bad, but who would really care if she didn't make it? Not her, that was for sure. It would just be an easier way to end things.

Now, with lights flashing purple and red in her eyes and throngs of prospectors leering at her chest, she wondered what she'd been thinking. This was a man's world—Doug's world—and she was trespassing. She wanted to know what he got up to every night while she drank alone in the west wing of the Varley mansion, but she also kind of didn't. Yet as her eyes adjusted to the dimness and her ears started to pick out bits of conversation from between the thundering beats, she heard his braying guffaw over by the go-go platforms and realized that, whether or not she still wanted to, she was about to get a glimpse into Doug's secret life.

Her husband lounged in a cluster of greasy-looking men, a Coors tallboy sweating in his hand. His teeth gleamed as he threw back his head and howled at something one of them said. But he wasn't looking at the men—his gaze was fixed above them, at a woman oscillating atop a go-go platform like something out of an old James Bond movie.

Janie tensed as a spotlight flashed across the platform, illuminating the glitter on Luna's face and the charms in her hair. Luna's eyes were closed, and a catlike smile played across her lips as she spun a lit-up hula hoop in figure eights around her body, the leaves on her tree tattoo shivering as she moved. Even from across the room, Janie could read the desire in Doug's eyes. It was a look she remembered from the old days, a look he'd given her across the cafeteria junior year, a look that had followed them through early groping in the backseat of his dad's car and into the first time they made love after junior prom, on a sleeping bag spread out in the bed of his truck under a chilly sprinkle of stars. A streak of possessiveness flared somewhere beneath the vodka fog, pushing her past the gaping prospectors and bellying her up to the bar. She hadn't seen that look from Doug in a long time, and she didn't like where it was directed.

A barstool materialized, and she perched on it, ducking under the curtain of her blond hair. Doug hadn't seen her yet, and she was thankful for that. She needed to formulate a plan, a way to make him realize what he was missing, how important it was for them to recapture what they'd lost. He wouldn't find what he was looking for with Luna, she knew that. No amount of longing on Doug's part would make her love him the way that Janie could. The way that she wanted to, if only they could find a way to turn back time and go back to the way things were.

She needed a drink, and she needed it that instant. She reached into her purse and waved a wad of bills at the two bartenders taunting a throng of prospectors down at the other end of the bar. At last, one of them acknowledged her with piercing emerald eyes.

"Cherry vodka!" She had to lean all the way across the bar and shout to be heard.

The bartender arched an eyebrow. "And?"

Janie felt herself flush. "And nothing. Just cherry vodka. In a glass. With ice, I guess."

She could feel the bartender's judgment in the feline arch of her back as she turned to fix Janie's drink, but once the glass was in her hand and the sweet liquid was on its way to her belly it didn't matter. She felt her uneasiness lift and her body relax into the relentless noise as she gulped it down, and with a satisfied sigh she settled the empty glass onto the bar and signaled for another.

"Rough night?"

The velvet voice came from the barstool to her left. The vodka made the whole room lurch as she turned, but then it was still again, and she realized she was looking at an angel.

Okay, not a *literal* angel. She may have been tipsy, but she wasn't *wasted*. Still, the boy on the barstool next to hers was so beautiful he was barely human, so perfect she wouldn't have been totally surprised to find wings sprouting from his back.

His skin was golden, his eyes the green of spring's first pass through the mountains. His cheekbones sat high on his face, delicate as robin's wings, and honey-colored hair cascaded to his chin in a curtain so lush and shiny she had to fight the urge to run her fingers through it. His smile cast a spotlight on her face.

"I'm sorry?" she croaked, realizing she still couldn't answer his question—couldn't even remember what he'd asked.

"You don't seem thrilled to be here." The words were a harsh dose of reality, but his tone was an invitation embossed on silken paper and awaiting a reply.

Still, she couldn't seem to speak. It felt like eons since anyone had noticed anything about her—unhappiness tended to blind those around you, to make them want to talk about anything but the big, sad elephant in the room.

Her silence didn't faze him. "I can tell you came here looking for something," he continued. "But it's something you already knew you wouldn't find."

"Maybe I did find it," she found herself saying. The green of his eyes made anything seem possible. "Maybe it wasn't what I thought I wanted after all."

His smile widened, refracting the bar's dim lights like a stained-glass window.

"So you're open to new possibilities."

"I guess." A million questions drifted through her mind, none staying long enough to let her form a complete thought.

"I'm Ciaran." He extended a hand, and she took it, noticing the way his palm sent spirals of warmth up her arm.

"Janie."

"Nice to meet you, Janie." Her heart beat a dozen more times before he released her hand.

"Same," she said, feeling dizzy and happy and way too warm.

"You lost someone recently." Ciaran rested an arm on the bar and leaned in close, so close she could smell pine needles and peat moss wafting from his skin. "Someone important."

Her mouth gaped. "Are you psychic or something?"

"Not exactly." His laugh was honey-tinged. "But sometimes I pick up on things other people don't. Especially when it's someone I find interesting."

The warmth seeped through her skin and into her bones. For the first time since her wedding, she felt special and singled out. She felt like she was glowing.

"You think I'm interesting?"

Once upon a time, she wouldn't have had to ask why a good-looking guy was interested in her. She would have known it was because she was cute, and fun, and knew how to crack a joke and a smile. But that was before her spark had gone out, before she traded a life in color for one etched out in shades of gray. That was before her baby died.

"Why?" She could barely choke out the word.

"Because I can tell how much you're suffering. It makes you more interesting, somehow. More alive."

She looked up at him in wonder, searching his face for signs that he was joking. But the way he leaned into her, so far forward that his barstool was in danger of tipping over, told her he meant it.

"That's funny." She allowed herself a small, ironic laugh. "It keeps everyone else away."

He shrugged. "Most people can't handle suffering. It freaks them out. They don't realize it's an essential part of life, no better or worse than joy."

The bartender set Janie's drink down in front of her, but for once she didn't want it. She didn't want anything to dull this moment, the fierce and sudden way this stranger, Ciaran, made her feel special and important.

He leaned closer, wrapping her in his forest-y scent. "So what was his name?" he asked quietly.

She drew back. "Whose name?"

"You know."

She felt her shoulders slump, dragged down by the leaden familiarity of her sadness. There it was again, big as before and twice as heavy. She should have known better than to try to ignore it.

"Jeremiah," she said stiffly.

"Janie." He clasped both of her hands in his. "It wasn't your fault. Jeremiah is in a better place now. It's time to let go."

A sob bloomed deep within her. She tried to stifle it, but it was too late. Tears flooded from her eyes, stinging a trail down her cheeks. She hadn't cried much since Jeremiah's death: It was like her tear ducts had turned to stone, and all she could do was retreat behind a thick pane of loss and watch the rest of the world go by while she stood still, waiting for something that never came.

Now all the tears she had never let herself cry, all the pain she had never let herself feel, poured from her. Ciaran held her hands through it all, an island in the ocean of her grief.

"It's okay," he crooned in her ear, a lullaby of forgiveness that she'd been waiting and longing to hear. His hands stayed steady on hers, cloaking the two of them in a bubble far away from the spilled drinks and laughter in the bar, in a secret space no longer part of the harsh world she'd known.

"I'm sorry," she blubbered. She could feel the tears loosening her mascara and knew she was getting raccoon eyes in front of the one person in the world who had actually made her feel pretty again. "I just met you—I shouldn't—"

"You should," Ciaran said firmly. "You need this. But it doesn't have to be here. Let's go."

The words brought her back to reality, to the sordid bar where she'd come to reclaim her husband. She glanced around, locating Doug in the mess of shadows, a string of saliva glistening between his teeth as he stared up at Luna grinding away on her go-go platform.

Ciaran stood and wrapped an arm around her, protecting her from the drunken, caterwauling crowd. She knew that as long as she could feel his touch, Doug would never hurt her again.

"Let's go," he said again, gently steering her toward the exit.

She went.

14

THAT LUNA SURE WAS SOMETHING else. Doug had wanted a piece of her ever since he first laid eyes on her at that bonfire back at the track, the night that . . . well, he preferred not to think about that night, at least not about what had happened later. He preferred not to think about any of the craziness with Janie, and so instead he thought about Luna's hips, the way they kept that hoop of hers going round and round and what they might feel like swiveling like that against him. The image made his mouth go dry, but he fixed that by chugging the watery remains of his Coors.

"Gonna need another one a' these." He crushed the can against his chest and tossed it in the general direction of the bar. "Who wants to buy the boss a beer?"

"You mean the boss's son," Dwayne grumbled next to him. "And you're the one with the cash, so shouldn't you be buying?"

"I'll get next," Doug assured him.

Dwayne, rolling his eyes, fished a few bills from the pocket of his oil-splattered Carhartts and headed to the bar.

He was all right, that Dwayne. In fact, most of the roughnecks were. Sure, they weren't the best-looking bunch, and they didn't exactly come from pedigreed stock, but they worked hard, drank harder, and always laughed at his jokes. Which actually meant a hell of a lot, now that Bryce and his buddies from high school had all turned into boring church freaks whose idea of a good time was throwing back a few Cokes and singing songs about Jesus.

Dwayne returned with a pair of sweating tallboys, and Doug clinked appreciatively. "To cold beer and hot women!" he toasted, eliciting a round of guffaws. Almost as if she'd been summoned, Luna squatted low on her platform, still swinging that hoop above her head, and favored Doug with a salacious wink.

"Aw, shit!" Doug looked around to make sure the guys saw. "Did you see that? She winked right at me!"

"She coulda been winking at any of us," argued Sid, whose heavy forehead and protruding eyebrows reminded Doug of a Cro-Magnon man from one of those Nat Geo documentaries.

"Nope." Doug shook his head forcefully, enjoying the way it felt like he was shaking his brain cells loose. "She looked dead at me. I know she wants it. She's always giving me looks like that."

"The hell she is," Sid snorted. "She works for tips, and she knows you're good for 'em. That's all."

A bubble of anger rose in Doug's throat, messy and bilious from the half dozen beers and handful of shots he'd already downed. "Shows what you know," he spat. "She happens to run this place, so tips ain't the half of it. She looks at me like that 'cause she wants it. They all do."

He looped his thumbs around his belt buckle and hiked it up a notch, just in case Sid's Cro-Magnon brain was too dense to know what "it" was.

His rig buddies howled. "Sure they do, champ," someone said.

"You're a regular ladies' man," another chimed in.

The back of Doug's neck grew hot, and he looked from the rig workers to Luna, hoping she'd choose that moment to prove them wrong. As if reading his thoughts, she locked her gaze on his, gave her hips an extra shimmy, and blew him a kiss.

"See?" he exploded. "She's been giving me signals like that for weeks! I bet I could get with her tonight, no questions asked."

Dwayne chuckled. "That's a wager I'm willing to take," he said. "Whatcha want to bet?"

It may have looked like harmless flirtation to anyone else, but Doug could tell from the passion sparking in Luna's eyes that this was the real thing. This was gonna happen—and it was gonna happen tonight.

"A Benjamin," he said confidently.

"Hell," Dwayne said. "Make it two."

"You're on." Doug wiped his palm on his jeans before grasping Dwayne's in a hearty handshake.

"Hey, man, how'll we know you really did the deed?" someone asked.

"What, you don't trust me?" He gave them a wounded look, his voice dripping with false innocence.

"Not as far as I can throw you." Dwayne grinned.

"I'll take a picture. Of her." Doug lowered his voice to a conspiratorial growl. *"Naked."*

"Damn!" the rig workers cried, laughing and slapping him on the back. Doug felt like a king: back on top, right where he belonged. By the next morning he'd have claimed the finest piece of tail in Carbon County and earned the undying respect of his coworkers in the bargain.

"Just need one more shot and I'll make this shit happen," Doug proclaimed, flagging down a cocktail waitress. As he ordered a fireball, he caught a flash of blond hair and a fuchsia shirt that looked exactly like one Janie used to have. In fact, the woman leaving the bar with some surfer-looking dude's arm over her shoulder could have been a dead ringer for Janie, at least from the back.

A small, cold fist of remorse socked him in the stomach. He was a married man, after all, and Janie wasn't doing so good as it was. He knew he was practically the only thing she still had to live for. Hell, he'd been the best thing in her life even before all the bad stuff went down. It would kill her to know that he cheated.

"Your shot?" The waitress handed him a glass and he tipped it back gratefully, hoping it would burn away the guilt. What Janie didn't know wouldn't hurt her, he rationalized. And with Janie in zombie mode half the time, it wasn't like she'd get suspicious and go asking questions. He'd just have a little fun with Luna, just this once, and then he'd go back to being a good husband.

At least, he'd try.

"You gonna do this or what, pal?"

Doug turned to find his buddies practically bursting with booze and excitement. He couldn't let them down. If he did, they would never let *him* live it down. Janie or no Janie, he had to finish what he'd started.

"Damn right." He slammed his shot glass down on a table and started for the go-go platform. "Time to go work my magic."

"Yeah, Mr. Smooth," Dwayne agreed. "You do that."

Doug could hear them laughing behind him and feel the shot still burning in his gut as he approached Luna's go-go platform. He didn't have a plan, exactly, but he didn't think he'd need one. He'd just hop up there, give her the ol' Varley charm, and she'd be eating out of his palm in no time.

He stopped for a moment, inches from the platform, and stared. Luna was even sexier up close. Her legs were sculpted bronze, her hair a serpent's nest of color that Doug would find revolting on anyone else, but it was somehow totally hot on her. He could practically smell sex seeping from her pores, inviting him to an all-you-can-eat buffet of pleasure that, to be honest, would probably be the best he'd ever had.

Because, okay, the truth was he'd never been with anyone but Janie. And even though Janie knew what she was doing, she was still just a kid. Luna may not have been any older, but she was a woman:

a woman who Doug was pretty damn sure knew how to please a man.

As the song dipped into a hard, driving beat, he placed a hand on the platform and leapt up behind her, ready to grind his way to a home run.

But he'd forgotten about her hoop. It whipped around her head and smacked him across the cheek, making him yelp like a kicked puppy and clutch his face, almost falling off the platform. He could feel his coworkers' jeers as he struggled to regain his balance, which he found just in time for Luna to turn to him, one hand on her jutting hip.

"And just what do you think you're doing?" She raised a provocative eyebrow.

"Hey." Doug spread his hands, hoping he looked bashful and charming. "No disrespect. Just wanted to get to know you a little better, that's all. Forgot about how hoops . . . well, go around." He chuckled manfully at his little pun.

Luna cocked her head, her eyes sparkling with mischief. "And how do you propose to get to know me, big guy?"

Doug knew it. He was in. It was all he could do not to turn around and flash a *V-for-victory* sign to his boys.

"Like this." He grabbed her hips and pressed his body against hers, moving the two of them to the music as one. Being so close to her was intoxicating. A spicy, earthy scent rose from her skin, and her hips were liquid gold under his hands, making his breath come quick and heavy. "I think we could have a real good time together," he growled in her ear. "Don't tell me you don't want this, too."

Revulsion flashed across Luna's face. Clasping her hands like iron cuffs around his wrists, she lifted his arms off of her and yanked him around so he teetered on the edge of the platform, a solid arm's length away. She was stronger than she looked, he realized, and as her nails dug into his wrists, she fixed him with a gaze sharp and jagged as broken glass.

"How dare you tell me what I want," she hissed.

"Whoa, baby, hey . . ." Doug started to say.

"That is not how this works," Luna continued. "*You* do what *I* want. Not the other way around. Now are you going to do what I want?"

She took a deep breath, and her eyes fluttered shut. A moment later they flew open, and an indigo light began to hover around her head like a halo, growing until it was larger than the disco ball hanging from the ceiling and twice as bright. Doug felt the light surround him, a cloud of brilliant blue. It dulled the music until there was nothing but the sound of blood pounding in his head, and then he felt it start to seep through his skin like a damp fog, creeping into his mind and burrowing deep in the crevices of his brain.

"You wanted me." Luna's voice sounded like it was coming from the end of a long tunnel. He blinked through the indigo fog, and it parted just enough to reveal her standing with her hands on her hips. She seemed bigger than the entire bar then, and brighter than the sun. She was magnificent in a way he was only beginning to understand, and he suddenly felt embarrassed for trying to get with her. Luna was clearly not the kind of girl you got with. She was the kind of girl you worshipped.

"And that means you will do what I want," she continued. "Understand?"

He nodded dumbly. Her voice tickled the furthest reaches of his brain. He felt it cascade through his veins, running through him like blood. She was inside of him, filling him with her glowing blue light.

His feet were rooted to the spot, his limbs frozen. His mind felt like it was stuck in traffic, with Luna in the driver's seat, navigating his thoughts. She could see all of him, his past and future, memories and desires, and he was powerless to stop her. Not only that, but he didn't want to.

It felt good to succumb to her, to be filled with her pulsing, calming glow. With Luna as his navigator he didn't have to be on his guard, trying to impress his father and the guys from the rig, worrying about Janie and wondering what the hell happened to his buddies from high school. He could take a break from the pressures of the world and just float. Just be.

"You'll do what I want?" she asked again.

"Yes," he found himself saying. He would do anything for her. He felt closer to her than he'd ever felt to Janie, to Trey, even to his mother while he was still in the womb. Luna owned him completely, and it felt so good to let her be in control, to simply let go.

Luna raised her head to the DJ booth. "Cut the music," she called. The bar quieted instantly, and Doug felt every head turn to look at him, sensed the mirth in their eyes. But he could only look at Luna, squinting into the indigo light to take in all of her, his retinas refusing to focus anywhere else. He'd be perfectly content to never look at anything else again.

"I have an announcement to make." Luna's voice was harps and angels. "This young man is going to lick my boots."

A tidal wave of laughter crashed through the bar, the loudest hoots and hollers coming from Dwayne and the boys. He heard it, but it meant nothing, the way everything meant nothing, everything but Luna. She was his whole world now, a bigger and more beautiful world than anything he'd experienced before.

"Well," she said, releasing his hands. "What are you waiting for?"

One of the busboys brought over a barstool, and Luna perched on top of it, above the crowd, where everyone could see. She stuck out her foot, sole facing Doug, as the cheering grew louder.

There was no question in Doug's mind. This was what Luna wanted, and it was what he would do. The indigo light guided him to his knees, and he cupped her ankle in his hands as reverently as if it were the Holy Grail.

Luna's boots were weathered imitation leather, the rubber soles two inches thick and molded into deep treads that seemed almost designed to trap dirt. Small gravel pebbles and even a cigarette butt poked out from the grooves, and the treads were worn in places and caked with grime, a graying wad of pink chewing gum winking at him from the left heel. As he drew his head closer he smelled oil and industrial cleanser, urine and dog shit.

"Lick it, lick it, lick it!" the crowd chanted, egging him on. But it wasn't for them that he stuck out his tongue and gave her foot a long, slow, thorough lick from heel to toe. It was for her.

He was aware of the bar's collective gasp, could hear the exhalations of disgust and even a few gagging noises, but they meant nothing. His tongue was on her heel again, wiggling into the crevices between treads, scraping against the detritus left there. He licked her soles over and over again, as enthusiastic as if her grimy boots were triple-butterscotch ice cream. It wasn't that he thought they tasted good—he knew they didn't. It was simply that his taste buds, his body, his soul no longer mattered. Every cell of him existed only to serve Luna, and this was what Luna wanted.

He realized dimly that the chant had broken off, and an uncomfortable silence hovered in the room. Even Luna, whose eyes he checked between each long, slow slurp, looked unnerved.

"Okay, you can stop already," she said with a small, silvery laugh. She yanked her feet away from him, looping them around the legs of the stool, and the indigo glow that had surrounded her abruptly vanished. Doug felt the light leak out of him, leaving him sick and dizzy, blinking rapidly into a crowd that was looking at him very differently than when he'd approached the go-go platform just minutes before.

He looked down and saw that he was on his knees, then looked up to find Luna smirking above him. She no longer exuded sex—in fact, she looked like she'd been sculpted from ice. His desire for her congealed into a clammy, unappetizing film that coated his skin like something you'd find inside of a Tupperware forgotten for months in the back of the refrigerator.

"What the hell just happened?" he asked, his face reddening.

Luna shrugged. "You wanted to clean my boots with your tongue. And, hey, thanks for that. They were actually pretty gross."

"What the fuck?" Doug stumbled back, off the platform and into the crowd, searching for his friends. But everyone he passed averted their eyes, and some turned their backs to him entirely, sniggering behind cupped hands.

"Dwayne." Doug approached him, stumbling a little, and held out his hand to steady himself on his friend's shoulder. "What's going on, bro?"

But Dwayne shrugged him off angrily, leaving Doug's arm swinging in empty air. "Don't touch me, you freak," he muttered. He turned and stormed out, the rest of the Varley rig roughnecks hurrying after him.

As Doug watched them go, a leaden revelation sank in his stomach. He still wasn't quite sure what had just happened, or why. All he knew was that he'd been humiliated bad—and in a way that a small town like Carbon County would never let him forget.

15

DADDY WASN'T HOME YET.

Daddy went out a lot at night. He liked to go to a place called the bar after he hung up his sheriff's hat and took off his uniform. He liked to spend time with women who painted their faces like clowns, with big red lips and too-blue eyes and shiny shoes that looked like they hurt.

But he always came home before sunrise.

Now the sun was up, and the big daytime trucks chugged up and down the road leaving whorls of dust in their wakes, and Daddy still wasn't home.

Charlie's body made a warm pocket of air under the blanket, but outside it was cold. Colder than it had been the day before, even with the sun peeking out from behind a pair of dirty gray clouds. He wanted to stay under the blanket and curl into the warmth—and since there was no Daddy around to tell him not to, that's exactly what he did.

He had just started to drift off again when a knock came at the door. He poked his head out from under the blanket and slid down off the bed, shivering when his toes touched the floor. Then he padded in his Tommy the Tank Engine pajamas to the front door.

Outside, standing on the faded welcome mat, was a fairy. Or maybe she was an angel—Charlie couldn't quite decide. All he knew was that she wasn't an ordinary lady. Ordinary ladies didn't look like this.

A swirling white skirt danced around her feet like snowdrifts. Stray sparkles caught the light around her eyes, and her lips were parted in a wide, sunny smile. Her hair was every color of the rainbow, full of toys and trinkets that jingled as she spoke.

"Charlie?"

He nodded. Her voice was like the high notes on a piano.

"I'm Luna." She knelt so they were eye to eye. "Do you know what happened to your daddy?"

He shrugged. "He went out, and he's not back yet."

"That's right." She nodded seriously. "Your daddy's going to be gone for a little while, and he asked me to take care of you. How does that sound?"

A twinge of fear made Charlie's tummy turn. "Where did he go?" His voice sounded small.

Luna took his hand. Her touch was warm and soft, and there was something about her that made the air around them look like it was turning blue. "He had to go on a trip," she said gently. "He might be gone a long time. But I promise I'll take very good care of you and not let anything bad happen to you until you get to see him again. Does that sound good?"

Charlie's stomach unknotted. He relaxed into the blue, a blue as pretty and easy as Luna herself.

"That sounds good." He thought for a moment. "Are you going to come live here?"

"No, honey." Luna gave his hand a reassuring squeeze. "You're going to come stay with me. But I'll make sure you have lots of friends, and you're never left alone, and you can have whatever you want."

"Okay." Charlie liked the sound of that. There was nothing he hated more than the nights his daddy left him with only sleepy old Eunice from next door for company.

He thought for another moment. "Are there chicken nuggets where we're going?"

She tilted her head toward the sky and laughed.

"Not yet. But I'll get some," she said when she was done. "Just for you."

"Okay." He liked her eyes and the sparkles around them. She looked like someone who should be in a cartoon.

"Is there anything you want to take with you?" she asked. "I can help you pack a suitcase."

Charlie thought for a moment. He thought about his toothbrush, and his Tommy the Tank Engine books, and his stuffed octopus with the big blue eyes. He thought about his socks and his blankets and the picture of Mommy on his nightstand and his little nightlight that was shaped like a soccer ball. He thought about all of that, but when he looked up at Luna he felt like none of it mattered. She was a fairy, and there were toys in her hair and sparkles on her eyes and music in her laugh. She would be enough.

"Nah," he said.

"Beautiful. You're a free spirit, just like me." Luna stood and held out her hand. "We don't need *things* to make us happy, right? We just need each other."

"Right," Charlie said. He slipped his hand into hers, letting her long, warm, fairy tale fingers wrap around his. With his other hand he reached behind him and tugged at the door, pulling it shut against his house, and all of his stuff, and the memories of Mommy and Daddy, and the life he was leaving behind.

16

THE KNOCK WAS GUNFIRE-QUICK, rattling the trailer's walls.

"Now who could that be?" Karen rested her wooden spoon in the bowl where she'd been mixing pink frosting and wiped floury hands on her apron. "Probably someone from the church, wanting something. They always do."

The knock came again, a gale-force demand.

"I'm coming!" Aunt Karen called, shaking her head as she ran to the door. The kitchen counter was covered in ingredients for the cupcakes she and Daphne were baking for the church social that evening, and the trailer was a warm oasis of butter and sugar in the unseasonably chilly afternoon.

A draft of cold air rushed in as she opened the door, making Daphne shiver into her hoodie. A pair of police detectives stood unsmiling on the doorstep.

"Ma'am." The skinnier of the two detectives nodded grimly. He was gaunt and hawk nosed, sporting a five-o'clock shadow that dotted his face like old coffee grounds. "I'm Detective Fraczek, and my partner here's Detective Madsen." He indicated a pale, towering hulk of a man with limp blond hair. "Is Daphne Peyton home?"

"Why, yes." Aunt Karen's smile trembled, then faded. "But—well, can I ask what this is all about?"

"I'm afraid I'll have to ask you to step aside, ma'am." Detective Fraczek's voice was cold as he brushed past Karen and into the trailer, his massive partner at his heels.

"What is it?" Daphne joined Karen at the door, putting a protective hand on her aunt's shoulder. She didn't like the rough way the cops spoke to her. "What do you want from me?"

"You're Daphne Peyton?" Both detectives looked surprised, like they'd been expecting someone else.

"Yes." She put her hands on her hips. "I am."

"Then you're under arrest on suspicion of manslaughter." Detective Madsen whipped a pair of handcuffs off his belt, the icy metal jangling in the air.

"What?" Karen sucked in the word like a gasp, her hand flying to her heart. "We've already been over all of this. It was self-defense!"

Daphne's heartbeat slammed in her throat as the huge blond man turned her around and slapped the cuffs on her wrists, their edges digging into her flesh. She flashed back to her arrest in Detroit, the exhausted city cop accusing her of committing murder against her abusive stepfather, Jim, and a twisted sense of déjà vu knotted her stomach. She squeezed her eyes shut, praying that when she opened them again it would all turn out to be a joke. But a moment later, the two unsmiling detectives were still there.

"What's this about?" she choked through the dryness in her throat.

A look of pity flashed across Detective Fraczek's eyes, but his voice stayed stern. "Last week you attacked a man and put him in the hospital. Now he's dead."

"He is?" Bitter bile coated the back of her tongue as she remembered her attacker's greasy hair and creepy, different-colored eyes. Now he was dead, and even though he'd attacked her first, she still felt the old unwelcome rush of guilt and helplessness flow through her and turn her limbs to concrete.

"You have the right to remain silent," the cop said in response. Daphne stood numbly as he recited the rest of her rights, trying to organize the thoughts ransacking her brain. What would this arrest do to her family, her community? Would her status as a prophet protect her, or would the townspeople of Carbon County turn on her yet again?

"We're going to take her down to the station for questioning." Detective Fraczek looked down his hawk-nose at Aunt Karen, who was practically hyperventilating, her face tomato-red. "She should be out on bail later tonight or tomorrow morning, if you want to come get her."

"*Tomorrow morning?!*" Karen shrieked. "You can't do that—she'd spend the night in jail!"

"I'll do what I can," he replied grimly. "But if this manslaughter charge sticks, she may be spending a whole lot more than one night in jail."

"No!" Aunt Karen fanned her face, trying to tame the color in her cheeks. "I'm calling Floyd—and Pastor Ted—and the press. You won't get away with this! Everyone knows she's innocent. She's a prophet, you know! She's been chosen by God!"

Daphne watched the detectives exchange glances.

"I'll be okay, Aunt Karen," Daphne said, forcing herself to stay calm. "I'll see you before you know it."

"How touching," Detective Madsen sneered, steering Daphne toward the door. The cold air slapped her face, making her shoulders shake as they stepped outside. She could hear Aunt Karen puffing and fretting behind them, already on the phone to Uncle Floyd.

"Watch your head," Fraczek said gruffly, opening the door to the backseat. Without the use of her hands, Daphne fell cheek-first against the bulletproof glass divider, the cuffs digging painfully into her back and making pins and needles tingle in her fingers. The detective closed the door behind her and started the car, and she watched its flashing lights slash the world outside with panels of red and blue.

Owen was out there in that world, probably getting ready to go to the Vein. She stiffened as she thought of her cell phone, back on her bedside table in Janie's old bedroom in the Peyton trailer.

Owen had said he'd text before he made the trip, and she'd wanted to wish him luck. Now she wouldn't get the chance. All she could do was hope he'd be safe. If all went well, she'd soon be out of police custody and he would come back from the Vein, and they could find refuge in each other's arms.

The squad car pulled up in front of the Carbon County Police Station, a squat, one-story building painted a depressing green. The inside was no cheerier. Dusty venetian blinds masked the paltry light, and a pair of scarred wooden desks faced each other, both piled high with paperwork and half-empty cups of coffee. A dark hall led away from the room, its shadowy recesses filling Daphne with dread. The police station was a fraction of the size of the one in Detroit, but she still knew what was back there: interrogation rooms and holding cells. Neither of which she'd ever wanted to see the inside of again.

Her thoughts beat double-time as the officers led her down the dark hall and into a small room, its smell so thick with dust and old coffee that she almost gagged. Dead flies fizzled in the bowl of a fluorescent light fixture above their heads, and the metal folding chairs on either side of an ancient table looked greasy and discolored from decades of handling.

It seemed fishy, somehow, that they had waited to arrest her until more than a week after the attack. When Sherriff Bates questioned her in the hospital, he'd seemed to accept that she was acting in self-defense. Something had obviously caused him to change his mind. But what—or who?

Detective Madsen locked the door behind them as Detective Fraczek undid Daphne's handcuffs and settled in across from her, nicotine-stained fingers resting on a manila folder. He regarded her with hazel eyes ringed with shadows of sleeplessness, and his voice sounded like a sigh.

"Daphne, we're going to ask you a few questions. It would be in your best interest to cooperate and answer everything with as much detail as possible. If you can do this, we may be able to get you out of here tonight. Do you understand?"

"Yes." Daphne rubbed her wrists where the cuffs had dug in. "Sir," she added, with what she hoped sounded like respect.

Detective Fraczek raised an eyebrow. "Well, that's a start, anyway." He opened the manila folder and slid a photograph across the table while his partner paced back and forth behind them. "Do you know this man?"

She shivered in disgust as she looked down at the greasy hair and bruise-mottled neck of the man in the photograph. One gray eye and one brown stared back at her, lifeless, unseeing. The picture had obviously been taken after her attacker died.

"Yes. That's the man who attacked me."

Detective Madsen stopped pacing and put his hands on the table, leaning close enough for her to see the broken blood vessels around his bulbous nose. “And you still allege that *he* attacked *you*? What you did to him there—the way you strangled him—was that in self-defense?”

“Yes, of course.” Daphne fought to keep her voice calm. She’d been over all of this before, with the sheriff. Where was the sheriff, anyway? “Why would I try to hurt him? I didn’t even know him!”

Detective Madsen opened his mouth to speak, but Detective Fraczek shushed him with a sharp look. Instead of replying, he opened the folder and took out another photo, inching it along the tabletop until it was directly under Daphne’s nose.

“How about this guy?” he asked. “Look familiar?”

The face staring up at Daphne was porky and sad-looking, with jowly rolls under the chin and a grim set to the eyes.

“That’s the sheriff.” She looked imploringly from one cop to the other. “Why are you showing me this? Where is he, anyway? Shouldn’t he be here?”

“That’s what we’d like to know.” Detective Fraczek sat back and crossed his arms. “He’s been missing since last night. And he’s not the only one. Have you ever seen this little guy before?”

He opened the folder one last time and handed Daphne a photograph. An involuntary gasp ripped through her as she took in the little boy with the sandy bowl cut, the one who had observed her with curiosity in the hospital room the night of the attack. She could tell from the sadness in Detective Fraczek's eyes that something was wrong, and a cold certainty twisted in her gut. Something had happened to this boy, something bad.

"You're upset," Detective Fraczek said bluntly. She raised her eyes from the photograph just in time to catch the two officers exchange knowing glances. "What are you feeling right now, Daphne? Sadness? Regret?" His eyes probed hers, a glimmer of triumph sparking in their hazel depths. *"Guilt?"*

"No!" The word erupted from her, unnaturally shrill. "I'm worried. You have to find him!"

"That's what we intend to do." Detective Fraczek said quietly. "We're asking you."

"Me?" The word echoed off the concrete walls. "Why?"

Detective Madsen sighed. "Because of this." He tapped a police file. "We found it on the sheriff's desk after he went missing. It's an investigation into the murder up at the drifter's camp, and it implicates you as the number-one suspect."

Blood thundered in Daphne's ears. The room around her felt airless, like it had been stuffed with wet cotton and was being slowly jammed down her throat. Everything she thought she'd escaped, the very crime she'd been finally absolved of once the town of Carbon County accepted her as a prophet, came rushing back at her, threatening to drown her. She wanted to bang her head against the table, to scream at the officers that they were wrong, to find the sheriff and shake him by the shoulders until he agreed to take it back.

Instead, she allowed herself one long, shaky breath before fixing her eyes solidly on Detective Fraczek. Her only chance, she knew from the past, was to get as much information as possible and hope that a good lawyer and an understanding jury would take care of the rest.

"Why me?" she asked with as much dignity as she could muster. "What makes him think I'd try to kill a man I've never met?"

Detective Fraczek twiddled a pen between his scrawny fingers, tapping it rapidly against the table with a clicking that made her want to jump up and bite his hand. She forced slow breaths through her lungs, trying not to panic.

"First of all," he said, "we have no evidence that you didn't know him. It's suspicious that you were up at the drifter's camp in the first place, and your coworker's story that you were quote-unquote 'acting weird' beforehand doesn't help your case. People often 'act weird' when they're about to commit a murder, don't you think?"

"But—" Daphne sputtered. "But there were witnesses! People saw him attack me first."

The detectives shook their heads in slow, perfect tandem, like a pair of hound dogs following the trajectory of a biscuit.

"Not so," Detective Madsen said. "We were up there earlier. There were witnesses all right, but what they saw were two people on the ground—and you had your hands around his neck. Nobody saw him attack you. They heard a scream, but they say now they're not even sure whose it was."

"But that's crazy!" Images from that night flashed in quick strobes through her mind: the knife glinting in the moonlight, the crazed look in the man's different-colored eyes, the greasy stench of his stringy hair and rancid breath, and the terrifying visions that overtook her when she thought all was lost. "He had a knife against my neck. I didn't even know what I was doing when I strangled him . . . I was seeing things, it was like I was in another world . . ."

She trailed off, suddenly realizing what her words implied. *Seeing things. In another world.* She sounded like a schizophrenic. In a flash, the line between being a prophet and being straight-up crazy narrowed until, seeing it through the detectives' eyes, she could barely discern it at all. In the religiously charged valley of Carbon County, her visions were accepted as truth and proselytized as gospel, but in other places, like police stations and courts of law, she'd be medicated and locked up. She needed to stop talking before she gave the cops more ammo to convict her for a crime she didn't commit.

"Were you seeing things when you murdered your stepfather, too?" Detective Fraczek leaned in for the kill. "What about when you murdered the sheriff . . . or his son?"

"I didn't murder anyone!" Daphne's words thundered through the tiny room, bouncing off the sweating stucco walls.

"Come on." Detective Fraczek laughed. "You have to admit, it's pretty suspicious that Sherriff Bates disappeared as soon as he started investigating you."

"But what about Charlie?" Anger blazed in her cheeks. "You really think I'd kill a child?"

Detective Madsen shrugged. "According to some, you already have. I'm sure the name Jeremiah Varley means something to you."

Daphne felt like she'd been kicked in the chest. The mention of Janie's stillborn baby always brought tears to her eyes, and now she wiped them away furiously, glaring at the detective's doughy face and suspicious eyes. "How could you even—you know that's not true." She struggled to draw a breath, but the pain had a stranglehold on her. It was like the detectives had found all the most horrible and agonizing moments in her life and laid them in front of her on the tabletop. Now they were burying her face in them, trying to smother her with the memories.

"All we know is what people in town tell us." Detective Fraczek steepled his fingers, and she noticed a mottle of black hairs like spider legs growing from his knuckles. "Some folks think you had a hand in baby Jeremiah's death. Others don't. Some think you killed your stepfather back in Detroit and that man up at the drifter's camp. Others don't. As for me—well, I'd bet a good chunk of change you're behind these other disappearances, too." He tapped the photos of the sheriff and Charlie. "We won't know until we find the bodies. Unless, of course, you want to save everyone a lot of time and trouble and just tell us where they are."

"I don't know." She twisted her fingers until they were white in her lap. "All I can say is that I'm innocent."

"We'll let the jury decide that." Detective Fraczek stood abruptly and gathered the photos, collating them neatly on the edge of the table before slamming the manila folder shut. "I think we have what we need for now. Detective Madsen will take you next door so the judge can set bail, but let me give you a piece of advice first."

He crouched so his eyes met Daphne's and his stale coffee breath was hot against her cheek. "You're gonna want to get yourself a damn good lawyer to beat these charges. Because this case is *not* looking good."

She felt the snap of handcuffs bite into her wrists as she watched him turn and saunter slowly out of the room.

17

OWEN COULDN'T SEE WHERE THE bonfire ended and the smoking red sky began.

"Come with us!" A woman danced close to him, her flimsy white dress falling over her curves like water. "Dance with us!" She held out a sinewy hand, fingers beckoning him forward, into the circle. Laughter spilled from her mouth, and her green cat-eyes glittered wickedly.

Behind her, others flailed to the ecstatic beat of an unseen drum. Their shouts mingled with showers of sparks, tiny blasts of light against the night's infinite darkness.

He could feel their joy in his veins, the hot rush of blood finally stirred to life. He was meant to be with them, doing the dance of life and death around the fire, becoming part of that circle of chosen ones born of the very core of the earth. His heart beat with the drum, with their footsteps, with their gleeful cries. They were the Children of the Earth, and he was one of them.

"Dance with us!" the woman in white spun in a circle, her hair a rainbow cutting the night. When she faced him again it was with

Luna's gaze, Luna's heat and life and emerald eyes. "Come, Earth Brother, be one of us."

He shook his head miserably, not trusting himself to speak for fear he would do as she asked, finally acquiescing to the longing that burned night and day in his soul.

"Come." The silver in her voice turned to lead.

He closed his eyes, unable to look at her, knowing the power in her gaze. If he went with her, took her hand and let her lead him to the fire, followed the flow of his blood, then he would lose Daphne. And if he lost Daphne, he would lose his moral compass, the core of goodness that kept him from falling headfirst into darkness.

A searing pain shot through his hand, and his eyes flew open. Luna stood above him, hair a nest of vipers writhing around her head, murderous rage in her eyes. Blood dripped from the dagger she brandished, and he looked down to find the pinky of his left hand severed, the joint bleeding out onto the dirt beside him.

"This is what it's like to deny your family!" she shrieked, bringing the blade down onto his ring finger, a slice through his flesh so swift and sharp he barely had time to register the loss. "It's like losing a part of yourself."

He let out a howl, twisted and ugly like the burned-out trunk of a gnarled tree dying in the flames.

"Please stop," he panted, dark spots dancing in his vision as blood gushed from his hand.

Her eyes flashed in the firelight as she brought the blade down again, severing his middle finger from its bed of tissue and bone. Owen let out a scream. "You are one of us, Owen. You are a Child of the Earth."

His face was a wet, hot mess of tears or sweat—he didn't know which. All he knew was the torture and the longing, the need to surrender to Luna and his brothers and sisters.

"You see what you're doing, Owen." Luna's voice was faint, and he sensed that soon he would pass out from loss of blood. When he looked up she was a shadow, a ghost flickering in and out of his vision. "Look at what you've lost."

She put her hand on his head and forced his eyes to the ground, to where his three lost fingers jumped and wriggled in the dirt.

"Stop it!" Owen kicked at the sheets tethering his feet to the bed, thrashing his way up from the panting, sweat-soaked nightmare. Pinpricks of heat spiked the three fingers on his left hand. He must have rolled onto them in his sleep, trapping them under his hip and cutting off their circulation.

He slapped his fingers against his thigh to wake them, waiting for his heartbeat to slow. The sky outside looked like steel wool, and it was cold in his room, so cold that his breath left his mouth in frosty puffs.

It was late afternoon, far later than he'd meant to sleep, but in a way that was a relief. It meant he didn't have to wait around, killing time until his trip to the Vein. Patience had never been his strong suit, and he was eager to have a mission for the day, eager to get answers.

He typed a quick text to Daphne as he waited for his truck to warm up, then rubbed his hands together near the thin stream of heat drifting from the air vents. He'd need to take it to be winterized, he thought—he hadn't realized how early winters came in Wyoming. And then he remembered, with a pang, that he didn't have a job anymore, and his savings would be gone by the end of the month. Winterizing would just have to wait.

Snowflakes started to fall as he drove up to the Vein, drifting from the sky in a lazy ballet. By the time he pulled in, they were starting to blanket the ground. He cut his engine and checked his phone again, but there was no return message from Daphne. Maybe she was busy on the rig, he reasoned. He knew how cranky Dale got when they looked at their phones on the job.

Still shivering from the cold, Owen steeled himself to enter. If Luna knew he was there for information—worse, information for Daphne—there was no telling what she'd do. But even more difficult than fooling Luna, he'd have to fool himself. It would be a battle against his own hidden desire to return to his family and succumb to the voice that bubbled from his subconscious and spilled out in his dreams. Being around them could be dangerous, seductive. He'd have to watch his back.

Before he could even knock, the door swung open.

"Owen!" Luna's dancing cat-eyes peered out at him. "It worked! You came."

Before he could ask what "worked," her arms were around him, submerging him in her familiar scent of patchouli and earth, a scent he hadn't realized until that very moment he'd even noticed, let alone missed. His arms went automatically around her slender back, her skin warm and alive under the snowflakes melting against her.

Behind her, a little boy stared at them with curious, chocolate-colored eyes. He was seated cross-legged near the bar, playing with a wooden duck whose feet thwapped against the dark, waxed floor and staring up at Luna like she was something out of a storybook. He looked familiar, Owen thought, but he couldn't recall where he'd seen the boy before.

"Come in. It's cold out. And meet Charlie, our nephew. Charlie, say hello to Owen."

"Hello to Owen." Charlie grinned fleetingly and went back to playing with the duck.

"He's shy," Luna explained, fixing the boy with a maternal smile. "But he'll like you once he gets to know you. Everyone will."

She still had a hold of Owen's hand, and she gave his fingers an extra squeeze as she ruffled the boy's hair. In the club's bleak daytime lighting he saw a damp glimmer in the corners of Luna's eyes, a touch of moisture on her lashes.

He struggled to reconcile this new Luna, the one who doted on children and got misty-eyed about seeing Owen, with the girl from his dreams. Since leaving her he'd come to think of his sister as cold and calculating, charismatic but disturbed. He'd forgotten that she had a warm side, too.

"Did you miss me?" Luna blinked up at him, her lashes still dewy with tears.

"Maybe a little."

"Is that why you're here?" She slid behind the bar, flicking a rag over its already-spotless surface, her eyes never leaving his.

"Not exactly." He took the rag from her hand and polished the bar until it gleamed like a mirror, reflecting their twin green eyes. "Actually, I'm looking for work. Got any?"

"For you?" Luna grinned. "Of course, Earth Brother. We're looking for an assistant manager. Your shift starts in an hour."

She named a salary that made Owen's head spin: It was close to what he'd made at the rig, for a fraction of the work.

"Say you'll take it!" Luna clapped her hands, and little Charlie clapped along with her, not understanding the negotiation but happy that she was happy. Owen nodded slowly.

"Excellent!" Luna held out a hand, and Charlie ran to her, clutching the swirling white bottom of her skirt. "Now come upstairs and meet your brothers and sisters. Are you hungry? Of course you are." She flitted through the maze of tables, leading him to a hidden staircase in the back of the bar. His curiosity mounted as they climbed the stairs, Charlie sticking close behind. He was close to meeting the Earth Brothers and Sisters he'd been forced to stay away from, close to unlocking the crucial information about who he was and where he'd come from, what his powers meant and whether others had them as well. Then he'd report it all back to Daphne, and together they'd figure out what to do next.

The loft over the Vein was a riot of color and noise, a hive of warmth and activity with snow falling fat and steady outside its windows. The thick aroma of fresh curry almost brought Owen to his knees. He realized he couldn't remember the last time he'd had a proper meal; life on the rig was a blur of canteen snacks and boxed mac 'n' cheese.

"Freya, get Owen a bowl of stew." Luna winked at a heavy-hipped girl with a long rope-colored braid trailing down her back.

Moments later, his hands closed around a heavy clay bowl, and thick steam drifted into his nostrils. Luna handed him a spoon and guided him to a purple velvet cushion on the floor where, surrounded by his brothers and sisters, Owen dug in and began to eat.

The snow kept falling, inching up the walls of the Vein, blocking the door with heavy, slumbering drifts. It blanketed Owen's truck and the wide, empty parking lot around it, falling with a steady determination that whispered to Owen to stay where he was and wait out the storm.

Time grew sluggish in the gray light of dusk, meandering through the tapestry of falling flakes, each fat as a gumball and feathered like a tiny bird. Owen no longer knew how long he'd been there in the welcoming nest of the loft above the Vein, snuggled into a mattress covered in a plush purple blanket as he downed bowl after bowl of Freya's stew and listened to the throaty melodies of Abilene's singing.

The Children of the Earth settled in around him, a kaleidoscope of shifting bodies and wide-open faces, an emerald sea of eyes just like his. They took turns sitting next to him, sometimes brushing a thigh against his or resting a head on his shoulder. Each of them had a story that began with dreams like his, a story that pulled them through the confusion of turning eighteen and the jumble of spaces between their home and Carbon County, a story that ended here and now, at the Vein with Luna and each other and, finally, him.

"We're so glad you're here," they said, taking his hand, looking him in the eyes. "You're our Earth Brother. You're one of us."

One of us. The words jogged a memory, something about why he'd come. His third helping of stew sat comfortably in his belly, but there was still a nagging question in the back of his mind. "What does that mean?" he asked finally. "What does it mean, to be one of the Children of the Earth?"

"It means you're special." Luna curled against him, taking his arm with one hand and circling Charlie with the other, pulling both of them close. "Powerful. Chosen. We belong to the God of the Earth, and he's given us powers."

"Powers?" He knew this part was important, maybe the most important of all, but he couldn't remember why.

"Yes, powers." Luna brushed his hair back from his eyes. "Special powers that other people don't have. It's because we're attuned to our earth and our gods, because we can feel the vibrations of other worlds and other universes."

"Rocks come when I call them," Heather said, drawing denim-clad knees into her chest.

"I control colors," Aura added.

"And I make *real* comfort food." Freya fingered the rope of her braid. "Food that makes you so comfortable, you won't be able to move or think for hours."

Owen looked from her to the empty bowl by his feet. He felt flattened by contentment, comfortable in the peace of finally being among his family.

These people were like him, and when they were together the thoughts and abilities that made them freaks in the outside world were a badge of honor, something to be celebrated. Here, it was okay to share his secret.

"I can change objects with my mind," he confessed quietly.

Little Charlie was sitting between him and Luna, so Owen couldn't see her eyes flash to life at his words. All he heard was her voice, velvet in his ear.

"That's a beautiful power, Owen," she purred. "You are truly special. Thank you for sharing."

Luna stroked his head, which felt impossibly heavy, like it was full of cement. He let his eyes drift shut. So this was what it felt like to not be alone anymore. These people were just like him: They had the same eyes, the same dreams, the same powers, the same restlessness. Restlessness that had never given way until they reached this place that Luna had created just for them. Until they came home.

Someone lit incense as the steel gray sky darkened to black outside, and Owen let himself drift atop the mattress, part of the tapestry of color and life inside the loft. The snow continued to fall in the still, dead world outside. Finally, he didn't feel like his blood was screaming to escape his veins, like the only way out of the prison of his mind was relentless speed and the deafening buzz of high-octane engines. Finally, he could relax.

It was good to know that he didn't have to fight his powers, that they didn't make him bad. It was even better to know that the Children of the Earth weren't evil or twisted, weren't out to destroy the world. All they wanted was to be together and be themselves. All they wanted was peace.

"I'm just going to take a nap," he murmured to nobody in particular, his voice already choked with slumber. "Just a little one."

"Just a little one," Luna echoed as he drifted off, surrounded by his new and ancient family, into a sleep that was finally, blessedly devoid of dreams.

18

"THERE'S A SEARCH PARTY ON for Sheriff Bates and his boy." Vince Varley stood in the doorless doorway to Doug and Janie's den. "They're missing, and the whole town's out looking for 'em. Are you two coming or not?"

"Coming!" Janie leapt from the couch, where she'd been trying to hold herself still as Doug downed beers and stared vacantly at an obstacle race on ESPN2. Ciaran had dropped her off close to dawn; even though she'd barely slept she felt charged with energy, like she'd been plugged into a wall socket until her internal battery thrummed with life.

It was all because of Ciaran. Ciaran with skin like a beach at sunset, Ciaran whose rainforest-green eyes brimmed with empathy as he drove her to the graveyard where her infant son was buried. Ciaran, who stood aside as she screamed and howled and cried until there was nothing left, until she was empty and clean and new.

Her mind felt clear and sharp, the cloud-cover of her grief wiped away by the cold front that had swept the town in the night.

All because of Ciaran: because he had looked at her and listened to her, unfazed by her sadness, willing to let her grieve.

She bounded to her piles of clothes and started pawing through them, looking for something to wear. Ciaran might be out there, and she wanted to look nice. She wanted to make him see her the way she saw him: as someone magical and lovely, someone who suddenly made life seem worth living.

"I need a shower," she said suddenly, abandoning the clothes. "I'll be quick, promise."

"Jeez," Vince grumbled as she brushed by him. "It's a search party, not a damn debutante ball."

Janie stopped midway down the hallway, his words registering for the first time.

"They're really missing?" She turned to face him.

Vince scowled. "Really. He never came into work, so they searched his house. No sign of him. That old bat Eunice from next door said he always asks her to keep an eye on things when they go out of town, but this time he didn't say a word."

"Oh. Well, I'll hurry up then. You guys go ahead—Doug and I can take his truck."

"Fine," Vince grunted. "Just be careful: It's snowing cats and dogs out there."

Kernels of worry began to poke at Janie's good mood as she stepped into the shower and shampooed her hair, shivering in the measly trickle from the mansion's overworked boiler. What would someone want with the sheriff and Charlie—Charlie, whose big brown eyes and tousled hair always tugged at something in her heart and made her think of the little boy she never got to raise.

But that boy was dead, she reminded herself. Jeremiah was dead, and as much as he would always hold a piece of her heart, she had to accept it and move on. And she could now, she really could, because she was stronger than she realized, stronger than anyone gave her credit for.

Ciaran had taught her that.

She wrapped a towel around her chest and padded back to the den, where Doug's unfocused gaze was still directed in the general vicinity of the TV.

"Damn it, Doug!" she snapped her fingers. "Didn't you hear what your dad said? Are you gonna help us find those guys or not?"

"Huh?" Doug's eyes were bloodshot, his jaw slack. Something was up with him—he wasn't usually this much of a vegetable, even when he was hungover. "Oh yeah. I guess I'll, like, put on a jacket or whatever."

"If you can be bothered." Janie rolled her eyes, waiting for Doug's retort, but none came. Instead he lumbered off the couch and shuffled to his room, his feet barely leaving the ground.

Janie didn't waste any more time worrying about Doug. He would be fine—he always was. Instead she dove for her phone and typed a frantic message to Ciaran. Then she turned back to her clothes.

↔

The search party was well under way by the time she and Doug pulled into the church parking lot. Flashlight beams danced in the thick, wooded area beyond the lawn, illuminating snowflakes that glittered in the darkness like stars. Through the truck's windows they could hear faint cries of "Sheriff Bates!" and "Charlie!"—strange nocturnal calls that made the forest seem at once dead and alive.

Janie shook her head, her hair settling in soft waves beneath her pink pom-pom hat. "I can't believe they're missing," she said quietly. Fear for little Charlie ran in a swift, cold current beneath her bubbling excitement.

"Unh," Doug agreed tonelessly.

"Here," she handed him a flashlight. "We should split up. We can cover more ground that way. And zip up your jacket, darn it. You're gonna freeze to death out there."

Doug looked down at his green puffer jacket, seeming to notice for the first time that he had it on. He was still toying with the zipper as Janie slipped from the truck and hurried toward the woods, following the bouncing beam of her flashlight.

Snowflakes brushed her cheeks, and her breath came in puffs like steam escaping a teakettle, but her insides felt warm, spreading in an even pink glow across her cheeks. She was going to see Ciaran again.

Her flashlight picked up the outline of the tree where they'd agreed to meet, the one with wooden slats on the side leading up to a hunter's blind. It had been her special place ever since she was a little girl, the place she escaped to when post-church picnics ran long into the afternoon and her pretty pink dresses started to scratch against her legs. She'd never shared it with anyone before, not even Doug.

Ciaran was already there, leaning against the trunk, his hands shoved into the pockets of a faded army jacket. He shielded his face against the glare of her flashlight, but the smile in his emerald eyes made her feet feel like wings, lifting her off the ground and carrying her toward him.

He laughed as she sank into his hug. He smelled like wood smoke and earth, like the autumn leaves decaying to dirt beneath their feet.

"It's so good to see you," she said into his chest. She wished they could stay that way all night, the heat from their bodies mingling through layers of coats and clothing. But after a few moments he pulled back and held her at arm's length, studying her carefully.

"Wow." His eyebrows inched up. "You're a new girl."

He brushed a snowflake off her cheek, and the feeling was strange and spicy, a bubbly mix of anticipation and longing that she hadn't felt about anyone in a very long time.

"It's because of you." She couldn't stop looking at his face, at his eyes. "Because of last night. Before that—I probably shouldn't tell you this, but I honestly just wanted to die."

"I know." His finger traced a path down her cheek, lingering beneath her chin.

"And then you helped me. Why?"

His eyes went dark, or maybe it was just a shadow passing through the woods.

"It doesn't matter why," he said quietly.

"What's wrong?" she asked.

"Nothing." He shook his head, and the shadow disappeared. "I'm just worried about that missing kid."

"Me too! We should go look for him."

"Okay."

But neither of them moved. Instead they stood still at the base of the tree, facing each other. She knew that they should search for Charlie, and she wanted to, but there was something she wanted even more.

She pulled Ciaran closer, and he complied, wrapping his arms around her waist, sighing as their bodies made contact. The tips of their noses touched, and a tiny spark lit between them, fueled by static electricity from the cold and maybe something else, something that had been inside of them all along. The shock made them leap at the same time. Then they collapsed against each other, smiling with surprise and nervousness and relief at the tiny joke the universe had sent them, a joke that somehow made it even easier to bring their lips together and lose themselves in a kiss as light and delicate as the snowflakes falling all around.

↔

Daphne's head ached, and her mouth was dry. She took a long drink from the thermos of steaming soup that Aunt Karen had brought to the courthouse, letting it warm her stomach as the headlights of Floyd's truck illuminated the fast-falling snow.

"Thanks again for paying my bail," she said as they pulled into the church parking lot.

"Stop thanking us." There was a grim cast to Karen's motherly tone. "We're family, and we have money now. It's the Godly thing to do."

"Are you sure you want to join this search party?" Floyd asked for what had to be the fifth time since they'd picked her up. "You've already had a heck of a day." His bushy white eyebrows were knit with anger; he'd nearly blown a fuse when he found out she'd been implicated in the sheriff's disappearance.

"I'm sure." Daphne pulled Floyd's old hunting cap down over her ears, grateful that he'd thought to bring a spare. She couldn't bear the thought of Charlie still being at large, missing or possibly worse. Joining the search party felt like the least she could do, even though part of her ached to run home and check her phone for messages from Owen, to see how he'd fared in his undercover mission to the Vein. "Should we meet back here?"

Floyd nodded. "Karen and I will check in the woods across the street. Here, take this." He handed her a small blue penlight. "It's dark out there."

"And be careful!" Karen added.

Daphne kissed each of them on the cheek and opened the door to the truck, her sneakers imprinting the fresh snow as her aunt and uncle started in the other direction.

The trees at the edge of the woods hovered tall and menacing. Dead leaves still clung to their branches, rustling coded warnings in the wind, and a trio of snowflakes landed in cold formation on her nose. There was still time to turn back, she thought as she stepped into the dark overhang. Nobody would judge her—she'd just spent the afternoon in jail. But she knew she wouldn't be able to rest knowing an innocent young boy was still missing.

The woods surrounded her, draping her in shadows. The penlight grew frigid in her ungloved hand, and dampness soaked through her canvas Chuck Taylors, nibbling at her toes.

A sound, startling in the dark maze of trees, made her freeze in place. It was faint but definitely there: a small whimper, followed by heavy breathing.

She froze, her pulse pounding against her neck. Those sounds could be coming from Charlie—and she didn't know who else was out there with him. She had to be careful; it was probably best not to let on that she was there.

Slowly, she raised her penlight and trained it around the woods, trees and shadows blending in the thin illumination of her beam. Then she saw it: something moving, a dark clump against one of the trees. Her light caught a mass of cornsilk-colored hair, and the clump broke into two figures, their breath coming in ragged ellipses.

Daphne's mouth dropped open.

"*Janie?!*" she gasped.

The figures broke apart.

"What the hell?" Janie squinted into the light, her big blue eyes hardening. Daphne's heart clenched as she glanced from her cousin to the guy who'd been kissing her—a guy who definitely wasn't Doug.

Where Doug was all size and neck, this new boy was elfin and delicate. Their eyes met, and a shiver went through her that had nothing to do with the frigid night. She knew those eyes, knew that too-bright-to-be-real shade of green. Janie wasn't just kissing a stranger. She was kissing one of the Children of the Earth.

Janie clicked on her flashlight, bathing Daphne in a sterile circle of white. Her mouth turned down when she made out her cousin's face. "What are you doing here?" Her voice was cold.

"Looking for the sheriff and his son." Daphne tried to keep her tone neutral. "Um, what are *you* doing?"

"That's none of your business," Janie said archly. "And if I were you, I'd keep my mouth shut about this. Unless, of course, you want everyone knowing about your little *thing* with Owen."

"What?" Daphne's hands started to shake, trembling the beam of her penlight.

Janie rolled her eyes. "I'm not dumb, you know. Even if you and everyone else think I am."

The boy placed a gentle hand on her shoulder. "I should go," he said quietly. "It sounds like you two have some things to work out."

"No, Ciaran!" Janie grasped his arm. "Don't. She can go. You stay."

Ciaran spoke so gently, Daphne had to strain to hear. "You care about each other—and both of you are hurting inside."

Daphne felt a jolt of discomfort. How did he know how she felt inside?

Janie shook her head. "I just don't want to deal with her right now."

"Janie." Ciaran caught her eyes and held them until she started to cave. "You need this. Like in the graveyard last night. Do this for you, not me. I'll meet you in the parking lot."

Her features softened as she looked up at him. "Okay." The word came out in a feathery sigh.

He took her hand and brushed her fingertips lightly before turning and walking toward Daphne, heading back the way she'd come.

Ciaran's eyes met Daphne's for a moment as he stepped past her, and she felt something pass between them, a subtle current of understanding. She sensed that he could tell that she knew who and what he was, and in turn he recognized her. He nodded once, the way an athlete would nod to someone from the opposing team. The way you'd nod to an enemy.

Daphne turned back to Janie. Her cousin leaned against the tree, her arms crossed over her chest and her eyes narrowed. The snowfall swallowed the silence between them.

"I guess he's right," Daphne said finally. "I guess we do have stuff to work out."

"Like what?" Janie's nose twitched. "Like you ignore me for months, and then as soon as something good finally happens, you come along and ruin it?"

Her words sliced Daphne's heart. "I wasn't ignoring you," she said quietly.

"Oh yeah? Then how come you never came to see me? I was up in that godforsaken house dying on the inside, and you couldn't even be bothered to stop by?"

Daphne sucked in a sharp breath. "I *wanted* to come see you," she insisted. "But you know how much the Varleys hate me. I wasn't even sure they'd let me in."

As the words fell from her mouth, she realized how pathetic they sounded. It made sense, suddenly, why Janie was so mad. So what if the Varleys weren't Daphne's number-one fans? That was no excuse not to be there for her cousin while she was in mourning, going through the most terrible grief a person could endure. Daphne should have tried harder. She should have been a better friend.

The truth of the matter was something she would rather keep hidden, something she could barely admit to herself. The truth was that she felt helpless in the face of Janie's grief, terrified by her own inability to do or say the right thing, to help when it seemed like her cousin was beyond help. And so she'd ignored it, that feeling of uselessness, caught up instead in her own relationship and her own life, too deep inside her own head to be there when Janie needed her the most.

"And you've been too busy playing prophet," Janie added, her lip curling in a sneer.

A small, hot thread of anger twisted through Daphne's core, burning at the edges of her sympathy. "I'm not playing!" she insisted. "Do you think it's *fun* blacking out? That I'm having these visions because I *feel* like it? Do you really think I'm doing it for the attention, Janie? You've known me my whole life. You know how much I hate attention."

Janie laughed bitterly. "Then why go around telling the whole world that *God* is sending you visions? What could you possibly have to gain, besides everyone making a big old fuss?"

Daphne shoved a freezing hand in her pocket, rubbing it against the lining for warmth. "I'm not doing it for the fuss. I hate the fuss. Something's happening, Janie. These visions are real."

Janie eyed her through slit lids. "And you *really* believe you're a prophet?"

Daphne felt herself shrinking under the weight of the question, a question she'd tried and failed so many times to answer for herself.

"I don't know," she said finally. "When I have these visions, it feels like someone is sending me messages, trying to warn me about something huge. I try to figure them out, but I can't. All I know is that they're important, and they feel like they're coming from a force that's greater than I am—than all of us are. Some people would call that God."

A long, slow breath escaped Janie's nostrils, turning to steam in the night air. "Yeah." When she spoke, she sounded resigned. "I used to believe in all of that: God, prophets, angels, the works. I used to think Pastor Ted was a goddamn genius. But look around you, Daphne. A child is missing. *My* child is dead. What kind of God would allow this? Can you seriously look me in the eye and tell me you still believe when the world is so fucked up?"

Daphne shook her head. "I don't know what to believe," she said.

A dozen scenarios unspooled in her mind. She knew that Janie was right about one thing: The world *was* messed up, full of cruelty and injustice. But maybe that was because God wanted it that way. Maybe all the terrible things that happened were messages warning people to change their ways. Maybe Pastor Ted was correct, and the only way out was through clean living and prayer, through getting right with God.

If only she knew for sure.

"Well, I'm glad we had this little chat." Janie stomped at the ground, trying to warm her feet. "But if you don't mind, I'm gonna take off now. There's someone waiting for me who actually has my back. And to be honest, I'd rather spend my night kissing him than talking to you."

"Janie, wait." The eerie feeling Daphne had gotten when she locked eyes with Ciaran came rushing back. Her gut screamed at her to keep Janie away from him, at least until she could talk to Owen to find out how dangerous the Children of the Earth really were.

"What do you want now?" Janie tapped her foot silently in the snow, impatient to return to the parking lot and her new romance.

"Will you promise me something?" Daphne wanted to take her cousin's hand, to wrap her in a hug, to say with a gesture everything she couldn't seem to say with words, but Janie's eyes held her back.

"Maybe," Janie replied. "Depends what."

"Just be careful around Ciaran," Daphne pleaded. "You don't know who he really is."

"Him?" Janie's laugh was incredulous. "I married *Doug Varley*, and you're telling me the long-haired hippie with the crystal around his neck is dangerous? Jesus, Daphne, you're even more delusional than I thought."

She began to walk away.

"Wait," Daphne started to say. "That's not what I meant . . ."

"I don't really care what you meant." Janie stormed past her, leaving angry footprints in the ankle-deep snow.

"Janie, wait!" Daphne cried. She trained her penlight on her cousin's receding back, but within moments Janie was just a blur between trees.

Daphne sank back against the tree trunk. She felt further from Janie than ever, and she was no closer to finding the sheriff and Charlie either. She snuck a glance at her watch and saw that the hour she'd promised her aunt and uncle was almost up: She'd have to hurry to meet them in time. The snow fell thicker and faster, and soon the roads would be impassible, keeping her from the warm bed and shower she suddenly desperately craved.

Heaving a long, loud sigh, Daphne pushed herself to standing and began the long, frigid walk to the church parking lot.

19

JANIE YAWNED AND STRETCHED, SIGHING with contentment. Chilly gray light filtered into the loft above the Vein, a sign that the snowstorm outside was still going strong the next morning. It was early in the year for that kind of weather, but who cared? She didn't—not as long as she could stay under the faded patchwork quilt with Ciaran, snuggled into his lean, tan body and smelling the mossy aroma of his hair.

"You awake?" His breath was warm on her neck.

"Mmmm-hmmmm." She turned over and found his eyes, her lips tipping into a smile.

"Good." He put his hand on her hip and drew her to him, making her twitch with longing. "Everyone else is downstairs already. C'mere."

Beyond the curve of his shoulder she saw that the loft was empty, its dozen-odd mattresses bare except for tangles of woven blankets and colorful quilts. Ciaran's lips met hers, gentle as butterfly wings, and a soupy desire coursed through her.

"*You* c'mere," she whispered into his mouth, pulling him closer. She kept her eyes open as they fell into a rhythm, not wanting to miss a moment of him. His lids fluttered open as if feeling her gaze, and he looked down at her, smiling. She grinned back, just happy to be there with him, as happy as she'd ever been about anything in her life.

"Wow," Ciaran said when they were done. He pushed a strand of hair behind her ear as she drifted back to reality, to the mattress and his clear green eyes.

"What do you mean, '*wow*'?" Janie pretended to be taken aback.

Ciaran's gaze drifted away from her, toward the door leading down to the Vein. When he turned back he looked almost pained. "It's just—I really like you."

"I really like you, too, silly." Janie sat up and kissed the tip of his nose. She felt loose, her cells still buzzing with pleasure. She felt like she would never be sad again. "I'd stay in this bed with you all day if I could, but it smells like pancakes in here, and I'm seriously about to die of hunger."

Ciaran's shoulders relaxed, and he grinned weakly. "We should go downstairs," he said. "Freya's pancakes are really good."

"Great." Janie dug under the covers for her clothes. "I can't wait to meet your brothers and sisters." A worm of nervousness wriggled under her skin. "Do you think they'll like me?"

It had been late when they'd come in the night before, whispering and giggling their way up the dark, narrow staircase, and the rest of the Children of the Earth were sleeping. It was rare that they got a night off from working at the Vein, Ciaran explained. Usually their days started early and went very late, and when they had the chance to get some extra shut-eye, they took it.

Ciaran's smile was almost wistful. "Oh, they'll love you," he said, getting up and heading for the stairs.

Janie heard voices and laughter coming from below, and they emerged into a room she barely recognized as the dark, seedy bar where she and Ciaran had met. All the lights were on, and the Children of the Earth had pushed the freestanding bar tables together to make a long communal eating space, where they sat with plates of half-eaten pancakes floating in pools of maple syrup. A round-cheeked girl with a deep mahogany complexion strummed a guitar and sang softly, her voice so beautiful that Janie wanted to reach out and wrap her hand around the song.

"Hey, everyone." Ciaran's words floated above the noise, drawing the chatter into silence. The girl with the guitar paused mid-note.

In the sudden quiet, Janie felt the flush across her face deepen. She looked down the length of the table at a dozen different faces, all with the same startling green eyes. They were family, she realized—and she was an intruder.

"This is Janie." Ciaran's hand was still in hers, and he gave her fingers a reassuring squeeze, sensing her sudden discomfort. "She's coming to stay with us for a while. Janie, this is my family: Luna,

Kimo, Abilene, Freya, Gray, Aura, Orion, Silas, Arrow, Cheyenne, Heather, and Owen. Don't worry, the test isn't until tonight."

He laughed, and they all joined in. Janie felt herself smile, but her eyes were still stuck at the end of the table, where Owen sat staring back at her in shock.

So Owen was here: He was one of them. Janie wondered if Daphne knew. And if she *did*, and she still claimed to support Pastor Ted's belief that the Vein was a hotbed of sin, and she still tried to stop Janie from seeing Ciaran, didn't that make her the biggest hypocrite who ever lived?

"Welcome, Janie." Luna came around the side of the table, her arms spread wide. She wore a long purple dress embroidered with tribal designs, and her dreadlocks were piled high on her head. For a moment, Janie's blood went cold. She remembered the way Doug had looked at Luna when she first blew into town, flaunting that skinny body and flinging hula hoops all over the place. She remembered hating Luna then.

But now it felt different. As she approached, Luna seemed to give off a soft blue light that wrapped around Janie like a fuzzy coat.

"Welcome," Luna said again. "Welcome home."

The blue light tickled Janie's cheek and snuggled into the back of her neck, and in that moment Janie realized that Ciaran, Luna, and the others weren't like the rest of Carbon County: They didn't secretly judge her for getting pregnant at seventeen, didn't resent her for losing the baby or look down on her the way Daphne did.

They seemed to see the person she could be, even under all the flaws.

She felt Ciaran's hand slip from hers as she accepted Luna's embrace, letting the warm blue light fill her until it seemed to glow beneath her skin. One by one Ciaran's family approached, literally welcoming her with open arms, telling her how glad they were to see her, how happy they hoped she'd be at the Vein.

Owen was last. She'd seen him hanging back from the rest of the crowd, a crease of confusion wrinkling his forehead. When everyone else had drifted away, he approached.

"Hi, Janie." He chewed his lower lip, staring down at his shoes.

"Hi, Owen."

Ciaran stepped forward. "You two know each other?"

"Oh yeah." Janie nodded. "We go way back."

"Yeah." Owen looked at her as if searching for a memory in her face, but finally he just shrugged. He seemed sleepy or something—definitely more out of it than when he first came to Carbon County and started causing trouble all over the motocross track.

"Great!" Ciaran put a hand on the small of her back, speaking to Owen. "Then why don't you take Janie into the kitchen and show her where we hid the breakfast? She mentioned something about being starving."

Janie turned and kissed Ciaran on the cheek, then let Owen lead her through a pair of double doors and into a bright industrial kitchen with big windows revealing the raging snow squall outside.

"So," she asked once they were out of earshot. "What are you doing here?"

"I belong here." Owen handed her a plate. "This is my family."

"Does Daphne know?" Janie took it, helping herself from a stack of pancakes steaming on a warmer.

"Daphne . . ." Owen trailed off, staring out the window.

"You know—your girlfriend?" Janie prompted.

Owen turned back to her. "Yeah, I know who Daphne is. My girlfriend."

"Does she approve?" Janie looked around for syrup. "Of you being here? 'Cause knowing Daphne, probably not."

"Yeah." Owen sighed, deflating against a countertop. "Probably not."

"She'd probably get all judgey on you, right? Tell you all about how what you're doing is wrong?"

Owen cracked a half-hearted smile. "You know her pretty well."

"Blood relatives." She located the syrup. "I know her just as well as anyone—or I thought I did, until she turned into Prissy the Prophet."

Owen shook his head. "She's just doing what she thinks is right."

"Yeah." Janie grabbed a fork. "Even though what she thinks is right is pretty crazypants. Like: prophet? Voices from God? Great battle between good and evil? C'mon." She shook her head. "Who even believes that stuff anymore? Just Daphne. And if you disagree with her, you're automatically going against God and should be, like, strung up on a cross or something."

Owen's hands balled into fists at his sides. "That's the thing—I know she wouldn't approve of me being here. But she doesn't understand: These guys aren't bad people. They're not trying to start an apocalypse or anything. They're just hippies. And they're my family."

Family. The word prodded at Janie's brain, reminding her of earlier, happier days, when her family had been her and Mom and Dad and Doug and even Cousin Daphne. But those days were gone—those people weren't her family anymore. Real families accepted one another and were there when bad things happened. Real families didn't let their loved ones practically die of grief.

"I get it," she said. Owen's cheeks flushed, and she wondered if he was embarrassed at how much he'd just confessed. "They seem pretty great to me."

"They are." He gave her a shy grin. "They're even better once you get to know them."

Janie started back to the doors. "I hope they'll feel like my family soon."

"They will." Owen reached out and patted her awkwardly on the shoulder. "You'll be surprised how quickly they will."

20

THE SNOWSTORM RAGED FOR TWO full days, which Janie and Owen spent snowed in at the Vein, sinking deeper into life with the Children of the Earth. Owen remembered, dimly, his promise to Daphne, but as the minutes melted into hours and the inches turned to feet in the parking lot outside, their pact grew fainter in the back of his mind. He was home at last, among his people and without worry or fear for the first time since his very earliest days. And with every bite of Freya's stew, beat of Orion's drum, note of Abilene's singing, and word from Luna's tongue the rest of the world faded further and further away until it, and Daphne, were nothing but a smudgy blur in the background of a long-forgotten photograph.

In the meantime, Daphne paced the claustrophobic Peyton trailer, biting her nails into nubs with each message to Owen that went unanswered. Something was wrong, but with the snowstorm raging outside there was nothing she could do. Jobs, schools, stores, and churches were all closed; even the rig shut down under the weight of the snow. The search party for the sheriff and Charlie was on hold, leaving the whole town on edge, and all Daphne could do was pace and pray and hope that when the snow cleared, Owen would reply to her texts and the sheriff and Charlie would be found and everything would go back to normal—or at least as close to normal as things in Carbon County could get.

On the third morning Daphne woke to the chug and scrape of the town plow clearing the road, and she opened her eyes to a blinding spray of sunlight. She tore out of bed and threw on the first clothes she could find, racing to the mound of snow burying her tiny hatchback to scrape and shovel until she was cherry-cheeked and breathless.

"Let me give you a hand with that." Floyd struggled out the front door with an industrial-grade ice scraper.

"I'm almost done." The car was on, puffing clouds of exhaust into the still morning, the engine's heat slowly melting the last stubborn bumps of ice from the windshield.

"Well, gosh." Floyd squinted into the sunlight. "Where are you on such a tear to, anyway?"

"Just out." She couldn't tell him the truth, and she didn't want to lie.

"Guess you're going a little stir-crazy from all that time snowed in with two old fuddy-duddies, huh?" He wiggled his eyebrows.

"Not at all." She kissed his ruddy cheek. "I'll be back in a couple hours."

"Grab some milk while you're out!" he called as she backed down the driveway, tires skidding. Even caked in sand and sprinkled in salt, the road was still like an ice rink.

Around the last bend in the road before town, a line of stalled cars blocked her way. She slammed on her brakes, the car fishtailing to a stop just inches from an SUV. Up beyond the line of cars she saw a small crowd of people huddled at the base of the flagpole outside the Carbon County police station. They craned their heads skyward, staring at something waving in the wind where Old Glory should have been.

"Oh no." Dread gathered in Daphne's stomach as she reached the station and got a better look. Someone was up there, strung up and left to die in the storm. What if it was Owen, and she was too late? She pushed open her door and ran along the row of smoke-stuttering cars toward the police station, ignoring the sudden stitch knitting her side.

As she drew close she heard the murmurs, soft mooings of disgust and dismay. "What kind of sicko . . . ?" ". . . some Satanic ritual . . ." ". . . just awful . . ." ". . . strung up like yesterday's laundry . . ." ". . . and to think, the boy is still missing."

The stitch pressed hard into her gut, and she doubled over at the edge of the crowd, her breath coming in gasps. Slowly, almost reluctantly, she followed the assembled gaze up the flagpole, craning her neck until the figure came fully into view and bile rushed her throat.

Dressed in a clean plaid shirt and pressed chinos, the sheriff had been carefully threaded into a harness made from nylon rope. Snow coated his head and shoulders, and his skin was blue and bitten by the wind, his eyes staring out at some unknown nothingness deep in the mountains. A single, glistening red teardrop had been drawn in blood on his forehead.

Daphne tore her eyes away from the corpse, fighting the dizziness that swam in her head. She hadn't tried hard enough to find him; none of them had. They shouldn't have let a storm stop them, even if meteorologists claimed it was the heaviest snowfall to hit Wyoming in September in over a hundred years.

Now it was too late for the sheriff. It was most likely too late for his son, Charlie, too. Daphne could hardly bear to think about what it meant for Owen. Was it too late for him as well?

"Daphne Peyton." Someone said her name, and the crowd under the flagpole turned imploring gazes upon her. She recognized them from Elmer's Gas 'n' Grocery and the new diners downtown, faces vaguely familiar in that small-town way, but mostly she recognized them from church.

"Who was it?" asked a string bean of a man in a plaid hunting jacket. "Who would do such a thing?"

"And *why*?" A woman cradling an infant asked plaintively, tears trickling in freezing rivulets down her face.

The crowd murmured, bouncing on their toes, silent, waiting.

She was their prophet, the one who supposedly had all the answers. Now they wanted to know why this had happened. They needed her to lead them in the face of this sudden dark stain on their community, this stark defiance of human life.

"I—" she began, and the crowd leaned forward. Out of the corner of her eye she saw something rustle in the window of the police station, a crack widening between two slats in the venetian blinds. The detectives were probably in there, she realized with a thought like a quick hiccup. And she was standing right outside, at the scene of the crime, their number-one suspect.

"Who?" The crowd persisted. "Why?"

"I don't know," she choked. Now Detective Fraczek was striding toward her, eyes locked on hers, a sneer drawn out over his coffee-grounds stubble. Detective Madsen waddled in his wake, trying to zip a fleece jacket over his stomach.

"I have to go."

She turned and ran, her feet sliding on the road's slick surface, each step threatening to send her sprawling. The last thing she heard was Detective Madsen shouting, "What the hell!" and then she was squealing into a one-eighty, swerving away from the police station, driving as fast as her little car dared to go up into the mountains.

↔

The door to the Vein swung open with a bang, and she stood for a moment in the doorway, breathing in the sudden warmth. The club had opened early that day to accommodate the town's hardest drinkers, and now they were bellied up to the bar nuzzling glasses of whiskey and foaming steins of beer, looking as if it had been years since they had a drink instead of just two days.

Daphne took a step forward, but a meaty arm blocked her way. "Miss, I need to see some ID," said a bouncer the size of a small cottage.

"I'm not here to drink." Daphne pushed past him and stormed into the bar, quickly scanning the room. "Is Owen here?"

"Owen? Sure." There was a smirk in the bouncer's voice. "Right over there."

She whirled, and there he was. Owen. Behind the bar, smiling as he wiped and stacked pint glasses. The look on his face was infuriatingly placid, as if three days hadn't passed since they last had contact, as if she hadn't been going crazy with worry and fear. As if nothing had happened at all.

"What the *hell*?" She started toward the bar, startling him. He fumbled with the glass he'd been cleaning but recovered it with a graceful swoop.

"Hey." He draped the cleaning rag over his shoulder and leaned a casual elbow on the bar. "How's it going?"

"How's it *going*? Owen, what happened? Why didn't you text me back?"

His face was different. In the club's slow-changing lights it took a moment to realize what it was.

He looked happy. The tension was gone from his temples, and his jaw no longer held that tightness she'd come to expect as if it were a part of him, something he had carried with him from the womb.

"I'm sorry." He shrugged, his smile fading but not disappearing. "I must have forgotten to charge my phone."

"Ever since you came up here?" She swallowed angrily, not wanting to lose it in the bar, with the greasy prospectors pretending not to peer at her over their drinks. "I'm confused . . . I thought you were on my side."

"Daphne. Hey." He came around the bar and put his hands on her shoulders. "This isn't about sides. You're my girlfriend. They're my family."

She stepped away. Something was wrong: This wasn't the Owen she knew. That Owen was a lot of things, but mellow had never been one of them. Something had happened to him, something to make him act the way he was acting. It was like he'd been drugged.

"What's wrong?" His arms still dangled in the air, searching for her touch. "Look, Daphne. They're not the monsters you think they are. They took me in and gave me work when I had nowhere else to go."

"And what about the tablet?" Daphne's whisper was tinged with fury. "We read it together. You know who these people are."

Owen shook his head. "Who knows about the tablet, what it really means or where it came from? I'm telling you, they're just a bunch of hippies. I'm happy here, okay? Can't you be happy for me?"

Daphne paused, torn. Why *couldn't* she be happy for him? Was she really so selfish that she'd deny him his right to be where he belonged, to be content with who he was? Did she really not want him to be happy just because he wasn't happy in quite the way she wanted?

But there was something fake about his happiness, something off. He wasn't the Owen she knew.

Taking his arm, she brought him into a dark corner of the bar, away from the prying eyes of the prospectors and bar staff.

"You remember why you came here, right?" she whispered.

Owen cocked his head, confusion clouding his eyes. "You wanted me to."

"*You* wanted to." She tried to keep the frustration, the pleading, from her voice. Maybe if Owen remembered why he'd come in the first place, it would jostle him back to reality, back to the world where he and Daphne were a team. "You wanted to find out about them, about what they're capable of. Remember?"

He shook his head. "They're capable of giving me work and making me feel at home," he said finally. "I hope you'll at least give them a chance."

Daphne felt something crack inside of her. Hot tears of anger and frustration gathered in the corners of her eyes.

"I don't understand. It's like you're a different person! It's like . . . don't you think it's possible they've . . . *done* something to you?" she pleaded. She took his hand, searching his eyes, and brought her face close to his so their lips were just inches apart. Maybe the closeness, the way their bodies fell naturally together, would remind him of who he was and what they had, even if words couldn't.

"Remember that night at the track?" she whispered. His eyes closed, and he pressed his forehead to hers. She could feel him starting to respond. "Remember . . ."

"Remember what?" Luna cut in, inserting herself into their corner of the bar. Gold dust glittered on her eyelids, and she was wrapped in a gold corset. She carried a hula hoop coated in dense gold glitter that sent pinpricks of light dancing on the club's dark walls.

At the sound of her voice, Owen instinctively took a step back, leaving Daphne standing alone.

She wheeled on Luna. "You did something to him," she said through clenched teeth.

Luna put a hand to her chest. "Nothing he didn't already want."

"I don't believe you." Daphne glanced at Owen placidly watching their conversation. "Look at him. He's just standing there, letting us talk about him like he's a child. He can't even think for himself!"

Luna's eyes narrowed. "I took away his pain. I made him feel at home. If you don't like it, you can leave."

"Not without him." Daphne drew herself up tall and clamped her hand around Owen's. But as quickly as she clasped it, he yanked it away.

"You don't get it, Daphne," he said quietly. "I want to stay. And I want that to be okay with you."

Prickles filled the back of Daphne's throat, stabbing as she tried to swallow them away. "Are you saying it's over?"

Owen shook his head. "I don't know why it has to be so cut and dried. Why can't I be with you *and* be with my family?"

"Because . . ." Daphne started to say.

But before she could get the words out, Luna fixed her with a piercing emerald gaze. Blue light poured from Luna's throat, and Daphne felt it coming for her, cornering her, bathing her in a feeling of warm relief like sinking into a sensory deprivation chamber where there was no more pain, no more blood, no more heart beating erratically in her chest.

"You want to leave Owen here with us." Luna spoke in the quiet, measured tones of a hypnotist, and Daphne felt herself succumbing. So this was what had a hold over Owen: this sense of peace. It was wonderful, she thought, sinking deeper. No wonder Owen wanted to stay. Maybe she'd stay, too.

Daphne felt the blue light enter her like water, stirring dormant longings that had slumbered in the back of her mind since her earliest days. She relaxed into the sense of peace, letting it take her. It was wonderful not to have to fight anymore.

Dimly, Daphne realized that just as Owen could change objects with his mind, Luna could change people's desires with her will. It was her power: the blue light, the hypnotic voice, all part of what made people do what she wanted. It was what had turned Owen to her side, and now she was trying to use her powers on Daphne.

Through the haze, Daphne suddenly understood how dangerous the Children of the Earth could be. They could control objects and minds—and probably other things—with their will. Between the thirteen of them, they likely held enough power to destroy the town . . . and possibly the whole world.

The thought broke a wave of blackness over her, and she felt her eyes start to roll back in her head. She had just enough time to feel for the door and stumble out into the snow before a third vision yanked her into another world, a world of booming voices and yawning chasms, of chaos, blackness, and fire.

Vision of the Fallen

Fear roots your feet to the earth.

A great pillar of fire rises

From the chasm dividing you

From good, and good from evil.

The smoke rises, and the people scream

And scaly beasts, ancient, giant,

Rise from the pits of Hell

To consume, to destroy.

An inhuman scream pulls your eyes away.

And lo, there in the great divide,

A dark figure in a dark chasm

Falls.

The body sinks.

The arms flail

And the eyes glow

An evil green.

And then it's gone, screams dead in the air.

Banished to the place where evil is born

And evil dies, a place more terrible

Than a thousand Hells.

21

DOUG ROLLED OVER ONTO HIS side and grimaced at the harsh sunlight seeping through the window. He guessed it had stopped snowing finally, which meant he was probably supposed to be at work down at the rig, which made him pull the pillow over his face and groan loudly.

The rig was the last place in the world he wanted to be. Ever since that thing at the Vein, the thing with Luna that he didn't want to think about but couldn't stop playing over and over in his mind, working at the Varley rig had been goddamn torture. In five drunken minutes he'd gone from being the golden boy all those roughnecks looked up to, to the grown-up equivalent of the little kid in middle school who always got picked last in gym class. He couldn't even walk by without those jerk-offs sniggering into their palms.

Even his dad was starting to look at him funny, but ol' Vince Varley was too much of a stick-in-the-mud to ask what was going on. Instead he'd turn his back quickly, always on the pretext of discussing some drilling BS with Dwayne or investigating a valve somewhere on the derrick. It was like he didn't even want to think that maybe his only son had done anything less than shit gold.

Which he was probably thinking right now, Doug realized as he ventured a peek at his alarm clock. It was nearly eleven, and he was supposed to report into work at seven A.M. sharp. If Vince wasn't his dad, he'd be *so* fired. As it was, he needed to get his ass down there before the ol' man decided that maybe nepotism wasn't his best bet.

Doug downed a few Advil as he struggled into his jeans. The snow days had been good: Not going to the rig meant not having to deal with his coworkers' bullying. He'd had the foresight to stop in at Elmer's Gas 'n' Grocery when the snow got bad, so he'd had a couple of cases of Coors to keep him company, plus all the crap TV he wanted to watch, with nobody around to tell him to change the channel. Janie hadn't been at the house; she'd texted him from that pointless search party to say she was going home with her folks that night, which probably meant she'd gotten her nose in the gossip mill and heard what happened with Luna at the Vein. She hadn't texted or anything since then, either, so he figured he was probably getting the silent treatment.

Hell, he'd be pissed if he were her, too. And he deserved it, in a way—she hadn't done anything to him except be weird and sad, and he'd tried to cheat on her. That was messed up. He kept telling himself that as soon as he felt like himself again he'd find a way to apologize, but so far that hadn't happened.

Doug blasted Slipknot as he drove to work, the music pumping him up for what was sure to be another miserable day of getting mocked, laughed at, and generally shat upon.

He had barely pulled into the parking area when Sid started in. "Hey, look who bothered to show up for work!" His thick Cro-Magnon lips sprayed saliva as he talked. "What happened, bootlicker, you need to put in a shift at the shoeshine stand first?"

The rest of the guys guffawed, and Doug put his head down, the back of his neck growing hot as he tried not to let the jeers penetrate. He was just there to do a job, he reminded himself. Eventually the guys would forget about what had happened up at the Vein. They had to, right?

But Doug knew better than anyone what a lost cause *that* was. Wasn't he the one who had teased Carl Boraca right up until high school graduation for the time he got an erection at the front of Ms. Tisdale's class in the seventh grade? He knew how good it felt to latch on to something like that and never let go. That was the bitch of it: He could actually *sympathize* with the people making his life hell, because for most of his life he'd done it to everyone else.

It wasn't something he felt so great about anymore, now that the tables were turned.

"Hey, Dad." Head still down and insults ringing in his ears, Doug entered the trailer where his father and Dwayne were bent over a complicated-looking geological map. Their heads jerked up, twin looks of irritation on their faces. "Uh, sorry I'm late," he soldiered on, fiddling with his zipper, pushing it up and down on its track. "My alarm didn't go off, and, uh, I guess I overslept."

"Jesus, son." Vince slammed a hand down on the table. "You gotta get it together. I got a rig to run here—I need folks who'll actually show up. I can't keep doing you favors just 'cause you're my boy."

"Sorry," Doug said again, his cheeks flaming. "I'm ready to get to work, if you have something for me."

Vince looked at Dwayne, who sighed heavily. "We're kind of in the middle of something, man." His eyes darted around the trailer, looking to settle anyplace but on Doug. "Can you gimme a sec? Just go sit over there or whatever."

"Okay." Doug lowered himself obediently into a cold metal folding chair in the corner, feeling like Bella that time Janie caught her shitting on the rug. As his dad and Dwayne turned their attention back to the map, he wished it were a snow day again. He wished it could stay a snow day forever.

"So *anyway*," Vince said to Dwayne, "you gotta make it deep—see, 'cause if we go *under* Floyd's supply, we'll not only get that oil for ourselves, but we'll choke off his share." His voice grew thick with glee. "Boy, I can't wait to see the look on his face."

"I dunno, boss." Dwayne scratched at the stubble speckling his chin. "I mean, it's a good idea, but it's not, like, totally the safest. You see this fault line here, on the geo map? We'd basically be drilling right through it."

"So?" Vince's look wavered between angry and perplexed.

"So—well, you don't want to disrupt a fault line." Dwayne sucked in breath, obviously uncomfortable. "It could mess up the plates or, like, even cause an earthquake. That's, like, Earth Science 101."

"Oh, is it?" A nasty edge crept into Vince's tone. "And you think you're so fancy, with your spankin' new earth science degree and that stupid foreman's belt of yours?"

"No, sir." Dwayne shrank back. "I just don't want to cause an earthquake."

"And I suppose what *you* want matters?" Vince took a step toward him, backing him up against the wall. "I suppose this is *your* oil rig, on *your* property, and *you* took out the loans to pay for it? Is that what you think?" His face was purple, set into the same glare of rage that had made Doug run and cower so many times throughout his life. He knew how it felt to have Vince Varley all up in your grill—it sucked, and even though Dwayne had been shitty to him since the bootlicker incident, he didn't deserve to get that kind of crap just for trying to do his job.

"Whoa, Dad, chill." Doug got up from his chair. "Maybe Dwayne has a point, y'know? Like, we haven't even tried drilling on our land yet. Maybe we should do that before we go and cause an earthquake or whatever."

Vince wheeled on him, furious. His hands were fists at his sides.

"Son, just who do you think you're talking to?"

Doug looked down at his shoes.

"You have *no right* to tell me how to run my rig!" Vince continued, as Doug had known he would. Once his dad geared up for a tirade, there was no stopping him. All you could do was stand there and take it. "First you go getting some floozy knocked up, then you lose the baby, and then you try running around on her in the most asinine goddamn way possible. You think I don't know about you licking that whore's boots up at that bar? You think I'm not goddamn embarrassed right now that you're my son?"

He paused, panting, his forehead glistening with beads of sweat. "*Do you?!*" he barked.

"I—I don't know," Doug finally stuttered.

"Well, I'll tell you." Vince's chest puffed out with rage and a touch of the old Varley pride. "If I could renounce you as my son, I would. You are a disgrace to the Varley name."

Something hot and unwelcome burned the back of Doug's eyes. *Oh god, please don't let me cry,* he thought, blinking rapidly. It would be too embarrassing, more embarrassing than one man could handle in a lifetime.

"But your mother would never let me do that, unfortunately." Vince Varley's voice was quieter now, although rage still simmered beneath the surface. "So listen, son, you have one job from now on—and trust me, it is *not* to tell me how to run my rig. All I want you to do from now on, son, is smile and nod. When I'm talking, when Dwayne is talking, when *anyone* is talking. Just smile and nod, son. Smile and nod. You got that?"

Doug, following his father's command, nodded. He tried to smile, too, but the smile just wouldn't come.

"Now get the hell out of here." Vince Varley turned from him back to Dwayne, as if he was exhausted by the subject. "The real men in this trailer have work to do."

Doug stumbled down the stairs, giving himself the small pleasure of slamming the door behind him. He trudged past his coworkers, their stale bootlicker jokes slashing at his ears, making his breath come in deep, ragged snorts. He could barely see by the time he got the door to his truck open and launched himself in, cranking the key in the ignition and getting the hell out of there as fast as possible, away from his horrible dad and shitty, fake friends.

He was still breathing heavily, his eyes still blurry, as he turned onto Buzzard Road and sped past town. It was like his whole world was coming down around him, and as he passed Elmers Gas 'n' Grocery he thought of the dusty shelf of DVDs inside. He and Janie used to spend hours in there, joshing each other and fake-arguing over what to watch, finally settling on the goofiest comedy they could find and watching it on his couch with a bag of microwave popcorn in their laps, giggling and holding buttery hands and sneaking makeout sessions whenever his parents were out of the room.

Impulsively, he turned into the lot and headed inside, brushing past the new display of fancy beef jerkies and the refrigerated beer cabinets and going all the way to the back, where the DVDs still sat right where he'd left them all those months ago.

He'd get something funny and surprise her, he decided, selecting a romantic comedy that he could give two shits about but knew would make Janie smile. It had been a while since they did something together—actually *together* and not just side by side in the twin closed-off bubbles their lives had become since the oil and the pregnancy and the wedding and the mansion and all the crazy shit that had gone down since. It would be nice to spend some time with her, to actually look her in the eyes and ask how she was doing, to tell her he knew she hadn't been all that great lately and that was okay because, hey, it turned out he wasn't doing so great either.

Janie'd had enough time to calm down over the incident at the Vein, he reasoned. She'd been at her folks' place for a couple of days, and now that the roads were passable he was almost positive she'd be there at the mansion, waiting for him to come home so they could talk about it and he could apologize and they could make up. To her, he was still the best halfback on the football team, the star rider at the motocross track, the guy in the cafeteria all the girls wanted to get with. He was still the star of her life.

This was gonna be good, he thought as he paid for the DVDs and the popcorn and an extra-large pack of Sour Patch Kids because, hey, why the hell not? He would show his wife some love, save his marriage, maybe even get her interested in sex again. Who needed Luna when he had a hot little number like Janie waiting for him at home?

He congratulated himself on his plan as he pulled out of the parking lot, Nickleback blasting in his ears while he hummed along in an offhand, off-key kind of way. He pulled into the driveway, cut the engine, and went running up the sweeping staircase, calling her name.

But his voice echoed back at him off the half-finished walls, and only Bella came running, yapping and pawing at his knees. He scooped her up and scratched absently at the soft fur behind her ears as he checked every wing of the house, even looking in the closets and beneath Janie's neatly folded pink sleeping bag, like maybe she'd shrunk to the size of a doll and was playing a game of hide-and-seek to amuse herself.

But Janie wasn't there. She wasn't in the kitchen, or the bathroom, or their bedroom, or the den. Janie was nowhere to be found, and he felt his stomach twist with worry and something darker and more bitter, something that leached into the lining of his gut with every place he thought to look.

Finally he sank onto the couch in the den they had once shared, opening the Sour Patch Kids and popping one into his mouth in defeat. He picked up his phone and stared at it as Bella nuzzled into his lap, knowing he had to call her, that it was on him to apologize.

Five more Sour Patch Kids, he decided, munching thoughtfully. Five more Sour Patch Kids, and then he'd make that call.

22

SNOW SEEPED THROUGH DAPHNE'S JACKET, chilling her until she felt heavy and immobile, as impermanent as the drifts that had cradled her fall. Fire from her visions mingled with the day's bright sunlight, orange and red and hot and cold and real and imagined. The world was all flames and sunshine, there were beasts and demons, the screams were both outside and inside her head.

A demon approached, scaly hands reaching for her, yellowed eyes burning. It opened its mouth to speak, to spew flames and lava down on her, and she shrank back, whimpering.

"Lady, you okay?" the demon asked. Its face swam before her, refusing to come into focus: She saw towering horns and scaly limbs rubbed gray by centuries of passing time.

She scurried backward, shielding her eyes from the sun, trying and failing to find traction in the snowdrift. Without the glare the horns turned to a Stetson hat, the scales to a case of dry skin. Was he a demon or a man in a hat? Fever burned at her, blurring the lines until she couldn't tell which was which.

"Just want to make sure you're okay." The demon (or was it a man in a hat?) squatted next to her. "Ain't exactly normal to come out of a bar and find a girl just lying in the snow."

A bar. A girl. The snow. Daphne looked past his wide hat to the glowing red sign that towered above him. *The Vein.*

The morning rushed back at her: the sheriff's corpse strung up outside the police station, Owen's strange behavior when she confronted him, Luna interrupting and filling Daphne's head with that otherworldly blue light, trying to bend her will.

"You faint or something?"

She remembered the vision then. It flooded her head, filling it with fire and chasms and that shadowy black figure falling into an endless void, its screams echoing off the walls. She clutched her forehead, trying to fight the searing pain there, a sudden and brutal headache.

"Miss." The man grasped her shoulder. "I'm gonna take you to the hospital."

Daphne rubbed her temples, willing the headache to subside. Instead it spread through her limbs, making her shudder against the pain. "No hospital," she said through gritted teeth. She didn't want to deal with doctors, with machines, with Pastor Ted showing up at her bedside to pick at her last vision before she could think it through. All she wanted was a glass of water and her bed. "I'll drive home."

She started to push herself to standing, but a wave of dizziness rolled over her, and she pitched forward, her cheek landing painfully on the snowdrift's icy crust.

"I don't think that's a good idea." The demon morphed into a man again, a man with concerned, heavy-lidded eyes. "I may've had two beers, but you're too sick to even walk. Tell me your address, and I'll drive you."

Ordinarily she would have known better than to accept a ride with a strange man. Ordinarily she would have crawled all the way home through the snow before giving in.

But the pain flooded through her, and images from her vision still pulsed in her mind. She was sick, she realized—definitely feverish, possibly delirious. "Okay," she said weakly. "But I carry pepper spray, just so you know."

He reached out a weatherworn hand and helped her to her feet. "You won't have to use it on me. Scout's honor."

The world rolled at her in waves as she stumbled, half-supported by the stranger, to his truck. She gasped out her address and collapsed in the passenger seat, scenes from her vision descending over her eyes like a stage curtain. Over and over again, a chasm opened in the earth—the same chasm she'd seen in her second vision, the one separating her from the Children of God.

Over and over, the ground opened up to release a pillar of flames, and just when it seemed like too much to bear, like the world was about to end in a rain of fire, she turned to see that dark figure falling, his screams echoing off the walls, being sucked down to a place that, the voice in her head had been clear, was worse than a thousand hells.

Where was that place, and who was the falling figure? She was dimly aware of the truck's wheels bouncing over Carbon County's back roads, the familiar scenery mingling with scraps from her vision as her eyes slit open and closed again, the lemony sunlight seeping through the clouds outside stabbing tiny daggers into her head.

"We're here." The man's gruff voice broke through her fever dreams, and she realized the car had come to a stop in front of the Peytons' trailer. "Told you you wouldn't have to use that pepper spray."

"Thanks." She fumbled for the door handle, but he was already there, opening it from the outside, helping her out. "Who are you, anyway?"

He held her elbow as they made their way slowly to the door. "Not much of anyone, really. Just another sucker drifting through Carbon County, hoping to hit oil and strike it rich."

Daphne's mouth fell open. So he was one of the drifters: those unsavory characters everyone in Carbon County was hardwired to hate.

"Do you live up at the old motocross track?" she asked.

He gave a single, doleful chuckle. "Don't know if 'live' is the right word for it, but yeah. That's where I stay."

They were at the door, and before Daphne could fumble for her keys, Aunt Karen opened it, took one look at Daphne, gasped, and collected her in her arms. Another wave of dizziness broke over Daphne, and she let her aunt lead her to the couch and tuck her under a warm blanket. She lay there gratefully drifting in and out of consciousness as her aunt clucked around her with hot tea and cool compresses and promises of chicken soup. It was only when she heard his truck pull away that Daphne realized she had never thanked the drifter who had helped her home. She had never even learned his name.

↔

The fever broke at dawn, but Daphne felt like she had broken with it. Still too weak to leave the couch, she let the afternoon sunlight slide over her face, pulling the afghan up to her chin and sinking deeper into the pillow, knowing but not caring that the plush corduroy would leave tracks across her cheek.

Did anything matter anymore? Owen was gone from her, different, holed up with Luna, and everything in the tablet was coming true. The Children of the Earth had arrived in Carbon County, and they had powers—powers that, if used properly, could bring Carbon County to its knees.

And what did Daphne have? Cryptic visions that turned opaque when examined too closely, visions that she felt—but did not know and could not prove—came from God.

In those visions Owen was a demon, drawing fire down from the mountains. The earth rumbled and divided, the Children of God on one side and the Children of the Earth on the other. There was a battle, with weapons, but she was on the wrong side. Why?

She shivered beneath the afghan. She couldn't shake the image of the figure falling, endlessly, into the chasm, couldn't ignore the sense of loss she felt whenever that image played over in her mind. She pulled the afghan over her head and closed her eyes, letting the hot, close darkness pull her back down into sleep . . .

↔

She woke from a fitful slumber at the sound of voices coming from the kitchen, low and thick with worry. Daphne shrugged off the last slivers of sleep and peered over the back of the couch. Floyd and Karen were huddled at the kitchen table, their faces worn and creased with concern. Opposite them was a wide, slumped back in a green fleece jacket.

A sour feeling rose in Daphne's stomach. She'd know the creased and reddened skin of that thick neck anywhere. Doug was in the trailer, and whatever he was telling the Peytons wasn't good.

". . . just can't find her anywhere." He spread his hands on the table. "I thought she was here, but when I called, you guys said you hadn't seen her, and then I got worried. I've been calling and texting her nonstop . . . nothing. I called Pastor Ted and Hilary and all our old buddies from high school. I even called the police. Nobody's heard a word."

"Find who?" Daphne climbed off the couch, tossing her fatigue aside with the afghan.

Doug looked up at her, surprised, and she recoiled at the sight of his face. His skin was rumpled and gray, his chin dotted with stubble too thick to be a five-o'clock shadow. His hair was greasy and uncombed, his clothes slack with the worn-in look of having been slept in. Or stayed-up-all-night in, given the broken blood vessels spreading across his eyes.

She expected Doug to bristle the way he always did when she was around. She knew she represented rejection for him, and Doug had never handled that like a man. Instead, he sighed and put his head in his hands.

"Janie." The word came out like a sob.

"Janie's missing." There was a sigh in Uncle Floyd's pale blue eyes as he looked up at Daphne, filling in the blanks. "We've been working with Doug to figure out where she might have gone, but right now—well, it's not looking so good."

"Oh, God." Daphne gripped the edge of the table, trying to steady herself.

"I know." Floyd's voice was grave. "It's disturbing, what with the sheriff and everything. We're trying to make the best of it, but we're all pretty scared."

"No." Daphne screwed her eyes shut to keep the world from spinning out of control. Her worst nightmares were coming true. Janie was gone, probably sucked into the vortex of the Children of the Earth. And it was all Daphne's fault. If she'd spoken up as soon as she learned that more of the predictions in the tablet were coming true, if she'd told her aunt and uncle about seeing Janie with Ciaran, then her cousin might be safe at home that very minute. She had to come clean with them now, before the Children of the Earth did to Janie what she now suspected they'd done to the sheriff. She didn't have any time to lose.

"I have to tell you all something," she said, taking a seat across the table from Doug. "Something about where Janie might be. And, to be honest, it's something I probably should have told you as soon as I knew."

Doug leaned toward her, hope burning in his eyes. "All I want is to get her home safe."

"I know." It was hard to believe that she and Doug finally agreed on something, but the pain in his eyes was too real for even a first-rate bullshit artist like Doug to fake. He was as worried as Daphne was—and somehow, underneath it all, it was obvious how much he loved his wife.

Daphne took a deep breath. "I think Janie's with a guy named Ciaran who works up at the Vein," she said shakily.

"That place?" Doug's face reddened. "Why'd you think that?"

"Because." She forced herself to look into his bloodshot, watery eyes. "I saw them kissing the other night. I'm sorry, Doug. I should have said something sooner."

"Oh." She watched him deflate in front of her, sinking low in his seat until his forehead hit the table with a soft bump. His shoulders started shaking, and wet huffing noises leaked out. "I guess I deserve it," he snuffled. "I wasn't good to her. I ignored her and used her. She was just so sad, and I was so scared. I didn't know what to do." He collapsed into another crying jag.

"We have to hurry," Daphne said, hoping it wasn't already too late. "We have to find her and get her away from the Children of the Earth. They're dangerous."

"The Children of the Earth?" Floyd jerked upright. "Like in the tablet?"

"Yes." Daphne looked down at her hands, realizing that she'd been twisting her fingers in her lap until they were the color of bone. "That's the other thing you need to know. The Children of the Earth are here—all of them. They're the ones who run the Vein."

"Oh, Daphne." Aunt Karen's eyes were pink-rimmed with dismay. "How long have you known?"

"Too long. I should have told you as soon as I found out, but I wanted to make sure they were really as dangerous as I thought. Now I'm worried it may be too late." Daphne's voice cracked. Betraying the Peytons' trust was the last thing she wanted, and disappointing them hurt more than she could bear. But she'd brought it upon herself, evading the truth like it was on fire. Now she had to face the consequences.

"There's another reason I didn't tell you." The words hurt her throat. "Owen's one of them, and I didn't want anyone to hurt him because . . . well, because I love him. I thought he was on my side then. I know better now."

She looked from her aunt to her uncle, but it was like a gate had fallen between them. She knew better than to count on them for comfort after keeping them in the dark for so long.

"I'm disappointed in you, Daphne." Her uncle's voice thrummed with regret. "I would hope that, after everything, you'd at least be able to confide in us."

Daphne shook her head. "I just didn't know what to do. I know I'm supposed to be the prophet. I'm supposed to lead everyone in this battle. But I barely know what to do myself."

Floyd placed a large, rough hand over hers. "We never expected you to have all the answers. We know you're still human, prophet or not. But it troubles me that, after everything, you still felt like you couldn't trust us. We're here to help you, even when you don't know what to do. That's what being a family is all about."

His words touched the tenderest places in her heart. She didn't know what to say, only that she'd been alone so long, so used to making decisions on her own, that it had barely occurred to her to talk to someone else about her problems. She was used to not having anyone to turn to for answers; she'd grown accustomed to trying to solve everything by herself.

"Oh, Floyd, maybe we were all too hard on her." Aunt Karen reached across the table and placed a soft hand on Daphne's. "We thought that just because she could talk to God, she'd turn into a leader overnight. We forgot that she's still barely more than a child."

"No." Daphne forced herself to look them in the eye, one after the other. "Uncle Floyd is right. I shouldn't have kept this a secret. I'm sorry I betrayed your trust. I hope you can forgive me."

"Guys, there isn't time for this!" Doug sat up suddenly, the skin around his eyes raw and puffy, his hair standing up at all angles. "We have to go find Janie. If she's with Luna and all them, that's no joke. I know what that girl can do—she can get inside people's minds. It's some scary shit. And if she does it to Janie . . ." He trailed off, shoulders trembling.

"You know about that?" Daphne asked. "About what Luna can do?"

Doug shivered. "She did it to me. She got inside my mind and made me do whatever she wanted. It was like being a puppet."

The Peytons looked from Doug to Daphne and back again, their mouths round with shock.

"It sounds crazy, but he's right," Daphne said, standing abruptly. She was still shaky from her confession to the Peytons, but there was no time to wallow. "The Children of the Earth have special powers. We shouldn't go up against them on our own."

Floyd nodded, already grabbing his coat. "Should we call the police?" he asked.

"No." Daphne bit her lip, thinking of the suspicion in Detective Fraczek's eyes. "They wouldn't even believe us, let alone help us. There's only one place we can go for help now."

23

FLOYD'S TIRES SQUEALED AS HE pulled into the expansive, newly paved parking lot of the brand-new Carbon County First Church of God. The building towered above them, its spire stretching proudly toward the heavens. It was done, finally, ready to host its first service that Sunday, to be a spiritual nexus huge enough to house all the worshippers who had poured into town to follow Pastor Ted and witness the Rapture.

They opened the church's heavy front door, and a blast of fresh varnish wafted out at them. Hilary stood in the lobby, tacking a flyer about the youth group's next bake sale to a virgin bulletin board.

"Daphne!" Hilary grinned, her curls shivering. "I'm so glad you decided to stop by! Wait'll you see the inside, it's so beautiful you'd think God designed it himself. C'mon, let me give you a tour."

"I'm sorry, but there isn't time," Daphne said. "Hil, Janie's missing. We think she's in danger."

"Oh no." Hilary's face went white. "I'll take you to Pastor Ted."

Daphne, Floyd, Karen, and Doug followed her through a side door and down a long corridor. She stopped at a door bearing a small gold plaque that read *Pastor Ted.*

The pastor's office was larger than Daphne had expected. It was carpeted in thick Oriental rugs and decorated with photographs from his TV appearances blown up to poster size. Boxes of books sat unopened on the floor.

"Daphne!" A smile spread across Pastor Ted's wide, easygoing face. "How lovely to see you. Come in, please, and have a seat."

"I'm afraid this isn't exactly a social visit." Daphne perched on the edge of a purple brocade wing chair. "I'm just going to be blunt, Pastor Ted: The Children of the Earth are here in Carbon County, and we think they have Janie. They're dangerous and powerful—I'm pretty sure they're the ones behind what happened to the sheriff. If we don't find Janie soon, they could do that to her."

"My God." The pastor sank heavily into his leather swivel chair. "Go on, my child."

Quickly and dispassionately, not wanting to linger on any of the sordid details, Daphne told him the whole story. As she spoke, the air seemed to leave the room, and she felt not only Pastor Ted but also Hilary, Doug, and her aunt and uncle leaning into her words. She saw Pastor Ted flinch when she explained her relationship with Owen, and she knew she'd let him down. She'd let them all down, all the people who had trusted her, who had viewed her as a leader.

But that was over now. Now she'd do whatever she could to bring peace to the town and to get Janie home safe and sound.

"So let me get this straight," Pastor Ted said when she'd finished. "The Children of the Earth are up at the Vein, and they've captured Janie. Now we need to go rescue her?"

"I think so," Daphne agreed. "Maybe 'captured' is the wrong word—it's more like 'brainwashed.' I've seen them do it before. I know how powerful they can be."

"It's messed up!" Doug cut in, his voice hoarse with emotion. "That Luna, she just gets in your head. She can make you do anything. And Janie was so messed up to begin with . . ." He took a shaky breath and buried his head in his sleeve, unable to go on.

"Is it time?" Hilary shot Pastor Ted a cautious glance.

"I think so." The pastor stood abruptly.

"Time for what?" Daphne asked, looking from one to the other.

But nobody answered.

"Come with me," Hilary commanded, her voice suddenly cold. She led the group out of the office and down the hallway to an unmarked metal door. The air grew chillier as they entered a stairwell, Hilary's corkscrew curls marching in time to her footsteps as she bounded down the stairs.

"We're still putting the finishing touches on the basement," Pastor Ted explained as they descended. "But there'll be daycare and rooms for all the Sunday school groups, a teen center with a rec room that has ping-pong and shuffleboard, even a movie theater for screening Bible epics. I'll tell you, Floyd Peyton, your money is being well spent."

Floyd grunted politely, but it was obvious that as long as his daughter was missing, his investment in the church was the last thing on his mind.

"This way." Hilary stopped at an unmarked black door and punched a code into its keypad, her movements crisp and efficient. The keypad beeped and glowed red, and she pushed open the door, ushering all of them through before snapping on the light.

"Whoa." Daphne stepped back, startled. Floor-to-ceiling racks covered the walls. They held every possible type of gun, from tiny pistols to massive, gleaming semiautomatics. Neatly labeled artillery bins lined the floor, and missiles like giant squid stood at attention behind locked cabinets.

"What is all this?" Daphne stuttered, blinking rapidly as she looked around.

"Weapons," Hilary answered matter-of-factly. "For the Rapture."

Pastor Ted gripped Daphne's hand, a burning fervor in his deep blue eyes. "We knew it was coming." His voice was urgent. "We knew it because of *you.* You're the one who translated the tablet, whose visions foretold a great battle between good and evil, the Battle of the Great Divide. And what's a battle without ammunition?"

"Look." Hilary led her to another door at the rear of the room. She reached into a cabinet and pulled out a pair of bug-like noise-cancelling headphones and protective plexiglass eyeshades. "Put these on."

Numbed into compliance, Daphne did what she was told, watching in shock as Hilary donned a matching pair. The youth group leader keyed a different, longer code into the keypad and pushed open the door.

Even with the headphones, the noise was deafening. Guns exploded in endless arcs before her, the sound ricocheting off the concrete walls, the air thick with the smell of hot metal and gunpowder. They were in an underground firing range, and as the shooters paused to get a look at the newcomers, Daphne realized that she recognized their faces. There was Mark from Cincinnati, and Monica, who had worn the cool vintage housedress to the church picnic and suggested a Roaring Twenties–themed party for a fundraiser.

Monica wasn't wearing a housedress anymore. Clad in camo from head to toe, the members of the youth group had abandoned their welcoming smiles. Adrenaline clenched their jaws shut, and their fingers were tight around the triggers of semiautomatics. They may have been separated from Daphne by bulletproof glass, but their expressions were unmistakable. No matter how or where it happened, they were ready for battle. And when that battle occurred, they'd be out for blood.

Daphne had seen this before. She'd seen these people, carrying these weapons, in her last vision. She shivered, realizing what this meant: The visions weren't just messages. They were *predictions*, foretelling what was to come.

Hilary pressed an intercom, and her voice boomed from speakers inlaid in the ceiling. "Hey, everyone!" she called. "It's time. Reload your weapons, stock up on ammo, and get ready to fight."

A joyful cheer rose from the shooting lanes, making Daphne feel sick to her stomach. These kids weren't just prepping for battle because they felt they had to, Daphne realized; they *wanted* to. They'd seemed enthusiastic about the community project and teen center, but this was what really got their blood pumping, was probably what had drawn them to Carbon County in the first place. Pastor Ted had preached on national TV promising a war, and, more than any other reason, they had come to fight.

"Take your pick, Daphne." Pastor Ted swept his hand across the room, indicating the stockpile of weapons. "Whatever you want, it's yours."

Her heart caught mid-beat as she scanned the crowd and realized she was the only one unarmed. While she had been in the shooting range Pastor Ted had donned a hip holster loaded with a pair of silver pistols. Aunt Karen ran her hands admiringly over the barrel of a compact Remington, and Floyd, scowling uncomfortably, hefted a hunting rifle over each shoulder. Doug cradled an AK-47, two ammunition belts crisscrossed over his puffy green jacket.

Daphne's throat constricted. Being in the armory made her uncomfortable—but not as uncomfortable as the way the people she loved seemed to morph into something cold and ugly the moment they had a weapon in their hands. She didn't want that to happen to her, too.

"Are you sure this is a good idea?" she asked. "I've been having seizures. What if I set it off by accident? Someone could get hurt."

"Someone's already been hurt," Pastor Ted said grimly. "Daphne, you're our prophet. I may be a figurehead, but you're our real leader, the one with the direct line to God. We need you to lead this fight."

The thumping in her heart traveled to her head, pounding in her temples. She didn't want to choose a gun, but she couldn't disappoint the people who heralded her as a prophet, the ones she was supposed to lead. "I guess this one." She picked up a shotgun that looked like it was made for a child and adjusted the strap uncertainly over her shoulder. Even through her jacket the metal was cold as death, a reminder of how out of control things had gotten, how much easier it would have been to speak up before it came to this. Before it turned into a war.

The room broke into spontaneous applause, and Daphne felt chilly sweat dapple her forehead, her mouth go dry.

"Now what?" Pastor Ted turned to her, and she realized they were all looking at her, waiting for her to speak. To lead.

"Okay." She gulped hard. "We believe that Janie's with the Children of the Earth, up at the Vein. We go up there, and we go in together, as a group. But . . . we talk to them first. We try to talk to *Janie*, to let her know how much we love her. That we're her community. That we're here for her."

"What if she doesn't want to come?" someone asked.

"Then we take her." The words sounded harsh and ugly in her ears. "Floyd and Doug and Pastor Ted, you'll be the ones to do it. Take her by the arms, put her in the car, and take her home. And be careful; The Children of the Earth have powers. Luna, the one with the dreadlocks, can get inside your head. But I bet if we're all in it together, we'll be too much for her."

The room filled with angry murmurs.

"When do we open fire?" someone shouted. An appreciative roar went up in response, along with loud cries of agreement.

"We don't," Daphne said curtly. "The weapons are just for show. We shoot only in self-defense, only if our lives are being threatened."

She ignored the disappointed rumblings and turned abruptly, stomping toward the door. "Now let's get going," she commanded. "We don't have a lot of time."

The makeshift army followed her up the stairs and into the sinking sunlight. She watched from Floyd's rearview mirror as they piled into a phalanx of church vans, weapons slung over their shoulders, boxes of ammo tucked into their pockets or strung in belts across their chests. The mountains loomed in the distance, dark and silent sentries standing guard over the valley.

"I never imagined it would come to this," Floyd said quietly. He started the truck and led the convoy down the road and up into the hills, his fingers a bloodless white on the wheel, the twin rifles resting in his lap. "I know the tablet said there would be a battle, but I guess I didn't think it would be this . . . literal."

Daphne stayed silent, the words shifting uneasily in her gut. None of this felt right, but neither did losing Owen. She couldn't lose Janie, too.

The Vein's sign glowered down at them, red and ominous atop its towering twin poles. Just looking at it made Daphne feel sick and lost, angry at this place and these people for robbing her of those she loved the most. She ran a hand down the length of her gun and wondered, just for a moment, how it would feel to fire it right between Luna's eyes, how it would feel to end this for good. The thought was almost too tempting. Without Luna, the Children of the Earth would have no leader, no direction. They'd go back to wherever they came from, confused hippies roaming the earth. All it would take was one well-aimed bullet . . .

She yanked her hand from the gun. Killing people couldn't be the answer. It couldn't be what God wanted.

Could it?

One by one the church vans pulled in after them, and the

Christian youth disembarked, silently adjusting their ammo belts and loading their weapons.

"Ready?" Pastor Ted approached Daphne, a grim determination in his eyes.

She nodded, a desert of fear drying her throat. "Yes," she whispered.

With Doug, the Peytons, and Pastor Ted at her side, and dozens of armed Christian youth at her back, Daphne approached the front door and pushed against it.

It didn't budge.

"Weird," she said, foreboding settling in her stomach. "It's dusk—they should be open."

Already the sky was gunmetal gray, blue cirrus clouds clustered over the mountains.

"Try again," Pastor Ted encouraged her.

Daphne pushed once more, grunting as her shoulder slammed up against the metal.

Still nothing.

She pounded on the door with both fists, the noise echoing through the silent parking lot. "Is anyone in there?" she called. "Janie? Owen? *Luna?*"

Only silence answered her.

"Okay." She took a few steps back and raised her gun reluctantly to her shoulder. "I guess we're doing it this way."

She squinted at the lock and took a deep breath, her pulse skittering like the wings of a dragonfly. Then she squeezed the trigger.

The shot exploded in her ears, the force propelling her back so that she tripped over her heels and almost landed ass-first in the gravel. She caught herself right before she lost her balance entirely and stood panting and sweating, staring at the smoking hole in the door, right next to the lock.

"What the hell?" she looked around to find Uncle Floyd smirking quietly.

"Never shot a gun before, have you?"

She wiped sweat from her forehead. "We used pepper spray in Detroit."

"Pepper spray doesn't have a kickback."

"Let's try this again," she muttered. The crowd held their breath around her, waiting for her next move. Any one of them probably could have shot the lock out on the first try, she realized—they'd been training down in the church's shooting range, and Doug and the Peytons had grown up hunting. But this was *her* plan, and she knew they would wait for her to get it right.

This time she expected the kick. She aimed the gun at the lock and steadied her hand, squeezing her finger on the trigger and letting her body absorb the power of the blast. There was the scrape of metal disintegrating and an acrid cloud of smoke, and then the door swung open.

Adrenaline took over as she shouldered the gun and pushed her way into the club, her family and community a solid mass at her back. So that was how it felt to shoot a gun and hit a target, to lead an army. It wasn't pride, exactly—more like pride's dark and brooding younger sister, a sense of accomplishment laced with uncertainty.

This was for Janie, she reminded herself.

She stepped across the threshold. The moment her eyes adjusted to the darkness, her heart sank. The Vein was deserted, lights off and chairs stacked neatly on tables.

The Children of the Earth were gone . . . and they had taken Janie with them.

JANIE STEPPED OUT OF THE van and onto the mountaintop, the wind making the delicate fabric of her gown cling to her legs and billow out behind her, a sail in the sea of falling darkness. The landscape around her was stunted, ravaged. Little vegetation could grow at this altitude, only small, twisted evergreens and gnarly-rooted scrub.

It was almost time.

She was a rock in the stream of Children of the Earth flowing around her, dredging objects she didn't recognize from Aura's van. She looked out across the jagged peaks of the Savage Mountain Range and down the length of the valley to the few sad, stuttering lights that were Carbon County. From the faraway mountaintop the town that had been her world looked insignificant, a postseason string of Christmas lights coiled and forgotten in someone's garage.

Abilene and Freya swept across the ground, digging their heels into the ashen soil to carve the sacred circle, a circle that would hold them all, with Janie in the middle, the newest initiate, the chosen one.

She'd prepared for this ritual, meditating with Luna and Ciaran, fasting until her body felt as clean and light as the stem of a feather. That morning her Earth Sisters had bathed her in rose water and rubbed her down with spicy, pungent oil, kneading it into her flesh until her muscles sang with pleasure and her skin gleamed. They danced and chanted around her, led by Abilene's throaty, bluesy alto. They braided her hair with wildflowers and painted her hands with henna designs so tiny and elaborate it looked like the brushes had been made for dolls.

"Are you ready?" Ciaran's voice was like the kiss of hot bathwater on her winter-chilled skin.

"Yes." She was more than ready. She wanted to feel the earth move through her feet and stardust settle in her hair the way Luna had described. She was ready to become one of them, one of the Children of the Earth.

It was almost time.

He stood before her and took her hands. "You know you don't have to do this."

Warmth coursed through her at his touch, but when she looked in his eyes, she saw concern. He was always thinking of her, always putting her first. She knew that the ritual would be powerful, and that afterward, nothing would be the same. She knew it was a decision that, once made, she could never unmake. She knew that it meant renouncing her friends and family, the life she'd always known and the world she'd always been a part of, forever.

She rose on her tiptoes to brush her lips against his. "I want to do this." Her breath made mist in the chilly mountain air. "I want to be with you. With all of you."

Ciaran's eyes darkened. "But," he began. His grip on her hands tightened, and he leaned in closer to her, his voice low and urgent. "Janie, there's something I need to tell you—"

"It's almost time." Luna materialized at Ciaran's elbow, and his lips clamped shut, his eyes glazing over in her presence. Luna had piled her hair into a towering crown held in place with massive steel clips, and she wore a halter dress of red and gold Indian brocade that ended at the tops of her thighs. Bronze gauntlets circled her wrists, held in place by rings around her middle fingers.

She placed her hand on their clasped palms, gentle but firm. The edge of her gauntlet was sharp and cold against Janie's skin, and she felt a flicker of unease somewhere beneath the layers of calm that had calcified inside her during her days with the Children of the Earth. Something wasn't right in Ciaran's tone of voice, the dark cast of his eyes, and the sudden, cold kiss of metal on her skin.

"Janie," Luna said, her gaze holding and penetrating her, the softness of her name on Luna's tongue snuffing out her whisper of unease like a candle, leaving only the memory of smoke. Ciaran's hands dropped limply to his side, and he drifted away, joining the bustling swarm of his Earth Brothers and Sisters. He left Janie and Luna alone, two women who would soon be sisters.

"Janie," Luna said again, and Janie nodded. The fasting made her slow to react sometimes, made her head feel full of clouds. "Are you ready to do your part?"

"Yes," she said.

The slow flame of a smile spread across Luna's face, and embers danced in her eyes. "Then let's do this," she said.

The cold bronze of her gauntlet warmed in Janie's hand as Luna led her past the van and into the center of the circle. Thirteen pairs of emerald eyes followed their progress, and she gazed back at them one after another: Gray and Kimo, Aura and Arrow and Silas and Orion and Cheyenne, Freya and Abilene. Heather looked stunned, as always, like she still couldn't quite believe what her life had become, and Owen's eyes twinkled with curiosity, drinking in this still-new way of life. Off to the side, not part of the circle but paying close attention, little Charlie gazed solemnly at her through chocolate-colored eyes. He had come to them seeking shelter when his father disappeared, Luna had explained, and they had taken him in and made him one of their own.

Finally, her gaze found Ciaran, and she realized with a small shock that he was crying. Maybe they were tears of happiness that she would finally become one of them; his empathetic nature made him sensitive that way. Or maybe it was the beautiful solemnity of the ritual, the silence that descended upon the circle as Luna lit a candle and held it aloft, touching its tip to the unlit wick of Owen's next to her and waiting for him to pass the flame in turn, creating a circle of light that glowed and flickered in the gathering darkness. The sun was a scarlet kiss sinking fast behind the mountains, leaving lipstick smears in its wake, and Janie felt her own eyes grow damp, the granite-heavy power of the ritual stirring her blood.

Circles of candlelight danced on their faces as Luna led them in a series of oms that resonated across the mountain peaks and vibrated at their feet. The sound lingered in Janie's chest as Luna began to speak, her voice low and hypnotic.

"Tonight, we call upon the Gods of Fire." The candlelight caught her beneath the chin, casting long shadows over her face. "We call upon them to burn this town to the ground, to right the wrongs we have done to this land, and to serve justice to those who scarred our planet in the pursuit of greed and riches."

Drumbeats began from the edge of the circle, slow and steady. Janie felt her heartbeat recede to their rhythm, felt it carry her pulse. Her body no longer belonged to her but to them, the drums and the night and the Children of the Earth.

Luna opened her mouth and began to chant.

"Gods of fire, hot and swift,
Bring your flames to heal this rift.

Heal the scars carved in our land

By mankind's cruel and greedy hand."

The chant picked up strength as it moved around the circle, mouths yawning open as the drumbeats gathered speed and the words gained momentum, voices bouncing off the stone mountain peaks and echoing back to Janie's ears.

Still holding their candles, the Children of the Earth began to slowly circle her, their feet a heavy counterpoint to the climbing tenor of their voices. Wind whipped their hair and flung candlelight across their faces, and she felt their energy enter her and fill her with a pulsing, dancing warmth.

Their eyes began to glow, green beams that moved hungrily over her body and set her skin aflame. She was candles and smoke, kindling and heat, a living embodiment of fire. And soon, soon she would be one of them.

Luna stepped forward, a hoop held before her in both hands. A dozen steel spines protruded from it, the ends wrapped in rags that glistened darkly with fresh, wet fuel. Her eyes stayed on Janie's as she approached, crouching low with each step like a cat hunting her prey, holding the hoop between spikes so that it circled her waist, ready to spin into orbit.

Her boots left soft prints in the snow.

"Now," she whispered. Janie could smell the fuel rising from each soaked rag, a scent as rich and metallic as blood. Moving as one, the Children of the Earth advanced, still chanting, the threads of their voices weaving a thick web. They held out their arms, each touching a flame to the gas-soaked rags on Luna's hoop.

Her wicks devoured the flames. Janie gasped as they sucked oxygen hungrily from the air, capering like demons to surround Luna in a circle of fire. Through the haze of heat she saw Luna's mouth open in laughter, her eyes glow with glee. She had never seen Luna so happy, so alive, as she grasped the hoop and bounced it up and down, making the fire expand into Chinese lanterns in the air.

"Gods of fire, hot and swift,
Bring your flames to heal this rift,"

The Children of the Earth linked arms and danced around her in a circle, clouds of snow swirling at their feet. The flames of their candles had grown bigger and brighter, as if touching them to Luna's hoop had fed them. They glowed with white-hot light, too bright to look at yet too beautiful to look away.

As bright as the flames burned, Janie couldn't take her eyes off of Luna, the crown of dreadlocks on her head and the feline smile on her face. Their eyes locked and, with an ecstatic laugh, Luna released the hoop and sent it whirling around her waist. The sudden rush of air fanned the flames until the dozen became one, a wall of fire rising between them, laced with sapphire threads of pure heat.

The fire spoke to Janie in whooshes of air, in the hungry crackle of flame burning swift and pure. It beckoned to her, spoke of a world where there was only pure energy and ever-burning life, where there was never any fear or hurt or pain. She had heard this voice before, fire speaking to her in flaming tongues, urging her into its world. She had seen this dance before, the dance of flame eating flame, of fire leaping and twirling and cartwheeling high into the sky. And she had been ready to join it.

It was the night of baby Jeremiah's funeral, when she and the rest of the townies had gone up to Elk Mountain to drink and forget. That night she'd danced closer and closer to their raging campfire, dancing away her grief and her pain and ready to join the blaze when it beckoned, to be its partner in this world and the one beyond. She had reached out her hands, ready to go to it, the heat entering her body as the candlelight did now, the light filling her until it spilled from her feet and she writhed like a wild woman being consumed from the inside out. She had been ready, willing, to join her life with the fire's and leave this cold, hard, unlit world behind. Only Doug had stopped her, yanking her away with brute force, throwing her to the ground and screaming at her the way the world screamed and her heart screamed and her womb screamed in its emptiness, in the shock of life being ripped from her with a pain that would never completely go away.

Doug wasn't here to stop her now.

The hoop whirled inches from her face, a vortex of flame that blocked out the rest of the world.

"*Gods of fire, hot and swift,*" Janie chanted, the words sparking from the place inside of her where desire burned hottest. Heat flashed through her legs until she was stomping in time to the drumbeats, until she was no longer Janie but a ball of whirling energy, the keeper of the flame.

The chant and the heat moved through her, and, oh, it felt good! It felt right the way being a slow human plodding through the world had never felt right, the way putting her son in a hole in the ground when she should have been holding him to her breast hadn't felt right. Fire flickered in her blood, and flame replaced her heart, and she was ready now to dance with the fire from this world into the next, to let it carry her to the place where Jeremiah had gone.

Her feet danced closer to the vortex of Luna's fire hoop. Flames brushed her nose, heating her face until she felt the skin swell and blister. Her eyes met Luna's through the hot orange veil, and she knew that Luna knew, knew that all of them knew. She was ready.

Luna's hand whipped out and stopped the hoop mid-spin, and the deafening whoosh of flames ripping through the air stopped, and the chanting stopped, and the drumming stopped, and the stomping, snow-kicking dancing stopped, and the night filled with a sudden, heavy silence. Smoke swirled around their shoes and the sky above them glowed the color of fire's white-hot core as Luna stepped out of the hoop and lowered it gently, lovingly, over Janie's head.

She didn't hold it in place. She didn't need to. The hoop rested in midair, held there by the fierce concentration of the Children of the Earth, by Janie's searing desire to let the flames consume her, and by something different and otherworldly, more primal and more powerful than anything she had ever known.

The Gods of Fire were there. Surrounding them. Ready to do what they asked.

As soon as Janie let go.

The pressure of their invisible force sent the hoop gyrating around her, dancing in faster, wilder circles until everything was a blur of blue and orange and blinding, blistering heat. The fire sucked air from her lungs, and she let it, wanting to feed it, knowing that soon it would take her away from this world and into the next, into the place of pure bliss and light where Jeremiah was waiting.

Soon she wouldn't be Janie anymore. Soon she wouldn't be alive. And she was ready. She was ready to let go.

Through the cyclone of fire she felt a disturbance ripple the circle, saw a shadow struggle from beyond the flames and lunge toward her, heard a voice shouting: "No!" For a moment, she caught a glimpse of oil-dark hair and terrified green eyes and felt a hand reach through the inferno, saw callused fingers grasp at her, trying to stop the helix of heat.

But it was too late. The flame within had taken over, and she was no longer Janie, no longer of this world. She felt something inside of her snuff out forever as the hoop dropped suddenly, the ring of fire extinguishing instantly in the thick layer of snow at her feet.

Janie followed, falling lifeless to the ground.

25

AS JANIE'S BODY HIT THE earth, Owen felt himself go still, the sudden fury that had made him break the circle and push his hand through the flames leaking out of him.

Silas and Orion released his arms, and he sank to his knees, spent and trembling. Ragged breaths shuddered through him, sending trails of snow skittering across the ground.

Luna knelt before Janie, her ear to her mouth. She pricked Janie's finger with the dagger she wore strapped to her thigh. Through the haze of smoke now thick on the ground, Owen saw a bead of blood bloom from her flesh. Gathering it with a fingertip black with carbon, Luna drew a single, perfect teardrop on Janie's forehead.

Hot bile rose in his throat, but he choked it down, gagging on the acidic spike but refusing to desecrate the ground where Janie had been tricked into giving her life, tricked by people she had trusted.

Tricked by people *he* had trusted.

So this was what it meant to be one of the Children of the Earth, to *really* be one of them. It wasn't just walks in the woods and meditation, wasn't all lentil stew and chanting and finally feeling like he was somewhere he actually belonged. It was *sacrificing lives.*

Dread ballooned inside of him as Luna picked up her hoop and sauntered away, calling to her brothers and sisters to pick up the candles, erase the circle, and remove Janie's body. They came to life as if awakening from a trance, Heather woodenly collecting the snuffed-out candles, Freya and Abilene kicking snow and dirt over the circle until it was gone.

He watched Ciaran stumble haltingly to Janie's body and crouch beside her, his eyes glossy with tears. He brushed Janie's hair back from her forehead and passed his hand slowly over her eyes, closing them forever, before gathering her in his arms and carrying her through the snow. Right before laying her in the backseat of his old Honda Civic, he ducked his head and touched his lips to hers, letting them linger there as her mouth turned blue beneath his.

The sight was too much. Owen turned and retched violently, his back heaving.

Daphne had been right, he realized as he wiped his mouth miserably with the back of his hand. She had warned him against getting too close to the Children of the Earth, had begged him to leave the Vein before it was too late. But he hadn't listened. He'd fallen under the spell of his family, and instead of listening to Daphne and trusting the strength of her visions, he'd followed Luna blindly, letting her powers of persuasion take control of his mind. It had started as curiosity, a need to know. And now he knew.

He had stood idly by as his brothers and sisters sacrificed a human life—didn't just stand idly by but danced and chanted, felt the power of the Gods of Fire course through him and touch him in a place deeper than the marrow of his bones.

He could still feel it, even as he sat back on his heels and ran clammy fingers through his hair. He felt the Gods of Fire swarming up from the south, racing through the air on tails bright as comets, bringing with them the fury of hot, dry winds that would bake the landscape to ash and ignite the mountains around Carbon County, turning the whole valley into an inferno.

He knew that the fire would scream through the foothills and down into the valley, thundering toward the oil rig. But he could only imagine the size of the explosion when the fire touched down on all that crude oil pumped freshly from the ground. It would definitely take down the Peytons' trailer; he knew that. It would probably wipe out the entire town.

As the sky turned red and tendrils of smoke began to wisp by his nose, he knew what he had to do. He stood quickly, ignoring the quivering in his legs and the nausea still churning his stomach. He was far away from the town of Carbon County, and without the Children of the Earth he'd have to walk.

"Where are you going, Earth Brother?"

Luna stood in his path, hands on her hips and the scent of fuel still swirling from her skin.

Owen didn't answer. He felt closer to her than ever, closer to all of them. The ritual had bonded them in a way he could never undo, no matter how much it sickened him, how wrong it was. Janie had thought the ritual was her initiation into the Children of the Earth, but she'd been duped; they both had.

It was his.

He brushed past Luna, the skin on his shoulder burning where they touched. With every step away from her he felt weaker and sicker, stretched to his breaking point. But he kept going, the image of Daphne flickering in his mind like a weak television signal that he struggled to hold in place, knowing it was the only thing that could keep him walking forward, walking away. The mountaintop was at least thirty miles from the oil rig, and he'd have to walk. In his broken state it would take hours—all night and part of the next morning. But he would do it. He would do what had to be done.

"You'll be back, Earth Brother," Luna called after him, unconcerned, a bird singing out a cheerful tune. "You're one of us now."

The tang of smoke choked the air, and he coughed, gagged, drew his shirt up over his nose and kept walking, away from her and them and the monster he knew he'd become.

It was too late to save himself. He had tried to fight his destiny, and he had failed. Maybe it couldn't have worked; maybe he should have realized that destiny couldn't be changed or altered by hard work or determination or even by love. He had felt the Gods of Fire penetrate his skin and activate the thing he was underneath, what he always had been and always would be.

He was a Child of the Earth, as much a part of them as anyone could be. He couldn't change that.

But there was one thing he could change, one thing he might not be too late for. If only he could get there in time.

↔

Ciaran arranged Janie's limbs inside the back of his rusting Honda Civic, carefully placing her hands in her lap and laying her head against the headrest so it wouldn't loll to one side. He couldn't stop the tears from streaming down his face and gathering in salty pools around his lips.

He would never forgive Luna for going through with it, or himself for letting her. If only he'd had a moment longer with Janie before the ritual—if only Luna hadn't shown up exactly when she did, just as he was planning to warn Janie what was about to happen—then maybe she'd still be alive. But he'd been weak, and Luna ignited the part of his mind that was still loyal, the piece that would do anything for the Children of the Earth, even sacrifice the girl he had unexpectedly come to love.

"Ready?" Kimo appeared at his side, all jangly energy and anarchy tattoos. His Mohawk looked taller, electrified by the ritual. Silas, the Vein's enormous bouncer, loped up behind him, a long coil of rope in his hand.

"I don't know." Ciaran still felt like his soul was being chewed apart. "I don't think I can do this."

"You have to!" Kimo squawked. "Luna says it has to be you."

Silas silenced him with a stony look. "C'mere, man," he said to Ciaran. He opened his arms, and Ciaran went to him, taking protection in the mass of his brother's embrace.

"We can do this," Silas reminded him when they broke apart. Ciaran wiped his eyes with his sleeve.

"We have to finish what we started," Kimo added.

Ciaran handed his car keys to Silas. "You drive."

They piled into the car, Ciaran struggling not to look at Janie's cold, dead face in the rearview mirror. But he couldn't help himself, and there she was, her lips already turning blue—lips that had been so full of life when she first kissed him under a snowy canopy of trees.

"I know this is hard for you, man." Silas had a leather-and-tobacco voice that filled the small car as he maneuvered down the winding gravel road. "But remember: She wanted to go to the other side."

"Yeah." Ciaran stared down at his hands. "I guess."

It was because of this that Ciaran had first approached her. As soon as she'd stepped into the Vein he'd known how miserable she was, how exhausted with life and everything in it. She didn't want to live anymore but couldn't figure out how to end it. It would actually be doing her a favor, making her their next sacrifice.

What he hadn't counted on was being able to change her. In the short time they spent together, he'd realized that all Janie had needed was for someone to look at her and actually see *her*, to understand and accept her pain, and the next thing he knew she was blooming under his nose, her thirst for life huge and overwhelming. She was beautiful and happy and bursting with life, and she loved him. And as hard as he tried not to, he'd found himself loving her back.

For the first time since his eighteenth birthday and the terrible dreams, he felt that maybe his powers of empathy could help people, people like Janie who needed to overcome loss or sadness and find peace with themselves and the world. Maybe his gift could be a blessing.

Silas slowed the car to a crawl.

"What's that?" he muttered, headlights catching a lone figure limping painfully along the side of the road.

"It's Owen." Kimo fidgeted in the backseat, trying to squeeze himself as far from Janie's corpse as possible. "I sensed him from a ways off."

Silas rolled up parallel to Owen and cranked down his window. "Hey, man, you okay?" he called.

Owen shook his head and kept walking, feet dragging in the dust, hands clutched to his stomach.

"Get in, man." The wheels barely moved as they kept pace with their Earth Brother. "Kimo can scoot over."

Kimo's face paled.

"C'mon." Silas rested an elbow on the window ledge. "Where d'you think you're walking to, anyway? We're thirty miles from anywhere right now."

Owen turned, glaring at him. His eyes were rimmed in red. "I'm not going anywhere with you," he spat. "I'll walk all night if I have to."

Ciaran wished he had the balls to do what Owen was doing—to walk away from Luna and the Children of the Earth, to follow the tiny, keening voice at the bottom of his heart telling him that what they were doing was wrong, that sacrificing people was not the answer.

For a moment, with Janie, he'd thought about it. The two of them could run away somewhere safe, and he could go to school for psychology, use his powers to help people overcome their pain. But there was never time, never a chance to get her alone and talk. Janie had fallen in love with the Children of the Earth, and Luna was always there, inside their minds, pulling at their desires until they no longer knew which thoughts were hers and which were their own. He had pledged his future to Luna, his loyalty. He'd signed over the deed to his car and invested his meager savings in the Vein. And now with Janie, his one chance for redemption, lifeless in the backseat, he had no hope left.

He was, and forever would be, nothing more than one of the Children of the Earth.

Silas shrugged. "Suit yourself, Earth Brother," he said to Owen, starting to roll up the window. "I wish you luck—it's hard out there without your family."

He stepped on the gas, and the car lurched forward, kicking up gravel in its wake.

"Do you think he'll be okay?" Kimo asked tentatively from the backseat.

"Oh yeah." Silas nodded, chewing on his lower lip. "He'll be okay—and he'll be back. Mark my words. He will definitely be back."

26

DAPHNE WAS INSIDE OWEN'S DREAM. She recognized the bonfire towering before her, clawing at the sky and spewing plumes of heavy black smoke, and the Children of the Earth whirling around it. They danced exactly as Owen had described: in a stomping, spinning, almost spastic frenzy. Occasionally one twirled toward her, flashing eyes that glowed phosphorescent green.

They danced to drumbeats that made the earth tremble beneath her feet, and with every revolution around the circle, the flames leapt higher and their eyes glowed with brighter, wilder abandon.

Daphne could feel the terror Owen had described, and she wanted to turn and run, but her feet disobeyed her and stepped forward. The heat from the bonfire made her face tingle, and she could feel the breath of her enemies warm and rotten on her cheeks.

"Come with ussss," the Children of the Earth hissed, tongues slithering from their mouths. In the smoky darkness their arms curled like serpents as they reached for her, scaly fingers trailing across her skin. "Join usssss."

She wanted to scream that she would never be one of them, but she found her tongue had cleaved to the roof of her mouth. It must be the heat, she thought dizzily, melting her insides together. The smoke entered her lungs, filling her with poisonous tendrils, choking the flow of oxygen to her brain. If only she could drop to her knees and cover her face, escape from the overpowering smell of burning pine. But her arms had melted into her sides, and there was nothing she could do, nowhere she could go, no way to escape the horror that had been Owen's, night after night after night.

The Children of the Earth advanced, locking arms and trapping her. Their eyes burned hotter than the flames, and she saw when they opened their mouths that their tongues were forked, their skin covered in scales.

"Come with usssss," they hissed again, and then they opened their mouths wide and screamed, a scream that turned her too-hot blood to ice, that echoed up from the fire and into the mountains and throughout the whole world.

The scream went on and on, an endless, anguished wail. Within it words began to form, unintelligible at first, then clear.

"No!" the Children of the Earth shrieked, forked tongues convulsing. "God, no! Please, no! God, why?"

But why were they invoking God? What did God have to do with *them*?

Daphne looked around the circle and saw the green glow of their eyes fade and disappear, the scales fall from their skin and their forked tongues vanish.

"What's happening?" she asked. "Is it me? Am I doing this?"

Her only answer was the Children of the Earth dropping to their knees, still crying, still invoking God. They shrank to the ground and beat the earth, growing smaller and smaller until they were no larger than granules of dirt. Then they were gone entirely, and all that remained was the fire, and the smoke, and the screaming . . .

↔

The screaming.

Daphne bolted awake, her hair wild around her face. She couldn't have been asleep for more than an hour. After driving around for most of the night, the Children of God had peeled off one by one, claiming exhaustion and vowing to continue the search for Janie the next day. Daphne had tried to keep going, to push through her exhaustion with Red Bull and coffee, but when Floyd caught her dozing in his passenger seat he insisted she get some rest. It had been almost five A.M. at that point, and dawn would be there sooner than they realized.

Now it had arrived—or at least some red and hazy approximation of dawn. Smoke choked the sky outside the trailer's small window, and the scent of burning pine filled the air.

The screaming went on and on. With dawning horror, Daphne realized she recognized the voice.

She shoved her feet into boots, not bothering to tie the laces, and stumbled through the trailer. The thin metal door felt hot to her touch as she flung it open, and sweat dotted her skin as soon as she stepped outside.

Carbon County was on fire.

The blaze consumed the mountains, blanketing them in red and black. Through the haze of smoke she could make out the charred stalks of pine trees lit up like candles. Bulbous black smoke roiled from the flames in clouds so thick they blocked entire mountains. The sky looked like it was bleeding.

Daphne ran toward the oil rig, in the direction of the screams, and the fire ran, too, thundering down the foothills, swallowing every living thing in its path. It was only a couple of miles away, the smoke heavy enough to make Daphne gag as she ran, her bootlaces flapping against the ground.

She saw the crowd first, the backs of her coworkers standing in a semicircle, clutching their hard hats in their hands.

She shouldered her way through to the source of the cries. Her heart contracted when she saw Aunt Karen on her hands and knees on the ground, her arms streaked with smoke and dust as she beat the ground. Her face was twisted in agony, and each ragged breath brought with it a fresh wail.

Daphne knelt beside her and put her arm around Karen's heaving shoulders. "Aunt Karen, what happened?"

With a trembling finger, her aunt pointed up. Up the length of the derrick, up the towering metal scaffolding to the very top, to a sight that made Daphne's blood stand still. Strung up on the derrick, skin dull and blue eyes dead, was her cousin Janie.

The sweat froze on Daphne's skin. Her cousin had been tied to the rig using the same white rope that had lashed the sheriff to the flagpole. A teardrop, drawn in blood, glistened on her forehead.

Daphne couldn't speak. Her legs gave out, and she pitched forward, face-first onto the ground.

She stayed like that, weak and limp and tasting dirt, powerless. She'd been too late to save Janie, too slow and stupid to help her cousin when she needed her most.

A sob ripped through her, threatening to split her in two. She didn't know if she was choking on smoke or dirt or tears, and it didn't matter. All she knew was that this thing had gone too far. It had gone too far, and she had let it.

The Children of the Earth had done this, and it wasn't enough just to stop them. She had to make them suffer as hard and as deep as the Peyton family would from this moment on. She didn't know how; all she knew was that she had to make them pay. She *would* make them pay.

She had God on her side.

She felt a hand on her back and turned to see Dale kneeling beside her, worry lines deep around his eyes.

"Daphne, I know this is hard, but we've got to get out of here." Urgency flooded his voice. "That fire's coming closer by the minute. We shut down the pumps, but there's still a ton of crude on this land. I don't have to tell you what that means."

Daphne looked from him to the top of the derrick.

"We have to get her down," she said. "I'll climb up and grab her." The thought of touching her cousin's corpse turned her stomach, but not as much as the idea of letting Janie's body stay to be consumed by the flames.

Dale shook his head. "I can't let anyone up there. The metal's too hot to touch. Everyone needs to evacuate. *Now.*"

"We can't!" Karen stopped sobbing long enough to look up at them with ashen eyes. "I won't leave my girl."

Daphne watched Dale dig for the right words, his eyes darting nervously from Karen to the wall of fire creeping down the foothills. Over his shoulder, in the distance, she saw someone running toward them, feet kicking up a long plume of dust. As the figure grew nearer she made out a shock of thick, dark hair.

"Owen." The name slipped like poison from her lips.

He came to a stop in front of her, speaking between labored gasps. "You were right. I'm sorry. I didn't know."

Carbon dust left thick smears on his skin, and his hair was a greasy, tangled mess. A sweat-soaked shirt clung to him like tissue paper, and the scent rising from his body was strong and animal, as if he'd been running all night. It reminded Daphne of their most intimate moments together, the times they had been as close as two humans could be, and a volcano of rage began to boil inside her.

"You did this." She struggled to keep her voice under control, but her hand shook as she pointed to the top of the rig, to Janie's body.

Pain clouded Owen's eyes.

"You're one of them. You're a killer. The tablet warned us about you."

A walloping crack thundered through the foothills as a burning evergreen hit the ground, sending a fireball the size of a house ballooning into the sky. The top of the downed tree lit the pine grove at the edge of the Peytons' property, igniting the tall, dry trees and carpet of pine needles.

"We have to get out of here!" Dale barked. "It's less than a football field away."

The crackling flames shut out all other sounds, and the heat beat relentlessly against Daphne's skin.

"He's right," she said reluctantly, grasping her aunt's arm and trying to pull her to her feet. "Karen, we have to go now. I'm sorry."

Dale grabbed her other arm, but Karen refused to get to her feet. "I won't leave my girl!" she sobbed again.

As Daphne and Dale struggled with her aunt's dead weight,

Owen took a step forward, toward the blaze. His eyes began to glow with that evil, fluorescent green, the dreaded light that Daphne now recognized as the Children of the Earth activating their powers.

He held up his hands, palms facing the burning pine grove, eyes blazing with determination. The fire, which had begun to lap at the grass between the pine grove and the oil rig, froze for a moment, looking like the paused frame of a video. Then it flickered back to life.

But instead of creeping toward them, it leapt upward, flames licking the sky.

Sweat poured from Owen's head, and his entire body shook with effort. The flames climbed higher and higher, until they looked like they were searing the stratosphere. He was controlling the fire, Daphne realized. But was he bringing it closer or keeping it at bay?

A sick sense of déjà vu washed over her. She had seen this image before: Owen standing in front of the rig, his eyes glowing that terrifying green and his hands held out to the flames. She had seen him control fire, seen his evil power spill out of him until he could manipulate the very elements of the world.

She had seen it in a vision, her first vision. A vision sent to her from God.

The picture in front of her went cloudy as, without warning, she fell back seizing on the ground.

The Vision of the Final Reckoning

The room is dark, the air close,

The window small and streaked with dirt.

Garbage trucks screech and chug

Through the Detroit streets outside.

You huddle in the corner of your bed,

Knees drawn to your chest,

Heart pounding, limbs shivering,

Alone, but not alone enough.

Here come his footsteps,

Drunk and heavy down the hall.

Here comes his breath,

Thick with drink and unwanted kisses.

Here comes his hand,

Knocking on the door,

Knocking down the door,

Splintering the cheap lock, kicking it in.

There is his face.

Chapped lips, bloodshot eyes

Emanating evil,

Wanting what you will not give.

You shrink back,

Protecting yourself:

The part of yourself he wants

But will never have.

This time is different.

Something silver flashes in his hand,

Reflected in the grimy yellow

Of the streetlight.

Something sharp, bone-handled, deadly.

A knife.

He approaches slowly, licking his lips,

Raising the knife above your head.

You have stopped trembling.

Inside of you, everything is still.

And as he brings the knife

Down upon you,

As the blade comes whizzing

Toward your chest

You lunge.

And grab it.

And turn it around.

It happens so fast.

You are just protecting yourself—

As yea, my child, my prophet,

Survivor of terror, seer of visions,

You must.

You must protect the world:

My child,

My prophet.

You must.

For when metal meets flesh

And life leaks from

This evildoer

In wet ribbons of red

When he falls to the ground

And gasps, and writhes,

And finally stops breathing,

The world is once again at peace.

Now look upon his face!
My child, my prophet,
Watch his jowls melt away
And his hair grow thick and black

Look upon his face
And see his eyes turn
Green.
See who he truly is.

The enemy has come to you
In many forms.
Yet this is the final one:
The King of Evils.

27

DOUG HAD BEEN DRIVING ALL night, drinking Red Bull to stay awake and looking for Janie. Now he was jittery and sleep-deprived, and his wife was still MIA.

He'd looked for her in all their old haunts: the woods behind the football field, the pullout where they used to make out after school dances, that all-night diner she liked up in Rawlins.

Then, when he returned to Carbon County, he noticed the red clouds hanging low in the sky and the smoke drifting down from the Savage Mountains. It wasn't the first time there'd been a forest fire up there, but it was the first time it had made his stomach clench in fear, for reasons he couldn't explain and didn't want to think about all that hard.

Now he was at work, bone-tired and worried as shit, practically gagging on smoke while his dad barked out orders to hurry up and get that pipeline in, drill faster before Floyd Peyton got wind of what they were doing and turned the tables to slap a lawsuit on *him.*

"Listen, Mr. Varley." Dwayne trotted behind him, clutching his clipboard with clammy palms. "I've been keeping an eye on those fires, and it don't look good. They're getting closer."

"What, you think *they'll* cause an earthquake, too?" Vince swatted his foreman away and kept pacing, yelling at the roughnecks to drill faster, to get a move on, he wasn't paying them an extra 20 percent to loll around like a bunch of barflies.

"Mr. Varley!" Dwayne tugged on his sleeve. His pale eyebrows were damp with sweat.

Vince whirled. *"What?!"*

"Look, I know you want me to just keep quiet and do my job, but this is messed up." Dwayne waved the clipboard at the rig, and the fire, and the guys struggling to keep up with Vince's orders. "We're already way deeper than any of the plans we submitted, and the guys've been telling me they're feeling tremors when they drill. I can't say for sure, but I'd hazard a bet it's 'cause we're hitting that fault line. Now there's a fire so close we can all *feel* it, and instead of having us evacuate you want us to stick around and maybe burn to death? That's just not right, Mr. Varley. It's seriously messed up."

Vince glared at him, his face the color of roasted giblets. "And just what do you intend to do about it?"

"Look, Mr. Varley, I'm just trying to talk sense here." Dwayne stumbled on his words. "You don't want to run a dangerous rig, do you?"

"You think I give a flying rat's ass?" Vince snorted. "I'm not doing this 'cause it's good for the community or any of that kumbaya bullshit. I want the oil that's rightfully mine, and I want it *now.*

It's either my way or the highway, buddy. I don't know how many times I gotta tell you."

Doug could hear Dwayne's gulp all the way over by the Quonset hut where he was pretending to stack sacks of drilling mud. "Then I guess it's the highway," Dwayne said finally. He trembled a little as he handed Vince his clipboard, but he didn't look away. "I won't work for someone who don't put safety first. I just won't."

Vince's nostrils flared. He reared back and hurled the clipboard at Dwayne, missing by several feet in his rage. Its pages fluttered as it clattered to the ground, dislodging a sheaf of papers and sending them swirling away on the swift, dry wind blowing down from the foothills.

"You have a contract!" Vince screamed.

"I'm breaking it." Satisfied that Vince had nothing left to throw, Dwayne turned and headed for the parking lot, unbuckling his helmet as he went. His face was grim, but something twitched at the corner of his mouth, making the blond hairs on his chin glimmer like filaments of fishing wire. At first, Doug couldn't tell quite what that expression meant. But as Dwayne drew closer, the slap of his boots angry on the dirt, Doug recognized it as pride. Pride at having done the right thing, pride at knowing that if something went wrong with the pipeline or the fire, his hands would be washed clean.

It must have felt good to stand up to Vince Varley like that, Doug thought. Maybe someday he'd have the guts to do it himself.

He paused, the piles of drilling mud at his feet, as Dwayne walked by. He wanted to salute or something, give the guy a pat on the back, but all he could manage was a half smile.

"Hey, listen bud." Dwayne leaned in as he walked past, barely breaking stride. "You try talking some sense into him. Maybe he'll listen 'cause you're his son. 'Cause if he keeps doing what he's doing, people are gonna die."

As punctuation, he took off his hard hat and tossed it to Doug, who caught it reflexively. Standing there, cradling the yellow plastic orb, he watched Dwayne drive away, his fourth-hand Dodge Dart disappearing almost instantly into a low-hanging cloud of smoke.

People are gonna die. The words reverberated as he set the hard hat slowly down and lifted another sack of drilling mud, barely noticing its weight on his shoulders.

It had come to that, and his dad didn't care. Janie was missing, lives were at stake, it looked like the whole damn town was about to catch fire, and all ol' Vince cared about was getting his piece of the pie. Dwayne was right: It *was* messed up. His parents had a fucked-up way of looking at the world. And, thanks to them, so did he.

He set the drilling mud down, trying to think of what he could say that would stop his father's madness. Vince wasn't exactly his biggest fan right then, but they were still family. That had to count for something, right?

Maybe he could organize a strike or something, get all the workers to walk out. Without anyone to work his rig, Vince would have to stop—no way he could do it all himself. Could he?

But that was crazy. Doug knew the guys hated him, and he realized, suddenly, they always had. Sure, they'd slapped his back and laughed at his jokes, bought rounds at the bar and pretended to listen when he had something to say, but that was because he was the boss's son, and they were in it for the paycheck. When it came right down to it, they'd never really been his friends, and they'd used the incident up at the Vein as an excuse to say out loud what they'd probably been thinking all along.

There was no rallying them, not in his position. He'd have to confront his dad on his own.

He eyed ol' Vince from under the yellow brim of his hard hat. The guy was strutting around with his chest puffed out like a Thanksgiving turkey, talking about how he didn't take shit from no one and who the hell needed a foreman anyway. It was probably the worst time to call him on his shit ever. But Dwayne was gone, and the fires were getting closer. If Doug didn't do something, who would?

Maybe it was better not to overthink it. He wasn't any bigger than his dad, but he had built up some muscle working the rig. Worse came to worst, Doug could take him.

He took a step forward, then another. He was about to call Vince's name when a red pickup coated with dust came careening down the road and screeched to a stop just inches from the Quonset hut. The driver jumped down and ran to the roughnecks still working on the rig, shouting at them to stop what they were doing and evacuate.

"Are you people crazy? What the hell are you still doing here?" Doug squinted through the haze and saw that it was Dale, the foreman from over at the Peyton rig. His voice thundered over the drill's grinding. "Where's your foreman?"

"We were just about to evacuate." Vince hurried over. His face was still purple, but his voice had regained the honeyed calm that Doug had always thought of as the "Varley charm."

Except that suddenly, it didn't sound so charming anymore. It sounded fake and smarmy. Like anyone with half a brain could tell Vince Varley was full of it.

Dale looked from Vince to the rig and back again. "How are you still drilling?" he asked incredulously. "I just risked my life to come over here and make sure all your people were gone. The fire may look like it's taking a break, but trust me, that won't last long."

"We're going, we're going," Vince muttered. "Thanks for the warning. We'll see you over on the other side of town.

Dale still looked unconvinced. "Are you sure? I'm surprised your people are still working."

Doug could almost hear the steam whistling from his dad's ears. "We were just about to pack up. You go on and get back to your guys. Trust me, we got this."

"All right." Dale turned to go, and Doug watched that crazy gleam of greed return to his father's eyes. He'd bet his left nut that ol' Vince had no intention of shutting things down. He was just waiting for Dale to leave so he could yell at his roughnecks to double down and drill harder.

Dale took two steps, then turned again. "Look, Vince, I don't want to burden you at a time like this, but there's something you oughta know."

"What now?" Vince was boiling on the inside, Doug could tell. One more word and he'd start frothing at the mouth.

"Is your son around? I'm afraid he should hear this, too."

Doug didn't like the sound of that.

"I'm right here." He stepped forward.

"Oh, Doug. Hi." Dale took off his Stetson and fiddled with the brim, looking down at the worn, scratched leather for support. Finally, he raised his pale blue eyes.

"Listen, guys, there's no easy way to say this, and I'm not one to beat around the bush. We found Janie's body strung up on our rig this morning. I'm sorry for your loss."

All the blood drained from Doug's head at once, leaving a rushing sound in his ears like a vacuum cleaner turned up high. The hazy world before him telescoped inward, and he stumbled forward, dizzy and nauseated and unable to think. Then the lightheadedness got the best of him, and he sat down hard and kept falling, coming to rest with his cheek in the dirt.

Janie. Body. Loss. Strung up. Sorry. Body. Loss. Janie.

The words knocked around in his brain like marbles in an empty room, bruising the inside of his skull. It couldn't be right.

But it had to be right.

Janie had been gone for days.

Janie had left and hadn't come home again.

Janie had been his wife, and now she was dead. Dead with her body strung up on an oil rig. Dead along with their son, the son he had only just forgiven her for losing.

The dirt around his face turned dark, then sticky, mud clinging to his cheeks. He realized he was crying, sobbing into the earth. He hadn't felt the spit of tears on his face in years. Now it felt like his cheeks would never be dry again.

There were so many tears.

All the tears he had never cried for Jeremiah.

All the tears he had never cried for his own shitty childhood, for the dark nights spent cowering from his father's belt and nursing bloody red whelps in the musty back of his closet.

All the tears he had never cried for his town gone sideways and his marriage gone wrong.

All the tears he'd never let Janie cry.

All the tears she would never cry again.

"You need my help getting him out of here?" he heard Dale ask Vince. Vince's voice was so tight Doug couldn't hear his reply—or maybe he was just sobbing too loud, no longer caring what his father or the guys from the rig or Dale or anyone thought, absolutely anyone at all. He had lost the one person who ever cared about him, who ever believed in him, who didn't abandon him when things got rough. She was gone, and he'd never even told her how much he loved her, how amazing she really was. He'd come damn close to not even realizing it himself.

He heard trucks start up and pull away, one after another, and he curled up tighter on his side, glad to be alone with his grief. Maybe the fire would come and take him and then they could be together again, him and Janie and baby Jeremiah, a real family at last. What a sweet relief that would be, to be with them for eternity and never have to face the world of the living again.

"Get up, son!"

Misery shuddered through him as he realized he wasn't alone. His father still towered over him, making Doug feel very small and very alone, the frightened little boy sniffling in the back of his closet.

"C'mon, you heard what he said about the fire. Get up now."

"Leave me here." It came out in a broken whimper.

"I'm not gonna do that, son." Vince sighed heavily. "You're a loser and a pansy and a freak, but you're my boy. My only boy. Now let's go."

"No." Maybe if he curled up tight enough, he would just disappear. Maybe he would melt in a puddle of his own tears. That would be better than anything right now. It would sure as hell be better than going with his dad.

"You get up or I'll make you get up!"

Doug knew what those words meant. He braced himself for a hard slap in the face or a kick in the ribs, steeled himself for the sting of his father's belt across his back.

But instead he felt a pair of hands wedging themselves under his armpits, heard his father groan as he struggled to drag him to his feet. He was so confused that he forgot to stay limp, to fight his father for his right to stay huddled and brokenhearted on the ground, in the only place that felt right now that his wife was dead.

Instead, he was on his feet, his father's arms tight around his shoulders, half-pushing and half-dragging him to the parking lot.

"C'mon, son," Vince was saying, his voice gruff in Doug's ear. "It's time to go home."

DAPHNE SAT BETWEEN AUNT KAREN and Uncle Floyd in the first row of the new Carbon County First Church of God, gagging on the scent of fresh varnish and lilies. The waxy flowers filled bathtub-sized urns flanking Pastor Ted's gilded pulpit and cascaded from baskets surrounding the coffin behind it, the coffin in which Janie's lifeless body lay.

As huge as the new chapel was, with soaring ceilings, pews that stretched all the way back to row JJ, and floor-to-ceiling stained glass, it wasn't nearly big enough to contain the Peytons' grief.

It had been two days since fires ravaged the hills around Carbon County, yet Daphne still felt burned inside and out, scorched to empty blackness by her cousin's death and tortured by memories of her last vision, reliving over and over again the moment that her knife plunged into Jim's heart only to have his face melt away to reveal Owen's. She'd barely slept since then, choosing instead to stay up nights fixing hot drinks and cool compresses for her aunt and uncle, to let them sob soft and helpless on her shoulder. They were broken now, their hearts trammeled beyond repair, and even though she knew she couldn't fix them, the least she could do was be there.

Her aunt and uncle clutched her hands through Pastor Ted's sermon, their skin as brittle as parchment. Floyd sat slumped and colorless to her left, a man aged twenty years in two days. On her right, Karen was a shivering lump, a steady stream of tears.

"Satan's forces have taken Janie Peyton!" Pastor Ted's words sizzled through the microphone. He was larger than life behind the pulpit, his eyes blazing blue over the crowd. Videographers crouched in the aisle, recording the funeral for his TV show. Pastor Ted addressed his next missive to them.

"Unless we fight back," he continued, pounding a fist on the lectern, "they will take more. We have to purify our souls for the End Times, because, my friends, my flock, the Rapture is coming! Soon it will be too late to get right with God."

Get right with God. Daphne glanced from her aunt and uncle to the larger-than-life Jesus staring at her in wavy stained-glass reproach. She was the one with a direct line to God, the one He'd chosen to hear His voice and receive His visions. She'd seen one of them come true before her eyes when Owen stood by the rig controlling fire with his mind, and she understood that they were predictions, omens of what would come to pass. If only she knew what to do about them, how to stop them. If only she knew what God wanted.

"It's time to confess our sins and cleanse our souls!" Pastor Ted's face gleamed under the layer of matte powder he wore for the cameras. "It's time to cast away all vestiges of doubt and open ourselves fully to God's glorious light!"

Daphne closed her eyes and prayed as hard as she could. But instead of feeling God's glorious light, she heard the echo of Janie's voice, cold and angry in the snowy forest, uttering some of the last words Daphne would ever hear her speak:

A child is missing. My child is dead. What kind of God would allow this?

Looking around at the miserable faces in the church, she had to wonder if Janie was right. Would a good and just God orchestrate so much destruction, so much suffering? Would He stand idly by and watch the mountains around Carbon County burn while one by one all the people she truly loved were torn from the face of the earth? Would a fair and loving God tolerate the years of abuse she'd endured at Jim's hand, an innocent child with nobody to turn to for help? And why would He send her a vision during one of the darkest moments of her life, reminding her how scared and alone she'd felt all those times with Jim and of the terrible night when she'd taken a life just to put an end to it?

The voices around her swelled in plaintive wails of "Praise be!" and "I believe!" It seemed so cut and dried for everyone else: Pastor Ted said to believe, and they believed. But *what* did they believe?

What was *she* supposed to believe? Was it enough to simply believe in God, or did she also have to believe that He was always good and always right, that His way was the best way, the only way? Because that was where it got tricky, where her belief began to slip and falter and fail. That was where she started to wonder if there couldn't be another, better way, one with less pain and suffering, one in which fewer innocents died.

"A great battle is coming, a battle between the Children of God and the Children of the Earth," Pastor Ted went on. "The tablet predicted it, and our very own prophet, our own Daphne Peyton, saw it in visions sent to her from God! It's coming, oh Lord, it's coming, and as God's chosen army it is our duty to fight."

Pastor Ted stared pointedly down the aisles. His youth group had stationed themselves at the edges of the church, guns cradled in their arms and ammo belts slung over their dark mourning clothes. Uncle Floyd had tried to protest, saying it wasn't seemly to have guns at a funeral—or cameras, for that matter—but Pastor Ted insisted. The End Times were so close, he'd said earlier in his office, gold cuff links gleaming in the soft light. They were so close, and the Children of the Earth were so nearby, and so unpredictable. There was no telling what they'd do and when. It was best to be armed and ready. The day of reckoning was at hand.

Daphne snuck a look at the young militiamen flanking her aisle. Their expressions were blank, a far cry from the clenched fury and tear-streaked faces in the front pews, where those who had known Janie sat. Hilary sobbed openly in her mother's arms, the skin around her nostrils pink and raw-looking. Elderly Madge and Eunice clung to each other at the edge of the second row, fingers trembling as they dabbed their faces with soggy lace handkerchiefs.

But starting in row E, the congregants' eyes were dry. They were newcomers drawn to Carbon County by the power of Ted's televised sermons, and most of them had never known Janie. They had never seen her apply blue mascara in the Peyton trailer's closet-sized bathroom or chase Bella through the pine grove. They hadn't heard the horsey warmth of her laugh or felt the soft ferocity of her hugs, hadn't played hide and seek with her as children or arranged her train before she walked down the aisle. To them, this was not so much a funeral as a call to arms.

Pastor Ted concluded his sermon to a thunderous round of applause sprinkled with shouts of "Amen!" and "I believe!"

"And now Floyd Peyton would like to say a few words in remembrance of his daughter," he said.

Floyd's hand stirred in Daphne's. He rose slowly and grasped the back of the pew for support. Daphne had always loved the way her uncle stood tall and proud, like he owned the world even when he had nothing to his name but his trailer and the land it stood on. She loved the way the skin around his eyes wrinkled when he looked at her—friendly and kind, even though she knew the squinting was from poor eyesight. She loved the broadness of his shoulders when he hugged her, and how it made her feel protected in a world that hadn't always been kind.

Now it was all gone. Floyd's shoulders hunched as he shuffled to the pulpit, his face slack and empty as a discarded plastic bag. His leg shook as he took his first step onto the dais, and his entire body trembled with such force that after a long, uncomfortable moment the preacher reached down a steady hand to help him up. With Pastor Ted's firm grip on his elbow, Floyd reached the pulpit looking like a sad-eyed hound dog half-drowned in grief.

"Well." Floyd's voice boomed hollow through the microphone. "This wasn't the speech I wanted to give my first time standing up here. But it is what it is. My daughter is gone, and my heart is gone with her. I hope you—all of you—I hope you never have to feel what it's like to lose a child. There are no words."

His voice cracked, and he bowed his head, revealing a bald spot that Daphne had never noticed before, ringed by a shivering nimbus of graying hair. There was rustling in the back of the church, and she turned to see parents pulling their children close, praying silently that they'd never have to grieve like Uncle Floyd.

"Yes." Floyd raised his head, noting them. "Hold your kids close to you. Protect them however you can. Nothing will ever be as important as your family. Nothing . . ."

He stopped, choking on the words. A thin, raspy cough threaded its way through the church's speakers.

"I mean, my God, what happened to this town?" His voice was a plaintive cry.

"Here we are in church, at a funeral, and there are *guns* here. And cameras." Floyd shook his head slowly. "I mean, they found my daughter strung up like an animal on our . . . on the . . . oh my God."

Floyd crumpled, his head hitting the microphone with a crack that resonated through the sound system in a squeal of feedback. The congregation hurried to cover their ears, but Daphne couldn't move. Her hand was frozen in Karen's, her heart suspended in her chest.

"You're not well." Pastor Ted grasped Floyd by the shoulders, pulling him away from the microphone. The squealing stopped, plunging the church into silence. "Would you like to sit down?"

"No." Floyd shook off the pastor's hands. "They found our Janie on the oil rig. That thing—nothing's been right since we struck oil."

Pastor Ted shot a nervous glance at the cameras. "You should sit down," he said to Floyd. It was no longer a suggestion. "This is a normal stage of grief, placing the blame where it doesn't belong. That oil has been nothing but good for our community and our church."

"It's been *everything* but good!" Floyd's voice shook. He shouldered Pastor Ted out of the way and slammed his palms down hard on the lectern, leaning into the microphone. "Listen, all of you, listen! This is important. It's something I should have realized a long time ago."

Daphne felt Aunt Karen stir next to her. Together they leaned forward, barely breathing, waiting for Floyd's next words.

"We were fine before we had that oil. We were poor, sure, but we were rich in spirit. We had everything that mattered: our faith and our family."

For the first time since Janie's death, Aunt Karen's shoulders stopped heaving. Tears glistened on her cheeks as she gazed up at her husband.

"Now my daughter's gone, and my grandson, too. And my faith? Well, that ain't doing so hot either." The sad plastic bag that was Floyd's face was inflating, filling with heat. "When we tapped that oil we released an evil that isn't going back in the ground. It drove us mad with greed and made us turn our eyes from what's important. I thought it was a gift, but it was a false gift, and we worshipped it like the Israelites worshipped false idols. But that wasn't the gift. The *real* gift was right here in front of our eyes all along."

His eyes landed on Daphne. "You were the gift, Daphne." His voice was coarse sand. "You're our family. You've been like a daughter to us, and now, with Janie gone, you're the only daughter we have left."

A ball of emotion rose in Daphne's throat, almost choking her. It was the validation she'd always wanted, the *only* validation she'd wanted: that she was important to her family, loved and treasured. But it had come at too high a price.

"And that's what's important. Family," Floyd said in a hoarse whisper. He turned back to the congregation, to the sea of mouths dropped open in shock. "People, stop worshipping the golden calf of the oil! Stop buying gilded pulpits and automatic weapons! Stop pretending that anything but love matters. Because it doesn't. It doesn't. And from now on, there will be no more oil, no more greed, no more false idols. I'm shutting down the rig. Enough is enough."

He paused to wipe a tear from his eye, and Pastor Ted used that moment to dive in front of the pulpit, blocking her uncle from saying another word.

"I'm sorry, my friends," he said into the microphone, a bead of sweat trickling down the bridge of his nose. "Mr. Peyton is not well. He doesn't know what he's talking about."

"I know what I'm talking about!" Floyd thundered, trying to muscle his way around the preacher. Two of the burliest youth group members bolted up the stairs and grabbed him by his elbows, practically dragging him back to his seat.

"I'm not done talking!" Floyd yelped, struggling in their arms. "It's my daughter's funeral, you could at least let me finish!"

He kicked one of them hard in the shin and twisted free of their grasp. Daphne wanted to cheer as her uncle made another run for the pulpit, but at that moment the church's doors flew open and every head in the room turned to gape at the newcomers.

A bolt of sunshine streamed down the center aisle, blinding Daphne as she whipped around in her seat. For a moment, all she saw were silhouettes: thirteen of them, dark against the tangerine sunset.

Then she saw their eyes. They glowed green, fiery beams that cut through the chapel and set the very air on edge.

"God, help us!" Pastor Ted screamed into the microphone, his fight with Uncle Floyd forgotten in the sudden cold terror of the invasion. "It's the Children of the Earth."

29

LUNA FLUNG OPEN THE HEAVY church doors and stepped inside. This was her moment, the moment she'd been feverishly working toward. The God of the Earth had whispered to her, promising that if she did everything he asked—if she found a sacrifice, if she chanted the words, if she did it all where the Children of God could finally see and understand—he would rise up and save them all. Before the night was over, she would accomplish what she'd been set on earth to do.

The God of the Earth was almost to the surface, so close she could feel it. She felt it in her belly like a flame, lighting her up from the inside, making her eyes glow green. She felt it in the vibrations under her feet, trembling the church's cement foundation. She felt it in the strength of her brothers and sisters hot as the August sun on her back, their powers at their apex, their bodies and minds moving as one.

Even Owen was with them. Poor, confused, broken Owen, whom she'd found half-dead from smoke inhalation after holding the forest fires at bay for what must have been close to nine hours, until either the smoke jumpers arrived or he collapsed from exhaustion. He hadn't spoken since she'd found him. All she knew was that he'd risked his life for the town of Carbon County and they'd left him for dead. That was simply the kind of people they were, hypocrite churchgoers now gasping and shielding their eyes from the glowing intensity of her stare.

If Luna hadn't spent the last two days nursing Owen back to health up at the Vein, he wouldn't have made it. Even now, she felt him at her back as the weakest link among his brothers and sisters. His head hung low, and the fire had turned his breath to labored wheezing. His weakness made it easier for Luna to use her gift of persuasion on him, to coax him back to her side, but it also worried her. She'd been counting on his powers, and his commitment, to draw the God of the Earth to the surface. With Owen half-broken, they would all have to work even harder to do what needed to be done.

Luna started down the church's aisle, her steps silent on the thick red carpet, her eyes glowing like fireflies.

"Is she a witch?" someone whispered, pointing a trembling finger.

"She's the devil!" another shrieked. "Get her out of here! She'll destroy us all!"

There was a rustling around the church's perimeter, and only then did she notice the militia lining the walls. They looked like children playing dress-up in their starched fatigues and gleaming black boots, cradling semi-automatic weapons instead of teddy bears, their faces twisted into tough-guy impersonations they must have learned from video games.

Luna bit back a laugh: Of *course* they were carrying guns in church, these false-faced people who claimed to want peace but secretly worshipped war. She was surprised they hadn't taken down the cross and hung a rifle in its place.

The youth army raised their guns, aiming them at Luna. The barrels winked at her like dozens of cold, steel eyes.

"Stop!" Through the sea of black-clad mourners, Daphne Peyton rose from her pew. "Everyone, stop. Luna, can't you see they have guns? We all know what you did to Janie. You have to leave before someone gets hurt."

Smiling, Luna shook her head and took another step forward. Guns were pitiful compared to her strength. She was blood, and granite, and fire, and she had the God of the Earth on her side.

"Luna, please." Behind her, Owen's voice was barely a wheeze. She turned to see him struggling forward, pain flickering across his face with every step. "Don't do this. Haven't enough lives already been lost?"

A bubble of anger rose in her throat. They were Owen's first words since she'd rescued him, and they were words of defiance. How dare he try to ruin this, after all she'd done for him?

"Silas." She snapped her fingers.

Her largest Earth Brother grabbed Owen by the back of his shirt. In one easy movement he had Owen's arms pinned behind his back and a hand clamped over his mouth. Owen squirmed in his grasp, trying to land a kick, but in his weakened state he was no match for Silas's strength. Luna knew it would be mere minutes until he was too tired to fight anymore.

She didn't have time for Owen anyway. She had a ritual to perform.

"One more step and they'll shoot!" It was the pastor this time, his voice shaking as it rang through the speakers. Luna heard the hard bite of safeties clicking off, the jangle of ammo belts maneuvering into place.

But guns were no match for the Children of the Earth. They were every element, an alchemical force strong enough to save the world.

"Abilene." Luna stared down the field of raised gun-barrels as her Earth Sister stepped forward to stand at her side. Abilene's mouth stretched wide, and a clear, bluesy note rang out across the church. It soared to the very top of the arched ceiling, bathing the chapel in song.

The youth army froze as the music gripped them, slithering into their ears and wrapping around their minds. Within moments, there was nothing in the world for them except Abilene's song.

One by one, they opened their mouths and joined in. Their voices were rusty and off-key, halting and stilted, but still they sang, zombies under the power of her voice.

"Aura." Luna's prettiest Earth Sister, no more than a wisp with a smattering of freckles across her nose and cheeks, materialized on her other side. Luna felt heat gather in Aura's eyes as she concentrated on the stained glass windows illuminating the church, drawing the essence of their color out of the glass and into the room. Strands of pigment danced through the air and expanded into clouds of violet, cerulean, and scarlet. They descended on the youth army, blanketing them in multihued fog, and Luna smiled as she heard panic creep into their voices, turning the simple melody of Abilene's song into a twisted calliope of fear.

In Aura's blinding fog, in the confusion of Abilene's music, Luna knew she was gaining the upper hand. All she needed was a finishing touch.

"Heather." Solid and loyal, her Earth Sister was there. Heather threw back her head and released a deep, animal roar. It vibrated through Luna's body and shook the church on its foundation.

The stones lining the church gardens were the first to respond. They clanked and groaned, rocking in their beds, dislodging themselves one after another and rolling toward the church. Slowly at first, they gained momentum until the first rock through the church doors barreled down the aisle with the force of a bowling ball angling for a strike. It hit one of the youth soldiers in the ankle and knocked her to her knees, her cry wrenching the song she'd been singing from its tracks. More rocks followed, pelting the stunned youth army in the shins and sweeping their feet out from under them, sending them tumbling, terrified, to the ground.

But Heather wasn't done. Another roar ripped from deep within her and tore through the valley until every rock, pebble, and boulder shivered in its moorings and knocked itself loose, tumbling toward the Carbon County First Church of God with the clumsy velocity of heat-seeking missiles.

The rocks crowded through the doors and sailed through the stained glass windows, raining jagged bits of Bible scenes down on the terrified parishioners. They ducked for cover, the notes of their song turning to high-pitched screams, and as they dove through the thick-colored fog to take shelter beneath the pews, their limbs collided with boulders, birthing bruises on their flesh. A grapefruit-sized stone arced through a broken window and knocked Daphne on the shoulder, sending her sprawling.

Luna wished she could bask in the chaos forever. She loved seeing the powers of her brothers and sisters at work, couldn't get enough of the way her ragtag band of hippies could bring a gun-toting army to its knees. But there wasn't time. Already, the bloody glow of sunset swept through the church. The God of the Earth demanded a sacrifice before the full moon rose.

"Ciaran." Now it was his power that she needed the most, and even through his grief and anger at losing Janie she could tell he was still loyal, a steadying force at Luna's side. "It's time. Find our sacrifice."

↔

The whimper was already in Ciaran's head, begging to be plucked from this world and sent soaring to the next, to be set free.

He heard it through the singing and the stumbling, could sense it through the fog and feel it through the low rumble of rocks rolling through the church. He let the song of sadness fill him until it drowned out all the other voices, and then he began to follow it. He traced it down the aisle, skirting the piles of rocks and falling bodies, until he reached the second row.

His eyes landed on a wizened china doll of a woman in an outdated pillbox hat. Mauve lipstick dotted the front of her teeth as she attempted to give him a trembling smile.

The woman was ancient, her back hunched into the telltale S-curve of scoliosis, her fingers purple and twisted with arthritis. Looking into her eyes he could feel the pokers of pain that shot through her limbs with every step she took, the dull throb of disappointment when she opened her eyes each morning and realized she was still alive. Unlike Janie (his poor, lost, beautiful Janie), she was truly ready to die.

"Her." He nodded to Luna.

The old woman had been singing along with the rest, her voice a creaky, quivering alto, but she stopped at his words and looked up at him, her eyes pink from allergies and tears. Ciaran could sense that deep down she understood what she'd been chosen for, and she was ready. Her husband was twelve years in the grave, and their one son out in Schenectady hadn't brought his family to visit for Christmas that year. She'd doted on little Charlie, the sheriff's young boy next door, but he had been taken from her, too.

Her only solace was the widow doddering next to her, clutching her sleeve in a haze of anxiety and cloying floral perfume.

"What does he want, Eunice?" Her voice shivered as she spoke. "Why is he looking at you like that?"

Luna stepped forward. Her eyes switched to high beam, their neon intensity making the old lady squint. She fixed Eunice with her most rare and special smile, and Ciaran watched her all-too-familiar blue halo radiate out from her, wrapping the old lady in its power.

"Come," Luna murmured, holding out her hand.

Ciaran couldn't tell if Eunice was trembling from fear or joy as she reached out and took it, but when Luna's fingers closed around hers, he felt the pain disappear from her joints and saw her smile open in amazement.

No longer stooped or shaking, Eunice followed Luna back down the aisle, around the downed youth army and the rock piles, and out of the church. Abilene stopped her song mid-note, Aura blinked away the colored fog, and Heather closed her mouth, causing every rock in Carbon County to stop rolling in its tracks as one by one the Children of the Earth followed them, Owen still struggling in Silas's grasp.

↔

Daphne crawled through the rocky rubble and pushed herself to standing. A bruise throbbed on her shoulder, and as she blinked away the sting of the rapidly dissipating purple cloud she scanned the church for her aunt and uncle. Panic tinged her voice as she called their names.

Her aunt was curled into a ball in the pew. Her red-rimmed eyes darted about in fear, but Daphne breathed a sigh of relief as she realized that aside from being shaken up, she was unscathed.

"I'm okay." Uncle Floyd limped toward her from the pulpit. "Just got a rock in the leg. What on earth *was* that?"

"I told you they had powers." Daphne's voice was grim. "We have to stop them. Let's go."

She started toward the door, dodging rock piles and brushing past the Children of God as they struggled to their feet, rubbing their eyes and grimacing as they ran hands over purple-spotted limbs. Most looked like they were still in shock. Pastor Ted's jaw hung open and for once he seemed speechless, a leader who didn't know the next step. He didn't understand what was happening, Daphne realized. None of them did. It was up to her to lead.

"Come on!" she commanded, her voice echoing through the church. Heads turned toward her as the disoriented congregation found their bearings, and she jumped onto the nearest pew to guide them. "We have to stop them before they make their next sacrifice!"

"Sacrifice?" She watched the people's gazes harden as her words penetrated.

"Yes! Like what happened to the sheriff . . . and Janie." There wasn't time left to explain. "Just follow me. We have to go *now.*"

Daphne leapt from the pew and pounded down the aisle, vaulting over the rocks scattered like an obstacle course in her path. As she burst through the doors she felt the congregation begin to pour out behind her, the youth army's boots pounding the ground and their cries cascading like war whoops down the hill.

She kicked off her pinching patent leather shoes, barely feeling the cold grass on the new church's sloping lawn as she ran full tilt to the bottom, where the Children of the Earth had drawn a circle on the ground.

"Stop!" she screamed.

Rusty razor blades of color slashed the sky, and she felt the earth heave beneath her. The Children of the Earth joined hands, the illuminated crossbeams of their eyes drenching the circle in light as they began to move in a slow, counterclockwise march, their footfalls heavy and deliberate.

God of Earth, come what may,

Rise and walk the earth today.

The chant thundered through the valley, echoing against the blackened mountaintops, and as the words gained strength the Children of the Earth became a whirling blur of white robes, ecto-plasmic eyes, and flowing hair. She glimpsed Owen among them, his eyes vacant and his body rag-doll limp as they pulled him along with them, his feet dragging on the ground. Through the spaces between them, in strobe-lit gasps, Daphne saw Luna place her hand on Eunice's forehead.

"Stop!" she cried again. Behind her, at the top of the hill, she heard Pastor Ted shout instructions to his congregation, pleading with them to get out of range so the militia could shoot.

Daphne lunged at the gyrating mass of bodies, trying to break through the circle in what felt like a twisted version of red rover. "They're going to shoot you if you don't stop!"

Their chant drowned out her cries.

God of Earth, come what might,

Overtake the world tonight.

Eunice looked up at Luna, her face like a dying star hurtling through the galaxy, full of fire and hope and the last bright vestiges of life. Then she went dark, and through gaps in the spinning bodies Daphne watched the old lady crumple to the ground.

Pandemonium broke out on top of the hill, the Children of God screaming at each other to get out of the way so they could shoot, as Luna knelt beside Eunice and drew the dagger from her thigh holster, pricking the old woman's finger and using the blood to trace a teardrop on her forehead. Seeing this, the Children of the Earth broke apart and fell to their knees, drumming their hands on the earth in a rhythm like fire crackling and buffalo stampeding.

"You killed her!" Daphne shrieked, just as the first shot rang out and ricocheted wildly through the valley, missing the Children of the Earth by several yards.

The earth shook again, pitching her forward. There was a deafening crack like thunder beneath her feet, and from up on the hill she heard the terrified screams of the congregation fill the air.

"The ground is opening!" someone hollered. She turned to look, and sure enough a crack had formed in the earth. Within moments it widened from a hairline fracture to a gaping wound. She stumbled backward, away from it, the ground still pitching and rolling under her until she lost her balance and fell onto one of the bodies beating the earth, into the achingly familiar scent of soap and motor oil.

↔

Owen grunted under the sudden weight. Silas had kept a firm grip on him as the ritual began, yanking him around the circle as his feet scrambled for purchase on the ground, but then Luna's blue light burned out every other thought in his head, and he found himself caught up in the power of the chant, pounding his fists on the earth until it shook on its axis and he forgot his reluctance, forgot the pain in his lungs, forgot everything but his destiny. In the heat of the ritual he could feel the God of the Earth rising, a presence vast and heavy that flowed through Owen's veins like smoke. Now he was eager to see his one true father—not whatever dirty hippie had impregnated his mother, but his *real* father, the father of them all: the God of the Earth.

The body rolled off of his and lay panting in the dirt, a tangle of dark hair and slim, muscular legs.

"Daphne." Her name broke through the chant and escaped his lips like a puff of steam. It jogged something in the back of his mind and cut the roiling rage and ecstasy the ritual had awakened. He reached down and grasped her, pulling her to her feet. Her arms were warm, making him ache for something he had almost forgotten.

"He has her!" The cry came like the scream of a hawk down the hill. Owen looked up to see Pastor Ted charging them, his suit jacket flapping in the wind, stumbling over the rippling earth. He stopped in front of the widening fissure, fear creasing his face as he stood shaking his fists.

A phalanx of youth group militia flanked him, guns raised.

"He's going to do to her what they did to Eunice!" Pastor Ted's scream was high-pitched and agonized as he shouted instructions to his army. "Take him down! Save our prophet!"

"No!" Daphne leapt to her feet, waving her arms. "He's just—"

Before she could finish, Owen heard the click of a trigger and felt the heat of a metal bullet.

He saw it coming in slow motion, a silver sphere revolving in lazy circles against the blood-red sky. He saw the way it changed the air around it, currents tumbling away in elegant curls. He saw the shooter's eyes widen in horror as she realized where the bullet was headed, and in slow motion he saw Pastor Ted's mouth flap open and Daphne drop to the ground, arms over her head.

Owen felt his mind clear and his eyes blaze green as he dove in front of Daphne, into the gunshot's path. He stared down the bullet, and in his mind he stretched the fabric of space and time, bending the air between them and forcing the bullet's trajectory just a little to the left.

Just a little more.

He trembled with the effort, his eyes glowing painfully hot, sweat pouring down his neck and soaking the collar of his shirt.

The bullet hovered, currents of atmosphere twisting around it like a waterfall. Owen squeezed a hot rush of breath through his lungs and felt every ounce of concentration explode out of him, smacking the bullet so that it grazed his shoulder, leaving a dazzling sear of pain on his clavicle before speeding away into the church parking lot.

From the corner of his eye, he saw Daphne climb slowly to her feet. He had saved her life, and he'd saved himself, too. But he could sense that the worst was still to come.

↔

Tears streamed from Doug's eyes as he peeled into the church parking lot. He left his truck idling in a no-parking zone, not even bothering to shut the door as he half-ran, half-staggered toward the sparkling white building with the steeple that scraped the sky.

It was his wife's funeral, goddammit, and his asshole parents had tried to make him miss it. They said it wasn't safe for him to be out in his condition, but he knew the truth: Ol' Vince Varley didn't want folks seeing his son cry in public. He was a Varley man, and Varley men were supposed to be tough.

But Doug didn't care what they thought anymore. His dad was down at the rig, drilling deep enough to hit that fault line and making the whole town shake, and when his mom took her eyes off of him long enough to go to the bathroom Doug grabbed the car keys and ran. He'd be late, he figured, but at least he'd get to see his wife's face one more time before they put her in the ground. At least he'd get to say goodbye.

He saw the people gathered on the lawn and ran faster, trying to conjure up the old Doug from his halfback days as the ground quaked just like Dwayne had warned it would, making it feel like he was running across the surface of a trampoline. The funeral procession must have started already, and he *had* to get there before they lowered Janie into the ground.

But as he got closer, his eyes narrowed in confusion. Something was going on in front of the church, something that looked more like a standoff than a funeral. There was a crater in the earth that he could have sworn hadn't been there before, and the Children of the Earth were on one side of it, on their knees in some kind of circle like they were praying or something.

On the other side of the crack, standing so close that his toes were practically over the edge, Pastor Ted raised his arms to the sky. But he didn't look like he was talking to God—he looked angry. And instead of wearing black and holding flowers, the people surrounding him wore head-to-toe camo and carried guns.

Doug ran, ignoring his confusion and the stitch of pain growing in his side until it exploded suddenly, hot and sharp. He clutched his chest, gasping, but he didn't think to look down until the pain forced him to his knees.

He glanced at his chest then and saw thick red liquid seeping out from around his fingers, a carnation of blood on the front of his shirt.

Did I seriously just get fucking shot? Doug asked himself before falling face-first onto the ground.

↔

Daphne heard the whoosh of the bullet change direction and staggered to her feet just in time to see Doug fall, blood gushing from his wound. She tore off her jacket and ran to him, stumbling as the earth pitched with another series of tremors. She half-sat, half-fell beside him, pressing the balled-up fabric against his chest.

"Call an ambulance!" she screamed, trying to staunch the blood. From the top of the hill she heard snatches of the congregation conferring, someone arguing that the paramedics were all out in the hills with the firefighters. "Just do it!" she screamed.

But Doug shook his head.

"Don't bother." His eyes were foggy, his voice laced with pain. "It's in my heart. I'm going to die."

"Don't say that." She shook her head, wiping sweat from his brow and pressing the soaked jacket tighter against his chest. "You'll make it, Doug. Just hang in there."

His face twisted. "I don't even want to," he croaked. "All I can think about is Janie. If there's an afterlife or whatever, maybe I can find her and . . . and make it up to her somehow."

He winced as a fresh spurt of blood trickled down his side. "Maybe, like, our son is there, and we can be a family for real."

The ground heaved. Daphne grasped his shoulders, steadying them both. The smell of sulfur filled the air, and the sky darkened to the color of blackbirds' wings.

"Daphne." A white film was spreading over Doug's eyes. "You have to stop my dad. All these earthquakes are probably his fault."

"Vince?" Daphne's forehead creased.

"Yeah." Doug could barely choke out his next words. "He's drilling . . . this pipeline and hitting . . . a fault. It's deep, Daph. Too . . . deep."

He fell back, panting. The film over his eyes was thick as cobwebs, and then his breathing slowed. Two labored gasps later, his hand went limp in hers.

Daphne looked down at him, at his eyes staring up into nothingness, the tears drying slowly on his face. He had only just turned into someone tolerable, someone she could actually stand, and now he was gone.

"I hope you're right," she murmured, gently shutting his eyes. "I hope you and Janie and Jeremiah really can be together again."

A fusillade of shots rang out behind her, and she threw herself to the ground. At the sound of guns reloading, she peeked out from between her fingers and confirmed what she'd already suspected: The guns weren't aimed at her. The youth group shouted instructions as they tried to take down the Children of the Earth, firing a fresh round of ammunition that filled the lawn in front of the church with the acrid stink of gun smoke. Owen stood facing the hailstorm of bullets, green beams of energy shooting from his eyes as he deflected one round after another, protecting the Children of the Earth. Some of the bullets dropped to the ground at his feet like discarded cherry stones while others ricocheted back to the youth group at full speed.

Daphne heard a shout of agony and saw a woman from the congregation fall, clutching her shoulder. She'd caught one of Owen's deflected bullets; the more the youth group shot at him, the more there would be.

She screamed for a ceasefire, but her voice was lost beneath the chanting and the gunshots and the grinding of the earth's plates below her feet. She had to get closer to the Children of God, to make them hear her, but it would mean circling the parking lot and approaching them from behind. It was the only way to circumvent the crack and the war zone of bullets filling the air with gunpowder and metal. She began to run.

God of Earth, open wide.
Release the power deep inside!

The chant spread like a storm, and the crack in the earth lengthened, blocking her way. The tremors had widened it to the size of a six-lane highway, creating a sinkhole in the concrete. She gasped as someone's Volvo tumbled into the abyss, its car alarm bleating in useless protest.

There was no way to tell how deep the crack went, only that its sheer rock walls extended further down than she could see. It divided her from the church, from Floyd and Karen and Pastor Ted, from the Children of God. Across the fissure the youth group stood in formation, guns still raised, eyes wide and mouths agog. Behind them, near the entrance to the church, the rest of the congregation huddled in a shivering mass, her aunt and uncle among them. Pastor Ted rushed back and forth from his flock to the front lines, eyes bulging above crimson cheeks as he exhorted the congregation to pray their hearts out, to pray as hard as they could, for the End Times were truly at hand.

But on Daphne's side of the crevasse, there was only herself and Doug's corpse and the Children of the Earth.

It was an image she'd seen before, a picture that had already seared itself into her memory. There was a great crack in the earth and a great battle raging before her—and she was on the wrong side.

Her second vision had come true.

30

THE CHILDREN OF THE EARTH bounded to their feet, cawing in delight as the crack widened, putting ever more distance between Daphne and the Children of God. Seeing her there, Pastor Ted screamed a command to the gunmen.

"Don't shoot!" he hollered, his voice carrying across the divide. "Our prophet's still there!"

A geyser of jaundiced steam poured from the crevasse, obscuring his face. It wrapped foul-smelling tentacles around Daphne's legs and steeped her hair in a primordial stench of rotten eggs and decay. As she brought her hand to her mouth she felt molten liquid slosh from the crack and scald the tops of her feet. She yelped and leapt back, leaving a slick black pool where she'd been standing.

Daphne wiped a viscous streak from her eye and stepped forward. A hissing sound came from within the fissure, trying to warn her back, and the stink made her gag reflex leap in her throat. But she needed to know what was in there, what they were up against. Holding her breath against the stench, she leaned forward and peeked inside.

A river of burbling lava filled the chasm. It bubbled and eddied, moving slow as mercury, blazing with molten igneous pustules. Black bubbles stretched across the surface, belching and sputtering before bursting into fireworks of hot tar.

Daphne watched, fascinated, as a single, scaly tentacle rose from the muck. Thick and muscular as a boa constrictor, it felt its way along the sheer rock wall before dropping below the surface in a chorus of slurping and gnashing sounds.

God of Earth, and minions, too,
Rise and let us worship you!

The chant throbbed in her head as a red-veined eye the size of a softball peeked up from the river of ooze. It disappeared, only to be replaced by the slimy, silver tip of a fin.

These were the minions, Daphne realized with nauseous shock. They had been shadows in her vision, but the Children of the Earth had coaxed them from the depths with their chanting. Now they were perilously close to walking the earth, and Daphne was powerless to stop them. It was only a matter of time before they got their bearings and made their way to land.

Behind her, the Children of the Earth kept chanting. She could no longer distinguish words, only the caterwauling of voices raised in ecstasy.

They surrounded her, clutching at her dress, breathing hot commands to join them, to succumb to them, to help them rouse the God of the Earth. Owen stood off to the side, hands on his knees, panting and gasping as he tried to catch his breath. He was dizzy from fending off the bullets with his mind, his lungs still clogged with smoke, and he barely noticed his brothers and sisters clawing at Daphne.

"Get off of me!" Daphne slapped their hands away, punching and kicking at the flailing tangle of limbs. She squinted against the incandescent green of their eyes until she found the person she was looking for, the person responsible for the chaos all around.

In the midst of the writhing mass of dancers, Luna stood perfectly still. She wore a scarlet robe with sleeves that brushed the ground, a band of pure gold circling her waist. Her hands were spread at her sides, and her head was thrown back, the pose of someone waiting to be taken. Bliss gleamed in her smile. Luna's dreams were coming true, Daphne realized; all along, she'd wanted this war, this chaos. She'd worked even harder to make it happen than Daphne had to stop it.

"Why?" It was the only word Daphne could choke out, and it was a question she should have asked a long time ago, a question that might have prevented everything. "Why are you doing this? What do you want?"

Luna laughed bitterly, her teeth glinting. "To save the earth. This is my father's planet, and we've let everyone destroy it for too long. Now it's time to listen."

It's time to listen.

The words stuck like a dagger. Luna had listened: She knew exactly how to reach her God, exactly how to fulfill his plan. She had gathered his children, opened the Vein, even killed people to please him. She had never questioned. Unlike Daphne, her mind had never been plagued by doubt.

Luna fixed her with a faux-sympathetic smile. "I thought you were supposed to be a prophet, Daphne? Where is your God?"

Daphne had no reply. Because Luna was right: She hadn't listened to the signs. She was supposed to be a prophet, a leader—but behind her, yet another corpse lay cold on the ground, and her God was nowhere to be seen. She'd hesitated and second-guessed and waited, and now it was too late.

It's time to listen.

Luna's laugh was rich and throaty as tarnished pewter.

"It's too bad your God never showed up, Daphne." Luna was looking past her now, beyond her shoulder at the fissure in the earth. "Because mine did. In fact, here he comes now."

↔

Owen felt a thrill course through him as the earth shook, its plates separating with a deafening crack as the fissure split into a gaping canyon. A pillar of molten fire exploded from within, brighter than the sun and twice as angry. It grew until it overshadowed the church's steeple. It reached the top of the mountains and then towered above them, higher than the highest skyscraper, so tall it seared black streaks into the stratosphere.

It pulsed red anger and white-hot light, so bright that Owen felt his pupils contract and saw dark sparks float behind his eyes. But he couldn't look away, and he didn't want to. This was his true father, the father of them all. This was the voice from his dreams and the force that had drawn him to Carbon County, that had controlled his desires and destiny ever since his eighteenth birthday—ever since his birth.

His true father was here, and he was more terrifying and magnificent than Owen had imagined.

The flames bent and contorted like a dancer wracked with pain, then straightened toward the heavens, torching the sky. Within moments they started to spread outward, whirling and dipping across the landscape, and in the depths of the inferno a form began to emerge.

First it was the outline of a mountain, the whorls of flame describing rugged rock outcroppings and a snow-dusted top. Then it shifted again, mutating into a great white whale that dove toward the earth in a graceful arc. The whale blurred and faded, and now it was a massive oak, its branches stretching over their heads as leaves made of sparks and flame trembled in an imaginary breeze.

Owen found himself dropping to his knees along with the rest of the Children of the Earth. This god, their father, was so huge, so powerful—it made sense that they had followed his voice wherever it led them, that they had sacrificed lives at his command. It made sense, even though he knew in his heart that it wasn't right.

Tears of joy shimmered in Luna's eyes, and Owen realized that the apparition blazing before her was an exact replica of the tree tattooed on her back. It was like Luna had remembered it from a long-ago memory, or a dream, and knew that one day she would see it again.

↔

It's time to listen.

Daphne had seen this pillar of fire before, in her visions. She'd seen it emerge and heard the screams that now echoed all around. She'd seen a pair of green eyes disappear into the open maw of the chasm before her as a dark figure spiraled downward to the center of the earth. She knew what the images *were*, but what did they *mean*? What was she supposed to do? What did God *want* her to do?

The fire shifted again, shaking off its leaves in clusters of sparks that started small fires in the grass. Flaming branches fused into a giant pair of arms, and the trunk split to become two legs, each ten stories tall. A flickering fireball expanded where the uppermost branches had been, and in the shimmering heat a nose appeared, then ears, then fire tendrils of hair that licked at the sky and scorched the blood-red clouds black.

The tree was becoming a giant man. A cavernous mouth sliced his head, and dozens of giant bats flew out, wingspans wide as an eagle's. They swooped, screeching, over the Children of God. One parishioner, a newcomer to town who ducked just a moment too late, was scooped up in a pair of fur-covered feet and carried off into the mountains, his cries a pitiful echo.

The man of flames opened his eyes, and Daphne felt her body stiffen and her heart pound in her ears. Across the divide, the Children of God flung their hands over their eyes, sobbing for mercy.

The monster's eyes were green and glowing, like those of the Children of the Earth. Within them, in vivid high definition, an endless parade of horrors played out. Forests were razed and children massacred, mountains of garbage grew into infinity and entire populations of fish flopped belly-up to the surface of polluted waters. Daphne saw cities choked with smog and rivers rank with chemicals, polar bears sliding off of melting ice caps and birds poisoned by fertilizers. And she saw gaping holes in the earth, scars across its surface that bled oil until they ran dry.

This, she realized, was the God of the Earth. He was here, just as Luna had promised he would be, to reap revenge for the destruction of the planet. And, just as Luna had predicted, Daphne's God was nowhere to be found. She still didn't know what He wanted of her, what she had to do to stop this insanity. All she knew was that, so far, she had failed.

She tried to focus on her visions, to put the pieces together as the God of the Earth raised a fiery leg high over their heads, emerging from the crevasse. Each footstep produced an earthquake of its own, sending shock waves across the ground and tossing the Children of God into the air like popcorn. He walked with slow determination, scanning the parishioners with his terrible green eyes, leaving smoldering bonfires wherever his feet landed.

"Satan is among us!" Pastor Ted dropped to his knees. "Kill him! Kill him before he destroys us all!"

The militia reloaded their weapons and advanced, filling the air with the echoing boom of gunshots, spraying the God of the Earth. The blasts would have left any human dead ten times over, but instead the bullets melted on contact, leaving wet streaks of silver running down his massive legs.

The God of the Earth threw back his head and roared, a noise that made the thundering gunshots sound like pennies dropped into a tin can. Daphne's ears rang in protest, and she clamped her hands over them, but there was no drowning out his cries.

The air around him turned to steam, shifting and melting as he stopped before a row of gunmen, the youth army's front lines. Visibly trembling, yet determined to stand their ground, they raised their guns—but before they could shoot he scooped a half dozen of them into a hand the size of an SUV.

Daphne caught the sickening aroma of charred flesh. She

watched the youth army's limbs blacken in his clutches, their hair turn to flaming haloes. Within seconds they were obliterated, the last of their cries dying into the scorched sky. He tossed their ashes aside, showering the heads of the living as he scanned the crowd for his next victim.

At his feet, standing no higher than the God of the Earth's ankle, Pastor Ted was a purple mess of tears, the knees of his new suit charred from the burning grass. "God, save us!" he begged, clasping his hands in prayer. "Deliver us from this evil and bring your Rapture down upon us now, that we may be saved and live in eternal glory in thy name!"

The congregation followed, falling to their knees as another tremor convulsed the earth. They pleaded with God for a miracle, for deliverance, begged Him to come back and fulfill His promise to lead them to freedom.

Uncle Floyd's voice boomed out over their prayers. "Don't be stupid!" He ran from one praying parishioner to the next, trying to drag them to their feet. "God isn't going to save us now. We have to save ourselves. Run for the parking lot and get in your cars! Drive away as fast as you can!"

Tears pricked Daphne's eyes as she watched him try to round up the hysterical churchgoers. Even Uncle Floyd had abandoned his faith in God, just as Janie had before him. Daphne had always admired the Peytons' faith, even if sometimes she had trouble sharing it. But now she had no choice: Skepticism had gotten her nowhere, and questioning hadn't led to any answers. God had spoken to her. He had sent her visions. It was time to put her doubt aside and listen.

As the congregation ran in crazed circles, the God of the Earth raised a foot the size of the Peytons' trailer and brought it down hard on a gray-haired couple clasping hands as they ran. They were squashed instantly, their bodies no more than outlines against the singed grass.

Thundering toward the church, the God of the Earth grasped its sloped roof and rocked the building like a child trying to loosen a tooth, shaking it on its foundation so that screams poured from its broken windows, the terrified cries of those trapped inside.

The roof began to glow scarlet with heat. As it started smoldering, the God of the Earth leaned forward and bit the steeple with massive fangs, yanking it from its roots and spitting it at the congregants still scrambling across the lawn. They leapt away as it arced from his mouth and landed point-down, the cross that had topped it so proudly now digging into the earth. The steeple incinerated instantly, oxygen rushing through its hollow core to fan the flames until they licked the sky with scarlet tongues.

Seconds later, the church ignited. The building, so new that the paint had barely dried on its walls, bloomed in a lotus of fire. Sparks and debris littered the air; Daphne watched as dozens of Bibles fluttered to the ground, pages flapping like a flock of pigeons.

She froze as the fire screamed its way to the church basement. It was only a matter of seconds until it reached the secret rooms below, until it caught the arsenal. And then . . .

"Duck!" she screamed, the wind carrying her voice over the divide. Bodies thudded to the ground on both sides of the chasm, and Daphne followed, protecting her head with her hands but unable to look away.

The underground arsenal exploded. A mushroom cloud of gunpowder, ammo, and broiling smoke engulfed the sky as bullets rained down in arcs of glittering silver. The earth seized from the explosion, shaking the ground in a series of epileptic spasms, and Daphne clutched at the grass, terrified of being pulled into the divide, her knuckles white and her fingernails bleeding into the dirt.

She righted herself, tears stinging her eyes. The church was gone, the families that had hidden inside along with it. Bodies lay scattered in the Earth God's wake. Beside her, the Children of the Earth sprang to their feet and joined hands, leaping and frolicking with the delight of schoolchildren released into their first day of summer vacation. They grasped at Owen's hands, but he batted them away, staring sadly at the destruction on the other side of the divide.

Luna clasped her hands over her heart and gazed at the God of the Earth with a look of unadulterated love. "He's finally here!" she crowed. "The work, the rituals, the sacrifices—it was all worth it."

The work. The rituals. The sacrifices.

Luna's words tugged at the edges of Daphne's visions, melting them together into one long loop.

Owen controlling fire.

The earth opening.

A pillar of flames.

A green-eyed figure falling into the chasm.

A knife plunged deep into Jim's chest.

Jim morphing into Owen before her eyes.

Owen controlling fire.

God wanted something from her, something she'd been unwilling to see before. He wanted more than her belief and devotion, more than praise and worship. And now, finally, she knew what she needed to sacrifice.

Dropping into a low crouch, Daphne gathered her strength, letting it pump through her veins and fill her muscles. She ran full-tilt at the Children of the Earth, lunging at Luna and tackling her to the ground.

They fell in a twisted ball of black and red and gold and flesh, Daphne's weight pinning Luna to the ground. Red glass beads and sandpapery dreadlocks slapped Daphne's face as Luna whipped her head from side to side, struggling to flee the iron of Daphne's grasp. Even with Luna immobilized on the grass, Daphne could feel the power in her sinewy arms. She sensed Luna trying to summon her powers and clasped a hand down over Luna's throat, blocking the first pale glow of her blue light.

"Help!" Luna cried. "Get her off of me!"

The Children of the Earth started toward them.

"Where is it?" Daphne muttered, feeling behind her, blindly running a hand up and down Luna's kicking legs. She knew she'd seen it when Luna's cloak fell open, the glint of something hard and deadly strapped to her thigh.

The Children of the Earth charged her, rage brewing in their eyes. She felt something cold and metal brush her fingertips just as Kimo's spidery fingers were about to close around her neck . . .

But suddenly they stopped. She looked up and saw that Kimo's fingers were locked in place in midair, his face contorted into a scowl. The rest of the Children of the Earth stood immobile behind him, suspended in a freeze-frame tableau.

Confusion clouded Luna's eyes. Something had stopped the Children of the Earth from grabbing her—some force greater than all of theirs combined.

It was Owen. Standing off to the side, he held his brothers and sisters steady with the fierce concentration of his gaze. He was using his powers on them, preventing them from taking another step. And he was doing it for Daphne.

"No!" Luna cried, thrashing her body like a scorpion's tail. She grabbed a chunk of Daphne's hair and yanked, sending rockets of pain through Daphne's scalp just as she managed to yank the dagger free and hold it above her head.

The blade glimmered inches from Luna's chest, winking at her, the same blade with which she'd drawn the blood of her sacrifices, marking them so the gods would recognize them as an offering.

Slowly, she uncurled her fist from Daphne's hair. For the first time, Daphne saw fear flash across her face.

"You won't do it," Luna snarled. "You wouldn't dare."

Daphne looked down at her, marveling at the destruction Luna had caused, the lives she had taken. All that misery and death from one girl, no older or bigger or stronger than Daphne herself.

"You deserve to die," Daphne said quietly, watching terror settle over Luna's features, making her lip tremble. Prone on the ground beneath Daphne's weight she looked suddenly vulnerable, like the lost little girl she must have been long ago.

Daphne shook her head, unable to go on. "But you were just doing what you thought was right," she sighed.

Luna nodded, a single tear leaking down her cheek. "It's what he wanted," she whispered. She nodded at the God of the Earth, who was stalking furiously up and down the church lawn, scorching wounded parishioners as they tried to crawl to the parking lot.

"Just because someone else wants it doesn't mean it's right." Daphne reared back and brought her fist down hard on Luna's face, the flesh connecting in a satisfying smack as blood sloshed from Luna's nose. Her eyes rolled back in her head, and Daphne used that moment to shove a knee hard into her stomach, knocking the air out of her so that she fell back, limp and gasping. "Even if that someone is a God."

Luna's eyes fluttered shut, and her breathing slowed. She was out cold.

Daphne turned and wiped the sweat from her brow, the knife still glinting in her hand. Now came the hard part: following her visions through to the end, letting God know that she'd pieced them together and recognized their message. She understood, finally, what God had been trying to tell her—and she understood, finally, what He wanted.

She understood the fear that had gripped her when she saw Owen huge as the hills, controlling fire. It was because God wanted her to be afraid.

She understood why she'd seen the earth open in a great chasm and release a pillar of flames, why she'd predicted being trapped on the wrong side of the fissure with the Children of the Earth. It was because God wanted her to know when.

She understood why He'd made her relive the awful night when she took Jim's life, only to have her stepfather's face melt into Owen's once she plunged the knife into his heart. It was God telling her what to do.

She felt the knife in her hand, heavy as time, swift as sorrow. Now she just needed the courage to use it.

31

OWEN RELEASED HIS CONTROL OVER the Children of the Earth and watched Daphne stand slowly, the dagger clasped in her palm. His brothers and sisters rushed to Luna's side, circling her frantically as they glared at him, the pain of his betrayal hardening their faces

"What did you do to her?" Kimo shrieked. Freya took Luna's hand as Abilene fanned her face and Aura ripped a section from her white skirt to staunch the blood from Luna's nose.

Daphne turned her back on them. She found Owen still standing apart from the others at the edge of the chasm, silently watching the scene unfold.

A hot breeze whipped his hair, and his shirt was scorched to rags, his skin slick with sweat and oil from the roiling river inside the canyon. Behind him, across the crevasse and through a thick haze of smoke, Uncle Floyd hustled Karen and the remaining Children of God into church vans. He climbed in after them and the vans screeched away, doors gaping open to reveal the sobbing survivors crammed inside.

Owen noted the dagger as Daphne approached, but he didn't run—didn't even flinch. He stood tall as the church blazed behind him and the God of the Earth pitched his head backward, emitting a roar that shook the mountains.

She stopped just inches from him, close enough to touch.

"You held them off." She nodded at the Children of the Earth. "Why?"

Owen's eyes never left hers. "I don't want this any more than you do. I thought if you could get to Luna, maybe you could stop it."

The sound of his voice stunned her. It felt like she hadn't heard it in a lifetime.

"I *can* stop it," she said quietly. Her throat, already parched from heat and fear, closed around her next words. Her body wanted to stop her from saying what she had to say next.

The world seemed to fall away around them, screams fading into silence, the flaming skies disappearing until everything was a pure, waiting white.

"I know what God wants now. I figured out what the visions were trying to say." Tears welled in her eyes, and her next words were a half whisper. "He wants a sacrifice."

Owen nodded silently. Beneath the glow of his eyes she saw someone broken, defeated, confused, and sorry. Remembering all of their days and nights together, for a second she let herself feel that thick bubble of love that filled her chest whenever they touched, that felt so huge inside her that she thought the world was too small to contain it.

"He wants you."

Owen looked around at the fire, the destruction, the terror, the sadness. "Will it stop all this?"

She nodded miserably, biting her lip. "I think so. It's what God's been trying to tell me all along. I just didn't want to hear it."

Owen sucked in his breath, his face wrenched with sadness, and pulled her into his chest, the butt of the dagger knocking him on the thigh. "I'm sorry I left you." He could barely choke out the words. "I didn't realize how wrong it all was until Janie was dead, and then it was too late. That day at the rig, with the fire, I tried to keep it away. To protect Janie's body . . . to protect you and your family."

Daphne let herself cry against his chest, breathing in the familiar scent of motor oil and earth. Finally, she collected herself, taking a step back from him. "I didn't listen to my visions because they painted you as evil. And I *know* in my heart you're not." She wiped her eyes with the back of her hand. "I always knew. Nobody is all good or all evil. Even Luna. We're all just human, muddling along, trying to do what's right."

A thundering bellow forced their eyes away from each other, toward the God of the Earth. He was coming for them, his footsteps like miniature earthquakes shuddering the ground. His mouth opened, revealing rows of black teeth sharp as swords. Plumes of flame shot from his nostrils.

Owen turned to her, urgency glowing in his eyes. "Do what you have to do—whatever it takes to make this stop. And know that no matter what, I love you."

She couldn't answer him with words. Her heart was too full, too heavy, too close to cracking in two like the ground they stood on.

Instead, she leaned forward and kissed him. Her lips burned with all the words they would never get to say, all the kisses they would never get to share, all the smiles they would never exchange—a future cut short by a pair of mad and vengeful gods and the zealots who followed them blindly into a battle that had no point and no meaning.

Owen's arms went around her, pulling her close as they poured their love into one another, letting it buoy them above the charred remains of Carbon County one last time.

When they finally let go, their faces were wet with tears.

Owen took a step back. He stood at the very edge of the yawning chasm, the dark river spewing oily geysers below him. Daphne took one last look at him, drinking in his features, the face she loved so dearly and would always hold close.

He smiled once—the same cocky half smile that had sent her heart skittering across a gas station parking lot when they first met, a smile that seemed to say that no matter what happened, he'd come out on top. Then she brought the knife down hard.

He stumbled back, his gaze never leaving hers. His arms cartwheeled, and the green of his eyes illuminated the entire sky before dying out entirely, leaving nothing but clear emerald irises shining with the innocence of a newborn. The river of oil melted away, and he fell into the crack in the earth, his body spiraling down and down and down until it was just a speck against the endlessness, a mirror image of the vision that had brought her to her knees. Far below she heard screeching wails and a gnashing, dribbling, lip-smacking hiss. Then the fissure began to shrink, the plates below them cracking thunderously as its walls pulled into each other. Soon it was the width of a highway, then a dirt road, then the dried-up creek bed behind the Peytons' trailer. Finally, it was no larger than a crack in the sidewalk.

Luna came to and howled, racing to the crack and flinging herself to the ground beside it, sobbing Owen's name. When she looked up at Daphne, her eyes were damp and smudged with makeup, her nose swollen and bleeding.

"What did you *do*?" she cried.

Daphne looked from Luna to the dagger in her hand. The blade was clean, she realized: Not a single drop of blood marred its glittering surface. But Owen was gone, and her heart felt like it was made of cement.

"I listened," she replied, wiping angry tears from her eyes.

The God of the Earth spun to face them. A blinding glow of anguish crossed his face, the scenes of destruction that danced in his eyes melting and blurring until they were nothing but static.

The pulsing molten flames of his body began to fade like a campfire going out after a long night. His skin dulled to the glow of embers dying beneath the pearly glimmer of dawn, and beneath the dwindling glare of his fiery skin Daphne saw that he was made of old twigs and chunks of mud, fossilized rocks and decaying animals and rotting pieces of wood.

The last bits of heat consumed these as well. Within moments he was nothing more than used charcoal, a towering mass of ashy gray.

Then the wind picked up, and he turned to dust, scattering across the lawn, landing on Luna's face and mingling with her tears until her cheeks were caked with soot.

Like an army of angels, dark storm clouds unfurled over the mountains, settling above the demolished church and blotting out the scorched red sky. They opened over the still-burning lawn, releasing torrents of cool, sweet rain that staunched the flames and put out the grass fires. Daphne stood with her arms spread wide and her face open to the sky, letting the rain wash the dirt and sweat from her face and intertwine with her tears. Within moments the raging field of fire that had been the churchyard was an expanse of mud, cool to the touch and squelching under her feet, twisted through with burbling streams that spoke of rejuvenation and renewal, the chance to forget and forgive and start again.

32

THE SCENT OF ROSES FILLED Daphne's car as she pulled slowly away from the Peytons' trailer, the puttering gurgle of her motor the only sound in the silent winter morning. They sat on her empty passenger seat, a bouquet of white blooms that matched the snow carpeting the ground where the oil rig had once been.

It was gone now, the machinery trucked away to a fresh well in North Dakota, Dale and his crew with it. Uncle Floyd had been adamant that the rig, and all the greed it stood for, be torn down. But that wasn't why they'd left.

According to the roughnecks on Dale's crew, the reserves had run dry the day the God of the Earth set foot on land. The machinery pumped nothing but dust, clogging the pipes and rusting the valves, and not one of the experts from Global Oil HQ could explain why. A month after that day, in the dreary November afternoon, all that was left of the once-bustling rig was a series of raised berms in Daphne's rearview mirror, scar tissue over wounds that had once gushed the earth's blood.

Her car glided smoothly over the road, her motor starting to purr as it warmed to the day. There were no more potholes, no more water trucks and construction vehicles and prospectors' RVs to cause them. Aside from her Subaru making its way to and from Elmer's Gas 'n' Grocery, where she did the bulk of the Peytons' shopping, there was almost no traffic at all.

Her heartbeat picked up, as it always did, when she rounded the bend in front of the police station. But despite the power of her memories there was no crowd of people under the flagpole, no body strung up there like a scarecrow with a glistening teardrop of blood on his forehead. Only the stars and stripes greeted her with a half-mast salute, bolstered by a light breeze.

Detectives Madsen and Fraczek had discarded her file after dozens of eyewitnesses testified to seeing the Children of the Earth perform the same grizzly death ritual on Eunice that had claimed the sheriff and Janie. And with the prospectors gone there was no need for a police presence in Carbon County beyond the state troopers' occasional passes through.

Still, she could almost feel the memory of the detectives' accusatory stares through the dusty venetian blinds, and as she cruised past the squat green building she flicked the heating dial on her dashboard so it blasted a welcome shot of warm air into her face.

She idled at the stop sign marking a fork in the road. The left prong snaked up into the mountains, to the low, empty building where the Vein had once stood. Its sign still glowed red at night, but cracks had formed in the cheap asphalt of its parking lot, and the padlock on its doors had begun to rust. The Children of the Earth had fled town as soon as their god abandoned them, pillaging the Vein's kitchen of every pot, pan, and sack of rice, even prying the industrial oven and dishwasher from the walls. Rumors flitted through the Carbon County gossip mill that they had gone west, picking up stragglers along the way with the promise of starting a new commune in Washington state, near where the old one had been. Someone had even claimed to have seen little Charlie's somber brown eyes peeking out from the window of their van, but that supposed eye-witness was often drunk and not to be trusted.

Maybe the rumors were true, or maybe they were idle speculation. Daphne tried not to listen to the gossip. It had no place in her new life, a life spent caring for her shell-shocked aunt and uncle, volunteering with the wounded at the hospital, taking correspondence courses through the community college in Rawlins, and trying not to get lost in yawning afternoon silences and restless dreams.

She turned right, onto the road leading to town. LED letters still trawled the window in Elmer's Gas 'n' Grocery, advertising *Hot Dogs 2 for $2.99* and *Firewood Special: $4/Bundle*, but in the once-packed parking lot there was just Elmer's tired Jeep, brooding under the steel-colored sky.

Across the street, the Sleep-EZ Motel was dark and deserted. Only a sign at the entrance to an empty dirt lot indicated that there had once been a bustling trailer park next door. The shops and restaurants along Main Street were shuttered yet again, the way Daphne had found them when she first arrived. Their signs, painted and hung just months before, were bright as carnival clowns against the town's gray facade. An old newspaper, its headline proclaiming *No More Oil?!*, cartwheeled down the empty street on a stiff breeze.

Carbon County was vacant again, quiet. It was exactly what Daphne had wanted when she'd escaped Detroit: wide-open spaces and fresh mountain air, nights where there was nothing to do but watch for shooting stars. But she had been consumed then, buzzing with a rage so great she could barely contain it, angry at the world for creating her stepfather and then blaming her for his death, wracked with guilt over the darkness in her past.

Now the darkness was gone. Like Carbon County, she was wide-open inside, white and quiet as the fields blanketed in snow. There had been no more seizures since she'd sacrificed Owen to defeat the God of the Earth, no more lapsing into another world where God filled her head with the thunder of his visions. She was no longer a prophet, but she was no longer a killer either, or a victim. She was simply Daphne, and that was enough.

She still had a role in Carbon County, but it was a simpler one. She brought soup to the dozens of parishioners still recovering from burned flesh and broken bones in the hospital, victims of the Battle of the Great Divide. She volunteered on the restoration crew to clear shrapnel and ammunition from the mega-church's explosion, some of which had flown as far as the Savage Mountains. She cooked for Aunt Karen and Uncle Floyd, made sure they were tucked in warm under afghans in front of the TV and had something uplifting to watch, a nature documentary or a show about how things were made, anything to help them through their grief. And of course there were her online classes.

That day, though, she passed the hospital, passed the turnoff to the Savage Mountains, and kept driving.

She pulled into the cemetery and cut the engine, the valley morning engulfing her in quiet. A hawk circled overhead, its wings nothing but a dark blink against the drifting clouds, but she was too far away to hear its cries.

She gathered the roses in her arms, their scent wrapping her in the faraway promise of springtime. She felt like it would never be spring again, and that was fine. The winter suited her; it suited the whole town. They needed time for things to be cold and dead, time before they could blossom once again. There was too much to process, and too much grieving to do, before the earth began to thaw.

The rows of new gravestones were cold, shiny slabs rising from the ground, granite polished until it reflected the weak sunlight. Most bore nothing but a name and a date of death. The congregation had grown so quickly and been so new; Pastor Ted's TV show drew them from all over the country to experience the End Times, but instead of a true Rapture it was their own End of Days that had befallen them, their untimely deaths in a flame-locked church or beneath the fiery footsteps of an angry God. Still, whether she knew them or not, Daphne put a single rose on each of their graves.

She paused when she got to old Eunice's headstone. It was white marble, as her will had requested, and covered from top to bottom in text: the names of her late husband and parents, son and daughter-in-law and grandchildren, quotes and proverbs that she had loved enough to keep in needlepoint on pillows all around her house.

Daphne lingered there, reading and rereading the words, thorns from the roses digging into her palms. She wanted to delay what came next: a trio of headstones that always hurt to look at but that would be even more unbearable to ignore.

They had all been so young. Doug Varley. Janie. Jeremiah, the baby who never took a breath. She placed the rest of the flowers on their graves and knelt in prayer, the snow soaking her knees and her tears watering the cold, hard ground.

She hoped that they were together again, wherever they were. She hoped that somewhere out there they could finally be the happy family they had never been in life. She no longer knew what she believed, had no idea if there was a heaven or an afterlife or anything at all. All she knew was that they deserved to be together; they deserved more in death than they'd gotten to experience in their short lives.

She stood slowly, her lips chapped from wind and tears. She smoothed a loose strand of hair into her wool cap and willed herself to leave the cemetery, to hurry to the hospital, where the sick and injured were waiting for her cool touch and gentle words.

But there was one more goodbye she wanted to say, a few last tears she wanted to cry.

There was no headstone for Owen in the cemetery, no acknowledgment of the sacrifice he had made, no cold slab of granite proclaiming his name. No place to rest her last rose.

Still, she could feel his presence. She could feel him in the dirt and the rain, when a hard downpour felt feathery light on her shoulders. She could feel it when she slipped on an icy patch in the Peytons' driveway and the ground caught her like a cushion, protecting her fall. She could feel it in the way the trees sang sometimes in the wind, and in the bite of a million cold stars when she tilted her face to the sky late at night, when she couldn't sleep and came outside seeking something she couldn't name.

He was out there somewhere, and she knew in the wide-open whisper of the future and the faint scent of motor oil that followed her everywhere that he wasn't gone for good. Someday, she knew, she would see him again. Someday she would kiss his lips and trace the calluses on his hands, and when that day came she would pull him to her and never let him go.

She didn't know how or when, but she knew it as sure as she knew the ground would thaw in the spring and the cold gray peaks around Carbon County would eventually mellow to green. Things weren't over for her and Owen. Someday, somehow, they would be together again.

Acknowledgments

A lot of awesome people helped bring this book to life. To my wonderful editor, Jessica Almon: *Children of the Earth* is as much your baby as it is mine, and I couldn't have asked for a better partner in rearing this little monster of ours.

Tina Wexler, I love bragging about my agent to anyone who will listen. Thanks for talking me off the wrong ledges and encouraging me to leap from the right ones, and for your sage (and notably un-slimy) advice about blurbs.

Casey McIntyre, the day you became my publicist is a national holiday in the Schumacher household. Thanks for everything from masterminding an unforgettable launch party to booking me on a packed panel at NY ComicCon.

Emily Osborne, you are a genius. The first time I saw your moody, mystical cover, it was like a punch in the gut . . . in a good way!

Ivan Anderson, your knowledge and attention to detail come through in every proofread: thanks to you, I will never inadvertently misuse the word "decimate" again. I'm also eternally grateful to

Kate Frentzel and Jenna Pocius for your tireless edits and keen eyes.

Ben Schrank, you've been a guiding force every step of the way. I couldn't have asked for a better team than your crew at Razorbill; working with you is always a dream.

I owe both enormous gratitude and a rather large apology to Joyce and River Higgenbottom, whose fascinating and down-to-earth *Paganism: An Introduction to Earth-Centered Religions* informed the structure (if absolutely not the sentiment) of the Children of the Earth's rituals.

Joan Burick and Annie Keating Schumacher, your support means everything to me (and, quite possibly, to my book sales). To my mom and dad, Zeke and Linda Hecker, I never would have written a word without you, and I hope you never forget that.

Tim Schumacher, I just can't even with how awesome you are. I literally can't.

Finally, I'm humbled and honored to be part of an amazing community of people who not only purchased my first book (often in multiples) but also recommended it to others, traveled from far and wide to attend the *End Times* book launch, and advocated for it as a selection in their book clubs. We are all lucky to have each other, and I'm especially lucky to have you.